PRODUCTION VALUES

This is a work of fiction. Names, characters, businesses, places, events, and incidents are either the products of the author's imagination or used in a fictitious manner. Any resemblance to actual persons, living or dead, or actual events is purely coincidental.

Cover Design by Victorine Lieske

ISBN: 1986974464
ISBN-13: 978-1986974462

PRODUCTION VALUES

LIV BARTLET

ALSO BY LIV BARTLET

Off Script

ALSO BY BECCA McCULLOCH

"A Fae One," *Mind Games* anthology
"To Mark the Time," *Something Lost* anthology

to those who have inspired and nurtured this dream—

thank you, gracias, danke schön

and, very Britishly, cheers

CHAPTER 1

"The world to me was a secret, which I desired to discover;
to her it was a vacancy, which she sought to people with imaginations of her own."

—Mary Shelley, Frankenstein

Kat

Yellow metal doors creak and then open wide to reveal my Elysium: the world of *21 Things*, my TV show. My baby. Cameramen greet me with cheeky grins, and a costume rack rushes by. The lead actors wave a hello.

This is the world I've hewn into existence, born as an idea on a sugar and clotted-cream soiled napkin in a Marylebone bakery four years ago. Electrified, animated life in a forgotten corner of BBC, the tiniest possible space granted, because the corporate suits wouldn't waste a real studio on a fool girl from America.

Someday, they'll choke on regret while I fill my shelves with golden statues—Emmys, BAFTAs, Globes.

Oscars.

Because I am a genius.

An evil genius, with an equally evil plan. I've decided to hire megastar Ian Graham as our major guest star this year so that I can ride into the production hall of fame on his very famous arse.

The only thing standing between me and über-success is Bea, my own best friend and business partner, an irony I can't quite grasp.

I stand outside our tiny production's studio door at the far edges of the BBC film studios and tap the cell phone in my hand before hitting the speed-dial icon that summons Bea. Maybe she won't answer and I can leave a completely empowered voicemail about why I'm right and she's wrong.

But I'm not that lucky. Bea answers. The beeps and blips in the background tell me she's still at the hospital, wrapped in scrubs and the past life she won't give up.

"I'm scrubbing up, Kat, so this better not be about Ian Graham. Whatever it is, it can wait a few more days. I'm back on Monday."

"No. It can't wait. It's been two weeks since you decided to play volunteer nurse—"

"I'm a mandated responder, Kat. Yell at the terrorists. They place bombs, I report to Royal Free's Emergency department. You want that not to happen, then work out a peace treaty with ISIS."

Bea fake-curses, a weird habit acquired during her upbringing in Mormon Idaho. She mumbles something to someone in medical-ese and I wish, for the thousandth time, that she'd quit her side gig. Who cares that she has two degrees in nursing? We're producers, not medical professionals. Well, Bea is technically the showrunner with a production tag, but she's better at money and schedules than I am so she runs the business side. And I need her to sign off on this detail right now.

"We're a week behind schedule, Bea. Losing money every minute that you're at the hospital instead of here." The whole of London's gone back to their real lives, real work. But not Bea. Bea won't leave until the hospital administration kicks her out.

Bea's voice is back, but not Bea's focus. "Just hold the phone, would you? It's slipping off my shoulder . . . I know it's not your job, but do you want another season of *21 Things* or not?"

The phone readjusts with a muffled shuffling and a squeak from latex-covered hands. Bea's voice is clear again. "Now you care about money? Then remember this: Ian Graham is a ridiculous expense that we can't afford. Tell his agent thanks, but no."

I draw two quick breaths and bang my head gently on the peeling yellow plaster wall before trying another tactic. "Bea—seriously—listen. Ian Graham is major star power. Word of mouth alone doubles our ratings. We want syndication, right? Wide coverage in America? That requires an actual marketing budget from the network. Ian Graham makes that happen—he's the ticket."

"No, he's not. He's just expensive. Anna, our current and *affordable* costar, is the ticket. John sent me her awards packet and she's going to get a BAFTA at least. That gets us—"

"A tiny bump in streaming numbers, at best! Bea—that's not enough. Trust me. Please."

"No. Do not hire Ian Graham. You'd have to fire the rest of the cast and film in our own bedroom closets. We can't cover that kind of expense."

A loud, ugly alarm sounds over the phone. "Aw, crap. Kat, I've got to go. The doctors need me more than you need to fangirl Ian Graham from the comfort of our own TV studio. I'm hanging up now."

The line goes dead and I kick the metal door to the studio. My toe objects with mind-popping pain. I hop and curse until the ache subsides.

Okay, so Bea's a dead end. I'll have to engage the evil in my evil plan. It's my production. I hired Bea. So what I say, goes. *I'm* the powerful and important Creative Genius and Executive Producer of the surprise hit of the decade.

And I have a plan.

I take a deep breath and push through the door to where Ian Graham waits, ready for filming. Sorry, Bea, but this is our future and I'm claiming it.

Each step takes me closer to the bright lights surrounding the actors and director. I'm totally prepared for this. For *him*.

Not like the other day. That was—well, I was rattled. It was the first time I'd seen Ian Graham in the flesh. But today I will absolutely not shake so hard that I accidentally toss a pen at a movie star and then try to clean up the mess on his shirt but then blush bright red at the reality of those muscles underneath his shirt. I will not turn every shade of red from crimson to vermillion and walk away mute, pathetic, and overwhelmed.

Nope, not going to happen. I'm calm and cool and professional. And I will stop thinking of Ian Graham as *eek! Ian Graham*. I will stop thinking about his overwhelming, high-wattage, sexy everything and focus on the assets he brings to *21 Things*—piercing blue eyes, a wicked eyebrow raise, long-fingered hands, the small unconscious gestures he makes that add an edge of vulnerability to his almost disreputable good looks, and all the women who love all those things.

Like me. Except I'm not thinking about that.

My nerves peak as I think about how much I have to prove. It's our first season without Meg, my mentor, at the executive helm. Our first season alone—the newbies, the young Americans, the odd ones out in BBC's hallowed halls. I know Meg believes in me, but insecurity skitters up my spine constantly since she left me the reins. Sure, she was mostly titular, and *21 Things* has always been my baby, but she was my safety net. Now, here I am, going for the creative skydive and uncertain about the hands that packed my parachute.

Chin up, my dad used to say. I push my chin up higher.

Lengthen your spine, my vocal coach used to say. I breathe and straighten my posture.

Smart. Radiant. Brilliant. Artistic. I mentally recite my aspirational adjectives and step past the lights. The set comes into focus.

Quinn, our lead actress, looks perfect in tighter-than-usual jeans, a sleeveless red top, and uncharacteristically heavy cat-eye makeup. She's perched on the pool table where she'll be snogging Ian this morning. Ian looks perfect, too—rakish in a tight t-shirt and a black leather jacket.

Ralph calls them to order. Quinn drops into place immediately. Ian messes with his cell phone up to the last possible second before his personal production assistant takes it off set. We'll be paying a young man to run items about for Ian—I can hear Bea's pencil scratching holes in her paper at the financial waste inherent in that young man's job description.

Ralph lifts his chin in acknowledgment when he sees me sit. His headphones plop on his ears. Go time.

The actors will do this scene cold because meticulous rehearsal leads to painstakingly boring kisses.

Ralph signals the scene for a single run-through before cameras roll.

Whoa.

Not a good *whoa*. This is—my stomach sinks with every passing second—awful. Pure cardboard. No emotion, no chemistry. Worst snog I've ever witnessed. I'm more uncomfortable than I was playing Spin the Bottle with the fat Harrison twins when my dad insisted I stay with them while he went to the base Christmas party. Two boys. Only me. No attraction. But, still—I'd rather see video of Timmy Harrison trying to French me than watch Ian slobber over Quinn again.

Ralph stops the scene. A good director knows how to motivate the actors, draw out emotion and character to get what the camera needs, so he'll fix this mess. He talks to Quinn and Ian with arms about both their shoulders. "Reckless," I hear. "Quinn, this is the moment of escape. Ian—take advantage of it."

They run the scene again and my stomach sinks further. *Zero* percent improvement.

Ralph talks to Quinn and Ian again. He rolls camera on the third attempt. I want to cry. How could it get worse? Seriously, we should find Timmy Harrison—it's a big day for him. He's now only the second worst snog in history. Ian Graham owns that title. Owns it like nobody's business. Ian Graham, grand master of the slimy snog.

Ralph leans over to me and I know what he's going to say. "Sorry, Kat, but this isn't Quinn's fault. Your bloke might be famous as sin, but right now I'd rather have a nobody who spends ten minutes finding character."

Ian has violated my first rule of artistic integrity: *always give your everything*. My expensive gamble is not paying out. Bea will have me killed by gypsies. Or pixies. Pixie gypsies with tiny little knives.

Ralph raises both eyebrows and speaks around the pen hanging from his mouth. "So, you want to chat with him?" This is so bad that Ralph wants producer pressure on Ian.

Shit. But that's my job.

"Yeah, I'll talk to him. Give everyone a short break."

Ralph calls the break. "Producer chat, you two," he points at Quinn and Ian.

I walk onto the set and pull Quinn aside. "Quinn, hon, you're doing great. We're going to get this," I whisper.

"I hope so. Thanks." She smiles at me, relieved, and I send her off set.

The PA has already shown back up with that stupid cell phone. Ian turns to walk away without so much as a word. Oh, the nerve. "No. You stay here and you listen." Frustration turns to anger. I want to curse and yell like I do at CEO Royce Rudkins's crony-brigade in budget meetings. The suits on the loose that never believed in us or our little show, but will soon be eating crow when *21 Things* becomes the network's top-rated comedy. Not third, not second—first. At the top. Someday, I will win an Oscar, and they will say that my award-winning career launched here, at the little show that could and did.

But I need Ian Graham to make it work.

"Right, then." He folds his arms and smiles at me with that famous eyebrow quirk. It would be charming, if he hadn't wasted everyone's time—and my patience—by undervaluing my show, my baby.

"Frankly, I don't care who you are right now. Right now, on my set, you're going to stop phoning it in. Quinn is the star of a successful TV show and deserves more than this blasé, half-here embarrassment of a performance. You have a character to play, and you're a very good actor. So give me the Ian Graham I hired." I manage not to yell, but I'm damn firm.

Ian's face changes completely by the time I'm done—the smirk settles into a scowl with deep lines across his forehead. I can't tell if he's surprised or pissed off, though—his eyes have gone blank and he says nothing.

My nerves ramp up as the silence stretches. I cross my arms. "Now go. And come back with your head in the game." Which sounds ridiculous. I do not do sports metaphors. Or sports.

He quirks an eyebrow at me though the deep lines remain. Dammit, I don't know if I'm going to have to tell Bea that I had to fire Ian Graham. I do not want to hear her say *I told you so* about "unnecessary expenses" like movie stars.

He taps a finger against one of his eyebrows. "My apologies, then. A monsoon set back my last project, and, you know, Leo is a perfectionist. Together, we were rather exacting. I barely had a day to get here."

"Ill-prepared isn't in your reputation."

"If you'll give me a few extra moments, I'll be right and focused. Promise. You've got something special here with this show, that's why I decided to squeeze it in."

"Well, thank you. How long do you need?"

"Half hour. Need to call my daughter." He waves his cell phone a little and I can see the notification light blinking.

"Forty-five minutes, then. You get one more chance." I pivot away. That's ten times more boss-lady scare tactic than I've ever employed.

I bury my face in my clipboard and pretend to do something important. Ian exits, tapping out a cigarette and punching keys on his cell phone.

"Well?" Ralph peers down at me from his perch at the main camera.

I don't look up. I'm too important to look up, right? "He's got one more shot. That's it. No more wasting time."

"Excellent." Ralph grins. "Hope you gave him hell."

"Just a little," I half look up and laugh.

The difference when Ralph calls action is palpable and beautiful. Every cell in my body sighs in relief as Ian grabs Quinn with lazy, heated intent. Their eyes connect and sparks fly.

This is it. This is the scene I envisioned. Slow kisses as his hands move up into her hair. She pushes the jacket off his shoulders and the desperation kicks in. He walks her back toward the pool table and they fall together into hot, desperate snogging.

It's so hot I can barely sit still. And there's not one little bit of awkward. Sorry, Timmy, back to the winner's circle for you. Ian Graham *can* snog the hell out of a woman.

Quinn digs her fingers into Ian's muscular back. Every cell in my body lights on triumphant fire. It's a lot of pennies for this snog, this extra edge of sexy on our little romantic comedy, but it'll be worth every damn one.

♦ ♦ ♦

Bea

Bea stifled her third yawn behind her blue-gloved hand without releasing her hold on the thread. She pulled the last stitch tight and looked at the woman in traditional black burqa and the man beside her, seated on an old-style yellow metal chair in a barely-funded refugee center on the wrong side of London. "So, the glass is out of his foot and it's all stitched up, but this little guy needs antibiotics. He'll have to see Joelle on Monday. Any questions?"

The translator repeated Bea's words while Bea yawned again. The parents' questions resembled so many others she'd answered—worries about being seen in dangerous days. Bea reassured them as best she could that they'd always be safe here. Joelle was a fierce mama bear. God himself would need a very, very good reason to cross the clinic threshold unannounced and would still get a firm lecture about confidentiality.

Bea tickled the boy's toes before slipping on a sock. "No more going outside without shoes." She rose and kissed the woman's cheeks, then bowed slightly to the father. "*Khuda afiz*."

Bea exited the exam room and tapped on Joelle's metal desk as she walked by. "I'm out."

The Southern Baptist woman stopped humming spirituals to rise and hug Bea. "Sweet mercy. First the bombings and then my panicked call. You must be barely half alive. But the good Lord knows we would've failed without you. When I opened the door day after the bombings, they were spilling out of the crevices. Some with real complaints but most just seeking asylum."

"As you've told me. Don't worry. They barely needed me on disaster response." Bea shook her head to stop another yawn.

"A lie! You arrived caked in gore. I'd wager you were on scene at the bombings, then did who knows how many alternating shifts at Royal Free."

"Can't waste that fine American education." Bea forced a grin. "But now, I return to television. This volunteer gig won't support my retail habits."

Joelle laughed, a loud unmetered sound that rattled the nerves of some clients, but defined the culture at the small, Southern Baptist charitable relief center in seedy London. "I'll see you in your off-season, as usual. We do miss you once filming starts. Oh—and your handsome boy, the photographer, he's waiting on you, girl. I made him cross the street. That large camera gives the clients the shudders."

"I'll remind him." Bea pawed through the clothes she'd been wearing when bombs rocked London's public transportation system. She'd run ten blocks to reach the first impacted station. Her Gucci blouse was splashed with blood and betadine and her Manolo Blahniks were destroyed. The scrubs that stunk of body fluids and her own sweat would have to do. Bea stuffed the clothes back in her bag and headed out the front entrance.

Matthias reclined against a brick wall across the street. He pushed longish brown hair out of caramel brown eyes and smiled at Bea. He was a small-time photographer in the most photographed city in the world. By day, he took tourist photos at the London Eye. By night, he scoured the city for stories worth selling to the tabloids. He was a useful friend for a producer-in-nurse-clothing. The dark spots of London hid nothing from him. More than once, his keen eye for celebrity trouble had saved Bea the headache of actor drama gone public. As *21 Things* grew more popular, Bea spent more and more time wandering streets with Matthias Perrini.

"Did you have to wait long?" Bea rubbed her arms against the cold damp of a London morning seeping through starched cotton.

"No longer than usual, *gattina*. I won't let you walk alone from here."

Matthias draped his jacket over her shoulders. "You look awful, like a forgotten victim that just stumbled above-ground."

"Ooh, good enough to start a zombie rumor?" Bea laughed at the idea.

"*Quasi*," Matthias chuckled. They started the five-block walk to Waterloo station—still hours before London would roar back to life.

"Did you have a good night?" Bea asked.

"You judge." Matthias handed Bea his digital camera.

Bea flipped through photos until she came to an image of an MI5 officer questioning a young mother. Matthias had captured the tears in her eyes and the child wrapped around her cotton-encased legs. Bea breathed out an appreciative *oh*. "Brilliant. You've an eye."

Matthias shrugged. He reached over and pushed the advance button. "The *Mail* doesn't pay me to take those. The useful pieces are further back."

Bea continued to scroll through photos until she reached the celebrity shots. "Wow. This is almost offensive after everything else you've taken. This rave happened the same night as the bombings?"

"Nothing stops the party, *gattina*."

Bea paged past the famous faces until she reached the bombings. Photo after photo of despair and fear. She saw herself working over a man in shock. Her hair had come free of her braid, whipping around in the breeze like updrafts in a tornado. She groaned at her unkempt, disrupted look. "If I look worse than that now, we'll get those zombie rumors. And the *Mail* also doesn't pay you for photos of unimportant producers."

Matthias ignored her half-hearted slap on his arm. "You're not as unimportant to some as others."

"Don't start on Kat. She's trying to do the impossible. That takes a little focus." Bea slipped the camera back over his neck. "I wish you'd focus on actual journalism. You're talented."

"Maybe, but I need *money*."

Bea scrunched her nose and rolled her eyes.

"To those of us who have lived without it, money is life. The *Mail* pays real money to people like me who are good at being at just the right angle. And then I will have more to offer a woman than the few quid I scrape into a pile these days. I'd think a woman who lists owning a Monet as a life goal would understand this."

"My goals are to have a baby *and* a Monet, and I work my rear end off to obtain them without burdening any man with the quest."

Matthias dropped an arm over Bea's shoulders. "Maybe a man will want to be along for the ride. At least with the baby half."

"That part's free. If a woman has substance, she'd find love in a hovel and work her way to success."

"Again, so says the woman with a closet full of designer rags. The man that takes you needs plenty of closet space and money to burn."

"The clothes make the woman, my friend. And I earn every rag I buy." Bea stopped in front of a barely-lit window. "I'm starved." She entered the small all-night market, grabbed a few self-serve items, and then sat at the single table. Bea grabbed a knife to slice her banana.

Matthias slid in beside her after paying the clerk. "So explain to me why Ian Graham has been on your set for three days and I don't have a single on-set to help me pay my rent?"

"Ian Graham. *The* Ian Graham? On my set?"

"Yes, *gattina*. Since Wednesday."

"Since Wednesday?" Bea shrieked and stabbed her banana. The clerk jerked out of her doze and fell from her chair. She shouted for calm as Bea murdered her banana in Kat's honor. She cut and sliced and smashed as she mumbled. "I can't believe she . . . I said no! No. No money . . . no . . . no, Kat. No means no."

Bea screamed again. She banged the knife against the steel table and cursed Kat to the soundtrack of Matthias laughing and the clerk's threats to call the police.

Then she plopped a chunk of mutilated banana in her mouth and chewed. "Thought we were past the whole *you work for me* bull-crap after I saved her over-budget second season from cancellation. Now she's over budget on her third season? Does she think I just pull advertiser revenue out of my rear end? I only saved the second season because I jumped in fast to the online syndication circuit. If Americans hadn't loved *21 Things*, we'd be yesterday's sad luck story. So what do I do now? Space broadcasting? In case E.T. is bored at home? But she's the grand, all-knowing artist. Her way or no way." Bea sighed. Deep. To her toes. "And I'm not. I'll just have to figure it out."

Matthias chuckled when a piece of banana plopped out of her mouth and landed on the paper placemat.

Bea stared at the slimy mess. "But not tonight. I can't even keep food in my mouth. Can I crash with you?"

Matthias grinned around his coffee cup. "You dare explore the seven smells of my flatmate?"

"For a few hours of uninterrupted sleep, I'd grab a bench in Hyde Park."

"My mattress has more lumps, and you'll want newspaper instead of our stinking blankets. Laundry day never comes around."

Bea lay her tired head on his shoulder. "Forget the vapid love and use the money to hire a cleaning lady."

Matthias kissed her hair. "A clean house is nice, but love is essential to life."

"You're as crazy as Kat," Bea said. She smeared her scone with jam and clotted cream and took a large bite.

Matthias snapped her portrait haphazardly. "*Punizione* for daring to criticize love in front of an Italian. Forever captured with cream on your nose."

"Ugh—I kind of hate you, Matthias Perrini."

CHAPTER 2

Er, der Herrlichste von Allen

He, the most glorious of all

—Robert Schumann, Frauenliebe und -leben

Kat

I try not to seethe too visibly on the Tube—nobody likes sitting next to a madwoman on their morning commute—but frustration crawls under my skin. Piano exercises tap out against the side of the closest hand pole to find center through repetition. Still somewhat madwoman-ish, though.

Mornings like this I can understand the appeal of killer high heels. When Bea's with me, her heels click with command down the sidewalk: Get out of my way, I'm in charge and I've got the footwear to prove it. I wear flats or trainers and let the sidewalk serve me quietly. But today there is no clack beside me.

Today, I'm on my way to work alone.

Because Bea is not back from nursing. *Monday,* she said. But now it's Monday and her usual noisy place beside me is eerily quiet.

I left a copy of the revised production budget and Ian's first dailies on her kitchen table and then hid in my apartment waiting for her to come home and scream and give me hell. But—nothing. Not a sign of Bea anywhere.

My hand tucks under my thigh. The lady next to me carries a snorting pig in a purse, but she's been looking at *me* with fear in her eyes.

In truth, I may have been humming.

Time to stop mulling over the mysteries of Bea and face the day. Ian will be on set and I'm still a bit out of control every time he's near me. That's got to stop. I must be contained. Calm. Professional. That's my new mantra.

The mantra resonates all along the route to the studio. I repeat it so often in my mind that I almost say it to the nice woman who greets me at the employee entrance.

Contained. Calm. Professional.

Confidence rises with each repetition, as it should. I'm flying by the time I round the corner and push open the door and—

"Oy, Kat," Ralph calls out from his chair, next to Bea's empty seat. "Did you bring the notes from yesterday's dailies? I've lost mine."

Ralph joins Bea in my frustration pool. He's been getting too full of himself. Losing or disregarding notes, playing king in an empire that already has a ruler—*me*.

My eyes open so wide they water, and I fist my right hand to prevent rhythmic tapping. I'm trying this whole not-swearing-at-people-who-annoy-me thing, but the words cram together on my tongue and I feel like Audrey Hepburn trying to sing about hurricanes in Hartford.

"Probably still in my office. I'll go get them," I mumble around obscenity-laden marbles.

"I'll send a PA." Ralph looks about for one of the younglings who do our bidding.

"No worries. I could use a walk." Another chance at mantra-chanting and not-swearing.

Ten minutes later, buried under a stack of folders and crinkled notepads, I'm prepping the most incredible scolding for Ralph. How could he have lost the notes?

I hear my name in front of me and then I smell *him*.

Ian.

Tobacco and juniper and—man. He's pure man. The smell of him short-circuits my—everything. Brain, breath, self-control. I attempt to deploy my longed-for, but mostly fictional, ability to stop a blush before it starts. Blood and heat fill my face.

We've stopped in front of the stage door. The visual of Ian Graham complements the scent of him. More than a clichéd roughness around the edges—with his well-trimmed beard and a voice soaked in Scotch and honey—he's rough on the inside and urbane at the edges.

He smiles—a win for me, considering the last time we spoke I called him unprofessional and threatened to fire him. I'm so dazzled that it takes me too long to notice he's not alone. A young girl with long blond hair stands a little behind him, a cautious set to her shoulders and her eyes hidden by bangs.

"Ah, good I caught you. Wanted to check with you, see if it's alright if Eden spends the day with ol' Da' at work." He tucks the girl under his arm and winks down at her, a gesture that reminds me of my dad at the flight hangar where he worked.

"Sure. I spent plenty of days hanging out with my dad." The girl's age escapes me. Nine? Eleven? Bea would know—she's got nieces and nephews of every age. "Anyone in particular she'd like to meet?"

"I like Jenny, she's beautiful. The other girl's you, right? The less-pretty one? That's what everyone says." Eden tilts her head at me. It's common speculation that I based Cate, Quinn's character, on myself, though it's not exactly true. She's more like my insecurity had a love child with Bea's sense of humor, but that sounds weirder than saying she's me. Still, the pretty thing makes insecure Kat quiver and long for a middle school bathroom stall for cover. An emerging mean girl's barbs hurt as much as the fully fleshed-out high school taunts.

I professional smile—my thank-you-for-coming-to-our-press-event smile—before I respond. "We'll be sure you meet everyone."

Ian opens the door and I take stride beside him, Eden on his other side. "Tight schedule today. I assume you're prepared?" Tight like his abs—the most ridiculous thought I've had in days. Yet, why not? He's a good-looking man, I might as well look.

Ian nods, solemn but with plenty of good humor. "I'm even more impressed than I thought I'd be when I said yes. It's well done, for the telly."

"Well, we aren't making a TV show. We are making a very long movie." Something I've said a hundred times. It's the banner on the damned official fan site.

"I've read that somewhere. Or everywhere." He winks at me and then his arm brushes mine.

Heat rises in my cheeks again as Ian grins. "Your work will only makes us better. We didn't just hire you for your looks." And I've done it. Embarrassed myself.

"But there's a reason for the number of fitted tees in my wardrobe."

I cough to cover up my lack of a comeback. Ian Graham flirted with me. I want to fangirl, to squeal and post online and obsess over every nuance for days and days and days. And maybe I live out that whole fantasy for long enough that I don't notice when Ian peels off toward makeup, leaving Eden to stick with me like yesterday's street food.

Ralph takes the notes with a raise of eyebrows and glance at Eden. I shrug and take my chair. What else is there to do? "Moodier lighting in general. The pub can't be as bright as the bookstore." I'm satisfied by Ralph's nod and save my lecture for another day.

Eden claims Bea's chair next to mine and leans in. "Do you know my mom? She'd be perfect for your show. Adelaide Andres. Isn't that the best name? Dad was with my mom almost the longest of anyone he's been with. Not as long as Tess, she has the most kids. It's hard to divorce the kids."

"Hm." It's not intelligent, polite, or conversational, but it's the only sound I can muster.

I suppose I wasn't much more graceful at that age, possessive of my father and the singular place I held in his life, with no clue what to do except chatter.

"I'm as pretty as Jenny. That's what my mom says. Do you think so?"

How the fuck do I answer a question so loaded shock jocks would change the subject? Feminist theory doesn't cover this, at least not anything I've read.

I really know nothing about children.

So, I go with honesty. The girl has excellent genes and while she's at that awkward stage—ten, I checked Ian's wiki page—she's still cuter than most girls, mid-pre-puberty. She has Ian's artist's eyes, pouty lips, and bright blond hair. Her features will blossom into real beauty if she doesn't spend them chasing approval and cultivating pettiness. "You've got potential."

Eden's face deflates and contorts with painful, young emotions. "My mother is very pretty," she says with a feigned flounce. "Everyone says I look just like her."

"No, you're going to be more beautiful than she ever was." I've seen her floozy of a mother—a tired tart forever in bright red lipstick, with over-processed hair to complete the stereotype.

Ralph rolls his eyes and holds up the schedule. As if I don't know what we need to get done today. It's not my fault Bea is MIA and I've been saddled with a prepubescent girl.

Eden peppers me with questions between periods of respectful cameras-rolling silence: *What did the book covered in coffee stains in season 2 mean? Will Jenny and Hugh get together? Is Cate going to leave behind Jack for the Englishman? She can't, Jack is so brill . . .*

By the time Ralph calls tea break, I'm more exhausted than after a full-day press event. I wonder if Marian, my dad's secretary, felt the same after any of those countless days or hours I spent talking her ear off when I was Eden's age. Marian, who listened because she cared. I wonder if I've done her example any kind of justice.

Ian strides down from set to retrieve her. "There's my gel." Ian grins and Eden lights up.

She hops down and tucks into his side, and I'm reminded of my dad, again, in that affectionate bond.

"Thank you for entertaining her, she's quite the fan."

"So I've discovered. She has some good theories. I think it's time she met the objects of some of those theories—what do you say, Eden?"

"I'd love to! Da, can I?"

"Course, right. I'll just be outside, then."

I need to ask Bea how I keep ending up babysitting. She's better with people. Somehow, nice turns out wrong when I try it. Ian's already retreating. I'll suppress my headache and growling stomach to shepherd Eden through introductions.

♦ ♦ ♦

Bea

Bea raced through the halls, her heels snapping along the hall like a runaway horse at a ticker-tape parade. The wise moved aside. The less wise got pushed aside.

She'd slept in. Missed her alarm completely.

In nine years of adulthood, Bea had never entered work one minute past start time, but her mother always said she slept like the devil's conscience if she got overtired. Kat was going to pitch a fit. Ten fits. Probably already had.

Bea extended her right heel to skid to a stop as she neared the production studio. She pivoted as though her stilettos had wheels to tuck herself into a small alcove.

Ian Graham. Right there. With a woman. She'd rehearsed how to say hello without a mental image of money flushing down the toilet, though she'd planned to do so with Kat in tow to actually do the small talk piece.

Ian Graham was everything Bea found grotesque. One billion children starved in abject poverty while Ian Graham raked in millions for a few days' work. He spent that money on little more than his own amusement and had amassed ex-houses and ex-lovers and ex-employees enough to fill the background on a disaster movie. He didn't even bother to have a pretend cause. His charitable contributions all poured back into the organizations that made him famous, the pseudo-charities that funded actors' guilds. No one mattered to Ian Graham, no one but himself.

At least one woman wasn't impressed. Two, if Bea counted the angry woman berating him outside the studio.

The woman with Ian stood like the wrath of God, her hands on her hips and strawberry hair waving with every word. Her full Irish brogue deepened to send each whispered word buzzing through the concrete and tile hall. "Ian, this has got to stop. You don't just toss her at me whenever you don't want to deal with her. And you don't summon me by text and then refuse to accept my answer. I'm the mother of your children—two of the three, at least—not hired help. So this be the last time—the very last time—I get summoned by the likes of you. Only reason I'm here now is to tell you what I already told you by text. Nah, I won't take her today. I've duties of my own. She's your daughter, she needs you. She's staying with you while I care for mine own. And you better be at family dinner on Sunday, so help me."

Ian's mouth puckered in a grimace. "I'm at work, Tess. And I've got plans later that Eden can't attend. I just need you to take her for the night. That gonna hurt you?"

Tess. Ian's first wife. He was divorcing his third, so family reunions must roil with complicated, drama-filled fun. Eden was the daughter he created by cheating on Tess. Ian Graham had turned Peter Pan syndrome into a full-blown lifestyle.

"Plans, eh? Ian Graham code for sex. How young is this one? Officially half your age? You've certainly found some fountain of feminine youth that spews lasses to do the bidding of the great Ian Graham, haven't you? They check their self-respect at the first raise of an eyebrow."

Tonight's play date better not be anyone Bea knew. Both Quinn and Anna were the perfect age for Ian Graham's wandering eye—and other body parts. Unbelievable that they'd spent this much money so Ian could avail himself of one, if not both, of their lead actresses. Plus, Bea somehow got dragged into every broken heart on set. Every pockmarked, distressed face found its way to her office—and usually her apartment.

Tess gave an exhausted, exaggerated sigh. "You've a little 'un that needs more than you're giving. You best be giving it or that Eden'll be another sad story in the papers. She's close to gone, Ian. So close."

Ian patted his pockets. Left. Right. Upper. Was he looking for cigarettes? This was a clearly marked no smoking area. It was in the contract. Well, it was supposed to be in the contract. Kat had given Ian the moon, maybe she'd also sold their lung health.

"I give what I can. Here for her more than I was the older two. I'm trying, Tess. Give me points for trying."

Tess withdrew a cigarette from an unseen pack tucked inside his belt. "But at your own convenience. She needs a father, Ian. A real 'un. Fully grown with all the responsibilities. You canna stay young forever."

Ian grinned at her. He dropped his head a few inches, raised his eyebrows. Oh, gross. Ian Graham flirting. "Sure I can, Tess. Done it so far."

Tess coughed. "I don't miss the smokes. Not a bit."

"But you miss the rest of me?" Ian smiled slightly when Tess shook her head at him. Then she pivoted and walked away. Bea liked her for that, liked her a lot.

One deep breath propelled Bea back out into the hall. She tossed her own long, red hair over her shoulder and then squared her shoulders.

Ian lit the cigarette and puffed, despite the No Smoking sign overhead.

Her usual reprimand over smoking violations echoed in her head to the time of her steps; medical training didn't disappear the moment she donned the heels. But as she approached Ian, the door behind him swung open and her cast spilled out.

Tea time.

She'd missed a full morning.

Ben dropped an arm over Ian, but his eyes centered on Bea with a look full of mirth. He was the class clown, a title he guarded as closely as the smokes in his own pocket.

Ben winked at her, though his words were for Ian whose back was to Bea. "Hey—healthy lungs per order of Saint Bea."

Jamie slapped Ben on the back. His voice came out in its usual half-whisper. Bea couldn't count the number of takes ruined by Jamie's preference for soft speech. "Don't call her that, Ben. Makes her sound awful. Bea's right to enforce the law."

"You all know I love my Busy-Bea." Another wink. Bea leveled her gaze and placed hands on her hips. Jamie mouthed, *I'm sorry*.

Ian still hadn't seen her, completely oblivious to anything happening further away than his credit card could reach. He took a deep drag. "I think she'll tolerate a little more this year."

"I think she won't," Bea said sharply. "Smoke outside if you insist. Inside, we breathe clean air."

Ian inhaled and exhaled around the rolled paper. "I'll keep the smoke to myself."

Ah, the game. Power and moxie locked in a death battle for set control. This was Bea's favorite part. Bea held every muscle still, impassive except for a subtle lift of her chin and eyebrow. Thus far, she'd had enough moxie to win any fight she entered.

A ripple moved through the cast. Ben grabbed at Ian's elbow. "I could use a cigarette, too. I'll show you where we smoke, just a few quick steps outside."

"Thank you, Ben. Be quick about it." Bea continued her course toward the door.

Kat stood inside, her yellow notepad already crumpled from the day's illegible hen-scratched notes and doodles. She looked up at Bea. "You sure you're ready to be back? I heard an old woman had chest pains in Derbyshire this morning."

A small blonde girl stood at Kat's elbow, peering with interest at the notepad. Eden. Unbelievable.

Bea let the door swing shut. "I noticed we hired Ian Graham. And became a childcare. That should help pay his keep." She stared hard at Kat, whose ears turned pink.

Kat held Bea's gaze despite her deepening blush. "We did. Hire him. Not become a sitting service. And he's great. You should see the dailies."

Bea grinned at Eden. "You're Eden, right? Your dad's just outside the first exit door on your right. Want me to walk you, or can you make it there on your own?"

"Oh, I can get there. I go all over London on my own." Eden grinned back. She was beautiful, not a surprise given the genetic package.

"Good. We'll see you after tea, then." Bea pushed the door open to let Eden out.

"Oh, thank you," Kat sighed. "I rather thought I'd adopted her. Where would I put her in our postage stamp apartments? My closet is full of mixing and recording equipment and your whole apartment is a closet."

"Now that I've taken care of your Eden problem, let's see those dailies. He'd better be amazing. I promised the dating service, Hearts Alive, that he'd be worth a substantial investment in *21 Things*. They're sending over brochures for product placement and enough cash to get you back in the black."

"You know I love you, right?" Kat's fingers fluttered in an erratic dance against her thigh, her eyes bright. Bea was a good worker bee, and the Queen was pleased.

Bea sat on the plastic chair, her silk skirt cinching in at the knees. Kat perched on the edge of the table in her owl t-shirt and jeans. Her tennies swung a wide arc under the desk. She handed Bea a tablet with pre-edited dailies.

"I have to go plead your case with Royce Rudkins, however, who is curious how we've funded this. So wow me with these dailies. I need stars in my eyes when I walk into his office."

"Better hold tight or you'll slip right off the chair. The sparkle gets intense." Kat was the artist in residence, and Bea was the heavy, both figuratively and literally.

Bea crossed her ankles and placed them on the desk to admire her emerald green shoes as Ian Graham pawed at Quinn. Kat wasn't wrong. He was a very good snog. If nothing else went wrong, Kat's plan might just work.

CHAPTER 3

Wie du auch strahlst in Diamantenpracht,
es fällt kein Strahl in deines Herzens Nacht

Even though you shine in diamond splendor,
there falls no light into your heart's night

—Robert Schumann, Dichterliebe

Bea

Bea collapsed on her couch after the weeks of nonstop filming. She'd earned a night off. But her cell phone disagreed as it shook and buzzed on the coffee table. One phone call. It only took one phone call before she had to don her heels and get back to work.

Bea finished undoing the last of her braid as she slipped out of the cab. Matthias waited, half-hidden in shadow, beside a long queue of hopeless normals wanting a chance to mingle with the celebs inside Warehouse 7.

The building shook with each pound of deep bass. Every so often, an unmarked door opened to flood the pier with light, which provoked photo flashes as paid paparazzi grabbed photo after photo. Later, they'd sort through the thousands of digital images to see who they could publish. Most of the photographers were on celebrity payrolls, paid to feed the tabloids the right photos per the celebrity brand. Matthias and a few others worked directly for the tabloids, paid to snoop out stories and capture public-enough evidence to skirt the strict privacy laws.

Matthias stepped deeper into his shadow after he nodded to Bea. Bea followed him out of earshot of the other gossip hunters.

"You're sure he's in there?" Bea asked.

"Absolutely. He went in with two women an hour ago. They've both come out, but he's still inside."

"So he's alone? That's worse. How I curse the day Ben met heroin."

Bea handed Matthias a brown envelope as payment for the intel. Then she unzipped the black cardigan covering her tie-wasted, silver snakeskin-embossed bodycon dress. She inverted her hair and shook hard, hoping to reinvigorate some volume.

When her head came back up, Matthias stared at her instead of the envelope.

"What? What's wrong? The dress? The hair? *Ten minutes ago, I was in pajamas* isn't exactly a style." The dress had enough sparkle to distract from everything else, but maybe it was too daring for a size-nine woman in a size-zero world.

"Nothing wrong. Nothing at all. You're front page material tonight." Matthias's eyes ran over her one more time before he shook his head and returned to the envelope.

He leafed through the perfectly untraceable full-size photographs ready for scanning. "Ian on-sets. About time. I was beginning to think you didn't care. I'll publish it with an unofficial *21 Things* spoiler alert. Buzz should be good." He flipped through and found Bea's personal favorite part of the package. "Ian with his hand on a PA's ass? That's gold, *gattina*."

"I can neither confirm nor deny any information about the *21 Things* set or family. And for the record, the unsanctioned record, they both claim it was consensual."

"Fully consensual, I'm sure. Must be good to be Ian."

Bea and Kat's administrative assistant emerged from inside the building. Her sparkle could blind airplane pilots. She wore full silver sequins on the tiniest dress ever created to cover a woman almost six feet tall. The plunging neckline almost showed her belly button, and her thigh gap commanded attention.

Nicola was one of the secrets to Bea's success and the first big favor Matthias had done her. She was his sister who had come to England after aging out as an Italian magazine model. Matthias introduced them soon after he and Bea met at the London Eye. He promised she'd be the perfect assistant, and she had been. Nic's modeling connections took her anywhere Bea wanted to go and her looks helped them when connections failed.

Nic kissed her brother on both cheeks. Then she leaned down a full foot to repeat the gesture with Bea. Having a former high-fashion model as an executive assistant had about a million perks, though being good on self-esteem wasn't one. No matter how hard Bea tried—and succeeded—with fashion, she became the ugly, fat friend the moment Nicola or Kat joined in. Not that Bea was badly put-together. She had high cheekbones and the right amount of muscle, but only her green eyes weren't covered in an unfortunate layer of fluffy fat. Among the beautiful elite of the entertainment world, Bea was definitely the least among them all.

Bea smiled at Matthias as she prepared to follow Nic back into the club. "Thanks for keeping an eye out for me." She stretched up to kiss his cheeks.

"Anything for you, *gattina*. There's a door behind the bar. That's your best bet for an anonymous exit."

Bea turned and grabbed for Nic's arm to keep tabs on her. The crowd grew more eager as fewer bodies were admitted to the rave. People pressed toward the door and shifted in excitement every time a sliver of light illuminated the border. The bouncers had been joined by three security guards in hopes of containing the crowd.

Nic leaned down to hear Bea despite Bea shouting at full volume. "Have you found him yet?"

"No. The crowd is madness. And we've another problem. Charlie's in there with Anna. He's drunk and mad that his latest album is *misunderstood by brainless fuckers*, as he's said a dozen times."

Someday, not-famous-enough guitarist Charlie Rood would dump Anna. Bea had lost any hope the breakup would go the other way. Anna practiced loyalty to a fault, and that fault line too often ran across her pretty face.

"We can't risk another bruised anything pushing back filming. Not with the money we've spent on Ian."

"I know. I'll go to Anna while you find Ben. She'll leave with us if we both insist."

Bea followed Nicola toward the security detail. The sequined dress hypnotized the bouncers and Bea did what she did best in a crowd: she slipped by unseen.

Nic hadn't exaggerated. Even inside, the crowd was insane. Bodies everywhere. The air was so thick that Bea immediately felt hot and sticky with sweat not her own. Her hair clung to the exposed skin on her neck and arms.

She pushed toward the curtained area in the back. She had no idea where she'd find a few days to dry Ben out again. Lead stars on drug holidays would ruin Kat's filming schedule. Ralph still wanted the fifteenth off for his son's birthday, so another lost day there. And Anna had a publicity tour in three weeks.

Her head began to ache as she faced another sleepless night shuffling details around the giant calendar in her office. Planning around Ben's errant decision-making and Charlie's temper and Kat's unpredictable creativity was always nearly impossible. The needs of guest stars and media had turned her worry canker into a bloody testament to overwhelming stress.

Bea followed her nose back into the vast space. Past the stench of nicotine and the sweet-grass of marijuana, and toward the smell her dolls had made when her brothers tossed them in the fire. Bea didn't pause until the scent of grass mingled with flowers and vinegar.

Heroin. Ben's hometown.

Gray Doc Martens with rock concert pins peeked out beneath a closed curtain. Ben always wore those boots when drug seeking—a paired association he swore made the highs higher.

Bea pushed back the curtain to find Ben alone. Relief flooded her, allowing her shoulders to unknot a little. In their first year of filming, she'd found him being serviced by a woman with big hair and very fast hands. Bea had bristled and yelled and been mocked in return—the birth of Saint Bea.

But tonight, it was only Ben and his first, truest love. The tight tourniquet cut harsh red marks in his skin. Bea counted four punctures. Only a few lumps of black tar lay scattered on the table. Bea could feel her mother's disapproval as she brushed the remaining black wad into her pocket, but sometimes Ben needed a hit and Bea needed him to work. Morals didn't make TV shows.

"Hey, Bea," Ben said when he saw her. His eyes remained half-closed as he rode through the peak.

Bea undid the elastic ribbon. Bea provided clean syringes, tourniquets, and a manager who was usually adept at removing Ben from danger, but Ben had given Rudy the slip at a karaoke bar in Bankside.

Ben's dilated eyes focused on her. "Hey, Bea! Just had a line. And a hit. I wanted to see friends . . . come to a party . . . where's everybody off to, ya think?"

Bea huffed at the lies. Ben likely hadn't seen anyone in hours. "I don't know. But you and I have a deal, Ben. No using while filming. Did you forget?"

It was an agreement she knew that Ben could never keep, but was useful for guilting him into leaving any rave. Bea sat beside him and helped Ben into the black hooded sweatshirt. She pulled a baseball cap and sunglasses from her messenger bag to obscure his identity. Yes, it marked him as someone with an identity to hide, but, more often than not, the press upgraded the story to include a celebrity with a profitable identity. Truth had little value when it came to good gossip.

"Sorry, Bea. Won't happen again. Never again." Ben's teeth chattered.

"Nope. It won't. Rudy is outside waiting."

"I fired that asswipe!"

"You can't fire him. He works for me. His official responsibility is to rescue your career."

"I don't need his help. I'm big again. My agent says I have offers. Lots of offers. I can manage myself. I was just leaving . . . soon as I find the girls." Ben's voice trailed off, his eyes unfocused again.

"Now, Ben. I need you to leave now. Royce Rudkins is en route. I can't have the CEO of the BBC find our romantic lead shooting up in a dark corner. He'd up our insurance premium or fire you—probably fire all of us. So I need you out now."

Ben nodded, but he was bottoming fast. A tear slipped down his cheek. She was about to have 240 pounds of immovable muscle on her hands.

Bea tugged his arm and begged. Eventually, Ben tried to stand, but he lost his balance and stumbled into Bea. She smacked into the table. The edge dug hard into her hip, and her hand went down on the hot spoon. She swallowed a curse as she rotated to land firmly on her butt, more frustrated than hurt.

Just once, she'd like Kat to be the one burnt and bruised in their show's honor. But Kat would simply fire Ben. She'd ruin the whole romantic arc of the show and leave Ben hopeless and destitute. So Bea endured her injuries. She sucked the palm of her hand as she scrambled to her feet, taking Ben's hand to guide him to the back door where Rudy waited.

"Three days max, Rudy."

"He'll be there." Rudy pulled Ben's arm over his shoulder, rolling his eyes as Ben launched a tirade of curses and complaints.

Bea slipped back into the crowd. For the first time, she took in the atmosphere. Laser beams flickered along smoke trails. Black lights backlit bars, stages, and platforms. Topless dancers gyrated on crates hung from the ceiling as lithe acrobats peddled lust with pole routines in suspended gravity. The last time she'd gone out for fun, party-goers pounded drums soaked in neon paint—a passé practice for at least five years.

Nicola waved, in a panic, from the dais. Charlie had upended a table. Tonight was definitely not about fun. Bea grabbed a soda on ice to soothe her palm and give her a weapon. A childhood defending herself against four brothers, all athletic and double her size, had given her wicked good aim and plenty of temper. Charlie would likely experience both tonight.

♦ ♦ ♦

Kat

This week has gone completely to shit. Quinn got the flu, then Ben went MIA, and Anna and Nic both took a whole morning off over some brawl at a nightclub. Even Corinne got in on it all when an attack of the shingles left her grimacing through every scene. Only Jamie and Ian have been fit for work. Bea handled all the PR and got budget and schedule worked out, thank the gods, but now I'm antsy. Ian's only on set one more week, and I'm not cutting or revamping storyline because the world got draped in a red and white tent and taken over by clowns with Ben as emcee.

Ben bursts into the conference room, ahead of the other actors, for a script read-through that will conclude this twisted-circus workweek. The great galumphing idiot sits on my lap and almost knocks me over with coffee still in my hand. "Come pubbing tonight. I found a cool new karaoke place full of bad liquor and worse women."

"Not today. We're both on set late, and then early tomorrow." I punch him in the arm. Stupid big brother I never had. He looks tired, though, even after a few free days. We're all a bit spent. Bea has us running at an insane pace to get Ian off set before we run out of money.

"But you've got to come. I've almost got Quinn agreed to give you a toss. It's taken some doing, because she's a bit distracted by Ian. But you're next in line. Says she won't be able to have you shagged good and proper for a few weeks at least, though, sorry 'bout that."

"She said no such thing, Ben. Never."

"She did." Jamie insists, then laments. "I'm fifth in line. Corinne bested me. Quinn will shag the old woman before me."

"You guys need to leave Quinn be. She's allowed not to have sex between relationships. It's what most of us do. Apart from that, Quinn and I are incompatible, so this fantasy of yours is never happening."

Ben pushes his armpit in my face and I huff-laugh while I try to push him away. My protests come out a garbled mix of giggles. Ben is an idiot, but I adore him over the moon and halfway back.

"Who needs compatibility in sex? You just lay down and let the fun happen. See, you're good at it."

"Maybe." I punch him again, this time hard enough that he stops goofing off. "Everything is so fluid. Tumblr tells me I have a new sexual identity every week."

Adorable, exasperating Ben. He pulls his feet up to try and sit quietly in my lap like a child even though he's almost a giant. The chair would tip over if Jamie weren't sweet enough to stand behind us and keep me from toppling. Behind Jamie, all the other actors file in.

"Quinnie could change your mind. She's hot," Ben says and licks my ear like a dog. He's super disgusting, so why am I laughing so hard?

But when he paws my shoulder, I can't help but wince. "Ouch!"

Ben stops goofing around. He pulls at the collar of my shirt. "Wait. Did you—is it done?"

"Yes." My biggest tattoo yet, a work of art, really. Three painful hours last night finished it.

"Ooh, show me, show me, show me." The chant rolls around the crowd.

"I hate you all," I gripe without meaning. I pull my shirt up and frame the tattoo with my hands.

I'm proud of my ink, the care I've put into the art of marking my achievements and dreams on my skin. There's a cluster of music symbols on my left shoulder blade, to commemorate graduating with my degree in vocal performance. The inside of my left wrist bears an infinity symbol edged on one side with Air Force wings, as a remembrance for my father. A delicate half armband of London's classic Thames skyline sits above my right elbow, because, well—London, duh. And my life's motto is written along my spine. And now I've added this—

The planets, in their order from the sun, starting at my shoulder. Saturn's rings graze my collarbone, and Pluto hovers below the inside line of my neck. It's covered by most tops, but will pop gloriously if I ever go strapless. It'll be the geeky edge to my future Oscar ballgown.

But the tatt reveal turns my perfectly respectable and boring script read-through into a sexy train wreck. Everyone starts talking tattoos and taking off clothes to demonstrate their art.

Sweet, adorable, gray-haired Corinne stands up and pulls down one side of her slim trousers to reveal a tattoo on her right hip—the color's faded, but it's a beautiful, elaborate floral design, just small enough to be hidden by a swimming suit and most underthings.

"Oh! That's lovely!" Anna exclaims. "And to think we all thought you so sweet and—"

"Old?" Corinne laughs. "We all have our secrets and surprises, darling."

Ben goes shirtless to flex his biceps and make his tattoo jump—a tribal armband that looks like rows of shark teeth, almost certainly the result of a drunken evening.

Quinn pulls up the side of her top to show a small flight of birds on her ribcage, elegant and well-hidden. "And that's all you get to see, you perv," she says to Ben.

"That hurts, Quinnie. Deep down."

Anna shuts Ben up when she pulls down the back of her jeans to uncover a butterfly tramp stamp. "Cliché, I know, but I love it."

Ian has been silent, sitting to my left with his finger rubbing his lower lip. I stare at Ian, wondering, hoping. He stares right back and it steals my breath—deliberate, long-held eye contact. He slowly undoes the buttons of his shirt and shucks it on the table next to mine. *Albu gu Bràth*—Scotland Forever—is written across the top of his right arm in sapphire blue. Is the text deliberately colored to match his eyes or did it magically match on cue?

If Bea ever arrives, she will eviscerate me on the spot, but I don't care. Ian Graham showed me his tattoo. Me. Not the whole room. I was—am—his singular focus.

"Only one tattoo on each of you lot? Sad, so sad," Corinne teases. "Kat's the only rebel soul among you."

"Not true. I've another." Ian pops the button on his jeans, and then pushes down denim and cotton—boxer briefs—oh hell—to reveal black lettering along the inside edge of pelvic bone.

fuck off

It's so deliciously, hilariously sexy. And provocative. Right there on that cut of muscle that exists on men just to make us think of following its path down, down.

Oh, I *want* him. More than ambition or artistry dictate. I want a memory. A hot, sexy, real memory.

Ian Graham slept with every female on the set of *Green Commando* between wives two and three, so why not me right here at the tail end of three? He's almost divorced. Just paperwork. What would be so wrong with having an on-set fling with Ian Graham?—what fun it would be, and the gods know I need some. I deserve it—I work hard, I've earned some pleasure.

And his eyes say he wants me, too, the way they travel up and down and linger on my tattoos while he touches his tongue to his bottom lip.

"Turn around. Let me see the words on your back," he says. My throat shouldn't be this dry, not in a business meeting. But Ian's voice dropped half an octave, an inviting octave, so I rotate on command. My skin pricks and pringles as though the look on Ian's face is being engraved across my thighs while I allow Ian to read *fear is the mind-killer* along my tingling spine.

A sharp rap against the glass behind me spoils my glow. Bea glares through the window into the conference room. Nicola stands behind Bea and next to her—oh, *shit.* One of the BBC suits from marketing and an exec from Hearts Afire.

If looks could kill, I would be so dead. Disgust flits over Bea's features before her imperturbable businesswoman face returns. She dismisses the suits with something pithy enough that the men laugh and give us a thumbs up.

The she pushes open the door, all seriousness. Stoic, controlled Bea.

"What about you, Bea? Got some ink to show?" Ben asks and I can barely stop myself from laughing.

"If I do, it's not for your eyes. Show and tell has ended. Clothes in place and script at the ready, please. Perhaps our Executive Producer would like to be first to set the example."

Clothes fall back into place as Nicola passes out stapled pages. Bea's furious eyes lock on me to give an entire shame-filled lecture in a single look.

She takes my usual place to start the meeting. "This is a working draft so there may be editing as we go. Just stay with us and it'll come together. Lots of set direction, so start on page three. Quinn, you're up first."

CHAPTER 4

Sonst ist licht- und farblos
Alles um mich her,
Nach der Schwestern Spiele
Nicht begehr' ich mehr,

All else dark and colorless
everywhere around me,
for the games of my sisters
I no longer yearn

—Robert Schumann, Frauenliebe und -leben

Bea

Bea barely made it through the meeting before her rage exploded. She walked out of the meeting, strolled out the main door of BBC, and continued on to the Tube and to her apartment. Of all the ridiculous, horrendous, and unprofessional moments in her ridiculous, horrendous, previously professional life.

Kat had blown their budget on her sex life. Their precious, barely-adequate, almost-running-red budget had been gouged so Katrine could play out a fantasy she'd held since she was old enough to think about sex. Maybe this whole damn season had been about Kat's sex life. The guest stars and the location shoots and the lusty, illicit Englishman were all Kat's creative doing.

The door slammed behind her as she stomped across the room to throw open the connecting door to Kat's apartment. Every concession Bea had made in the past five years tumbled over each other to ignite new burns in a forest of resentment. *Live in London, Bea, thousands of miles from family. Leave your career, Bea. Make TV with me, Bea. Do the business-y stuff I hate, Bea. Rescue Ben and learn how to score street drugs, Bea. Make deals with tabloid reporters and know every sordid detail and goings-on in London to keep our business safe, Bea. Help me succeed, Bea. Because I want to screw Ian Graham, the most gag-worthy man to ever sink between a woman's legs. So give up your life to make it happen, Bea.*

Designer clothes and a brand new iBook covered in paranormal TV show stickers were the only testaments to her high-stakes job title. She lived a pauper's life behind her expensive fabrics. The apartment walls and floor were bare except for a gray sofa, a Kitty-Cat clock, and an old projection-style TV attached to a DVR. Otherwise, she was the sad single girl in a big, cruel city. No, she was worse off than that. She was the supportive best friend to the plucky single girl—the most forgettable role in any romantic comedy.

Kat entered the apartment more than two hours later. There had been after-work drinks, judging by Kat's flushed cheeks and loose-limbed movements. She sang to herself as she put her bag away and then crossed to the couch to flop on her back with a giggle.

She *giggled.*

Bea walked through the connecting door and banged it off the wall with a satisfying boom.

"What is going on with you, Katrine?! That spectacle in the boardroom? What in the world were you thinking?"

Kat sat up. Her head popped up from the couch like a mole in an arcade game. Bea half-wished for a mallet.

"Huh? Didn't see you there, did you leave right after the meeting?"

"Yeah. I left. Didn't want to get in the way of whatever the hell comes after naked boardroom games."

Bea leaned over the side of the couch. Kat stared back, eye-to-eye despite their different postures.

"What are you—the tattoos? Nobody was naked." Kat gave a *pfft* of dismissal.

Bea's tight voice hissed through clenched teeth. "Go to the bathroom, Kat, and look at that bra in the light. Then try that statement again."

"What are you on about? It was just silliness, a bit of fun. Harmless." Kat stood up and towered above Bea.

Age-old anger at being so short whipped Bea's fire like a fierce west wind. "A sponsor and the VP of Marketing saw your little stunt! That's not harmless. That's a million miles from harmless. We could lose our tiny amount of support from the network if we're nothing but a group of sex-crazed buffoons standing around naked in a conference room."

"They laughed. I saw it. Both the stupid suits laughed and gave us a big thumbs up. So what's the fuss?" Kat crossed to the tiny galley kitchen without a glance at Bea.

Icy tendrils shoved aside the rage. How could Kat be so foolish? "We can't look like the young, dumb women ninety percent of them think we are."

"It was fun," Kat countered. "I got a few compliments on my ink, by the way. Fun and compliments happen when you're not always trying to be *the boss.*" Kat retrieved a glass and slammed a cupboard.

"Especially important not to be the boss when Ian is around, right? Can't be the boss then or he might not be willing to screw you before he goes."

Kat whipped around from the fridge, slamming a bottle of wine down on the counter. "Do you understand the kind of career bump people get when Ian Graham decides he likes them or their work? The kind of career bump *we* can get if Ian enjoys *21 Things* enough to want to work with us again? That's what I'm after. So I flirted with him, and I will keep on flirting. Because he is a career maker." Kat poured a large glass of wine.

Bea shook her head. "When did you become this person who gives a guy anything he wants—starting with the crazy salary and ridiculous on-set accommodations and ending with you in his bed."

"Maybe it's who I've always been." Kat shrugged and took a sip of wine, projecting an unsettling and unfamiliar cold insouciance.

"I thought I was used to all-different London you, but I believed there were some lines you wouldn't cross. We're supposed to be building a career together, the right way, not with loads of Machiavellian crap."

"God, Bea. You've got to grow up, sometime. I'd hoped getting you out of Utah would teach you a little about how the world really works. There's nothing devious about like-minded artists helping each other out. And if there's time and space for a little extracurricular activity . . ." Kat smirked over her glass.

"I imagine there will be. *Later.*" Bea said the word purposefully. Exaggerated. As Ian had done when his shirt went back on.

"Oh, my god. Ian committed sexual *entendre*. Put him in the stocks right now." Katrine flopped down on her couch and set her glass on top of a stack of books that served as a side table catch-all.

Bea forced her rage at Kat's nonchalance into something more metered—yelling at Kat never helped. "And that tattoo. Who puts that on their pelvis? Either he needs to inform the unfortunate souls who find it of his intent or he's just enough of an asshole to send that message to the stupid girl who screws him."

"My hell, Bea. Get a sense of humor."

"It's not funny. How could that be funny? And now you're going to sleep with him. I can't decide which is worse—that you're going to do it for career advancement or because you actually want to. I have never met such a raging asshole in my entire life. And you like it. I'm living a nightmare, an absolute nightmare."

"You don't have to like it. I like it. And I like him, and the twenty thousand new followers we got after Ian raved about us on Twitter. If that's a crime, then put me in the stocks, too." Kat put her hands out, wrists up, as if waiting for handcuffs.

"Fine. Do whatever you want. Just not on my boardroom table in the middle of a business meeting."

"It's not *your* table. And I'm doing this for *us*, for our show, for our careers."

"No, I don't think you are."

"Think what you want. Ian will be gone in a few days, anyway. But watch our ratings soar when this season airs. You'll thank me then for hiring him."

"Highly. Doubtful." Bea bit out the words and stepped with purpose toward her own space.

"Why do you have to be so damn self-righteous about this?" Bea kept her trajectory as Kat continued to rage. "You know what—just—fuck you, Bea. Just—"

Bea slammed and locked the connecting door. Through the door she heard books hitting a wall and Kat screaming curses.

Bea moved beyond the reach of the sound to her bedroom. Let Kat curse. Let Ian get paid for those Twitter followers. None of this was real anyway, only a stupid side stop on the way to her own ambitions: a baby of her own. A life freed from the need to please Kat or get permission from anyone. She'd have a comfortable, stable life doing good somewhere with a baby on her hip. She'd exist for herself, not as Kat's accessory. Never again as someone's accessory.

So let Kat be Hollywood and wrap her legs around who she thought would best promote her. Bea sat against a wall, surrounded by Dior and McCartney and a dozen other designers to work herself step by step toward a life she'd earned.

♦ ♦ ♦

Kat

The argument sticks to my apartment walls. Headphones won't block its endless repeat. Every time Bea makes any kind of noise, a spurt of bile restarts my desire to scream at her. She had no right to shame me. None at all. I don't need her small-town morality. I'd rather be hung than spend a minute in Bea's hometown.

So, no. I'm not ready to make nice and be professional. Let Bea hang on her own super-rule-following plans laid out by the suits. I didn't get here by following the rules. I got here by breaking them all. I networked my way through BBC at thirteen, worked on set design by the time I was fifteen, sent a homemade audition tape to the top performing arts high school in Los Angeles in lieu of application—before my dad had secured a transfer to

Edwards—and then I used my singing talent to get a scholarship so I could make Meg follow through on her *get a degree and I'll give you an internship* promise. And then I wrote a series that no one could ignore. I don't need rules, Bea. I need creativity. I need wild. I need art.

I'm not ready to give up on my über-ambitious plan or the fire in my heart. And fuck Bea for making a little flirtation with Ian feel wrong. So it's heart versus gut, split like a comic-book hero, with a splitting headache to boot. I resent the hell out of the idea that I shouldn't do what I need to get what I want, and Bea for calling me on it. The knot bounces around, twists me into a restless discomfort.

My dad's flag sits on the shelf next to my phone. At times like these, he calls for me. When he calls, I go. The only rule I follow, the only label that sticks: I'm daddy's little girl.

A lamp lights my stumble to the bathroom as quietly as I can to clean up the mascara smeared under my eyes, brush my teeth, and decide my hair will do fine if I put on a beanie. A couple outfits stuff into a bag along with my laptop and usual messenger bag stuff. *Dune* comes off my pile of comfort books to join the laptop.

By the time Bea wakes, I'll be on a train from St. Pancras, heading to Kaiserslautern. Germany, the next closest thing to home, where my dad was stationed until we moved to England in my preteen years.

I message Nicola and Bea, *Taking a retreat, need inspiration. Ralph has all the notes.* It's known code for *Kat will surface from her latest artistic fit when she's good and ready.*

Bea doesn't respond, but Nic sends me back a revised production schedule. Another one. This season has degraded from circus to poorly run carnival at the mall. But that's Bea's problem to solve right now.

The train speeds southeast into a wan late autumn sunrise. England rushes by as I scroll through music, trying to find a suitable sound to play against my frazzled edges. Finally, an old playlist from college hits me just right. It's the soundtrack of an easier life when I was a student musician, my father was alive, and I had just met Bea Douglas, my soon-to-be best friend.

The day I met Bea replaces the countryside as landscape for this trip. I was practicing my French when I first saw her. French, the impossible language, with its nasal vowels and endless rules—ugh. I was standing in front of a mirror to rehearse Debussy, with focus on shaping my mouth while maintaining a legato line from word to word.

A pile of unpacked DVDs sat next to the entertainment center in my last college apartment in the now-forgotten town of Logan, Utah. Not my first choice, but a scholarship is a scholarship when your dad is in the military, and this one was a good one. Full ride. Plus travel expenses for events and a small living stipend. All I had to do was pretend that I intended an opera career.

My other roommates had gone to the grocery store to stock up on basics, mainly the all-essential ice cream, for Girls' Movie Night. This was supposed to be our stellar senior year, an apartment full of music and musicians, but then one of our planned quartet up and married on us over the summer. She'd only gone on one date with the guy before school ended in May, but Utah girls rushed to marriage. Turning twenty-two unmarried was the greatest of all earthly sins. So my other roommates and I had a drink and a laugh at the game of matrimonial duck-duck-goose constantly underway. Then we pinned up a *roommate wanted* ad in the lobby.

Bea pulled that ad and seemed a great fit. I only hoped she'd not be bothered by three people who sang all the time and had a box of wine in the refrigerator.

As I finally mastered a tough word in French, a commotion at the door demanded attention—a chorus of male voices as if an entire frat house had come to visit. I rushed to the top of the small set of stairs down to our door and counted them as they entered—nine people, a conglomerate noisy unit of obvious family, each carrying something, all talking over each other, like something from *The Sound of Music*.

"Hey, I'm Kat." I always felt awkward meeting new people, roommates especially, since my quirks made me a less-than-desirable housemate. All I saw were parents and boys, until the shortest member of the troupe stepped forward—short, red-headed, laughing.

One of the boys spoke over her, his elbow rubbing hard into her head. "This is our little sister, Bea. We're here to help her settle in and make sure she knows where her classes are. Do you have chocolate milk? Wittle thing is thirsty from the drive."

Another boy—brother—interrupted my attempt to shake Bea's hand. "I'd be happy to show you around. I'm a business major. The name's Alex. I live in the next building."

"Oh, business. Nice. I'm music. We all are. Except, sorry—Bea, like the letter?" Large families often threw me off-balance. I had such a small one: Dad, me, and my sister, Rachel.

"Oh, shut up. Everyone. She's trying to meet me. I'm Bea. B-e-a, like Bea Arthur."

"Actually, it's Beatrice. Like Shakespeare." A lovely, older woman stepped forward. She was so like Bea that they even mirrored posture. "Nice to meet you, Kat. Ignore my boys. I failed them as a mother." She looked at the boys. "Get your sister settled. You insisted on coming, so be useful." The group filed past. Bea's father shook my hand with both of his, sincerity radiating in his eyes.

When we were alone, Bea rolled her eyes. "Sorry about them. Good intentions and all."

"They seem really nice. So, what's your major?"

"Nursing. Final year, taking max credit hours. I won't be around much, so don't worry about bothering me." She grinned and headed up the stairs, shouting directions and taunts at the handsome giants unpacking her things.

Max credit hours, studious, and driven. Bea was going to be a great roommate.

When she passed my room later, I called to her. Her flaming red hair that had been pinned up when we met fell in a long braid that licked her bottom rib.

"Hey, it's movie night. Want to join us? We're doing Bollywood."

"Great dance sequences," Bea said.

The red-headed brother draped over her. "Bea's a dancer. But she's too old now. She's got a rheumatism in her hip."

Bea elbowed her brother. "I'd love to, but I need to grab dinner with this crew. I'll stop in and say hi once I've had the police escort them from town." Her arm linked her sibling's and they started to pull faces at each other.

Bea's dad's head poked around the door frame. "Good to meet you. Do you need help with anything?"

"Oh. No. I'm good, thanks."

Then they were all gone. Come and gone in twenty minutes. The Douglas family hits hard and fast and you're never quite the same.

A few hours later, after too much chocolate and Bollywood, all I wanted was the approval of the sharp, smart rookie who loved movies and TV almost as much as I did. Bea sat with me on the couch, her legs pulled under her and an elastic in her teeth as she rebraided her hair for the third time.

We were the last ones up, still exclaiming over favorite shows and mythologies in between sharing histories and family stories. Bea had that weird thing I'd never understood—everyone who met her became her immediate friend. We'd had to pause the movie three times because one or the other of us couldn't stop telling Bea some vital detail of our lives.

"So what's next for you, Kat? Where you off to after Logan, Utah?" Bea smiled around the rubber band and I wanted to tell her all the things.

"I love music, I love singing, I really do. But my real love is film—screenwriting, actually. When I graduate I'm moving to London to work in TV. Promise not to tell my advisor, even if we end up mortal roommate enemies?" I bit my lip and waited for Bea's response. Then I told her all about Meg and Marian and my big plans.

"That's incredible. All my contacts would get me as far as the grand metropolis of Idaho Falls."

In that moment, I realized that Bea had listened to everyone's stories and told none of her own. I knew what I'd known in a single glance. She was short, red-headed, nice, and had a good sense of humor.

I looked at the clock. Two a.m. Over the next months, it would become our magic hour. Bea never slept and I'd sleep 'til midday so we could talk a few hours when everything else was silent.

After my dad died, Bea moved into the hole marked *family*. My sister had distanced herself from our family a long time ago, but Bea had never failed me. Not once.

And last night I'd cursed and screamed at her, all in defense of a plan more mercenary than even my music performance scholarship had been. That had been about paying for school, graduating without any student debt so I could run off to London and work for beans to make my dreams come true. Ian, though—my pursuit of Ian Graham is a tangle. It's part ambition, part lust, and all thoroughly disapproved by the one person who really matters.

The cool glass where I rest my head calls me back to the present. The train ride has offered no solutions, unfortunately, only an arrival at a destination I always forget is fraught until I'm here.

A funny thing happens whenever I come back to Germany—I start looking for my mother. I never knew her; she left us mere months after I was born. She was an artist, and the life of a military *Hausfrau* was not for her. I could find her, it wouldn't be that hard—some kind of online profile at the least. But I always stop before hitting *go* on a search for Renate Erbe. Instead, I scan crowds and look for my older, traitorous doppelganger.

The taxi driver delivers me to the *Gasthaus* with the best schnitzel within 20 kilometers, as requested. I pay for a tiny room and a generous meal, and then I people-watch, scribbling down impressions and overheard snatches of conversation from locals, tourists, soldiers, and airmen.

A lightning bolt of inspiration sparks an idea for a new story to tell—a show about the off-base lives of a close-knit group of military friends. The intertwining tales unfold in my head, full of humor and love and everything that drives good TV.

The rest of the days that Ian will be on set pass with me buried in a laptop, writing a pilot good enough for an American network because the next stop on my journey is the big-time: Los Angeles.

CHAPTER 5

"I feel my heart glow with an enthusiasm which elevates me to heaven, for nothing contributes so much to tranquilize the mind as a steady purpose—a point on which the soul may fix its intellectual eye."

—Mary Shelley, Frankenstein

Kat

A week later, I knock on Bea's open office door and close it behind me before she can look up from her computer. "So, who wants to be friends again?"

It's been too many days with the combatants retreated to their respective corners. I've knocked on Bea's apartment every night since I returned from Germany, but she's not there—she's been at the refugee clinic, where she goes when life turns bad. When I'm not writing like a dervish, I'm full of abject misery.

Which is why I've practiced an apology that I hope will tumble the wall between us. "The tattoo thing was stupid. No matter how it started, I know it looked terrible. I did everything you said. I spent money on a guest star to chase success in all the wrong ways. If we can't make it on our merits, it's not worth it. You were right."

Bea blinks at me, the only crack in her neutral nonconfrontational face. Then she melts. She won't make this hard. She never does.

"We've worked so hard, Kat. If the rumor reaches the board, they'll shut us down. We can't be that show." Bea sighs—deep, from her soul. "But I'm sorry, too. I overreacted."

I hug her without warning. I want it all the way over. Bea's not a hugger, not unless she's applying comfort like medicine, but she takes none herself, so this kind of mutual affection feels like cuddling a street cat.

Bea pushes back and holds my shoulders. She looks at me, reading me, her head tilted to the side. "And how was Germany?"

"It was fine, I'm fine. Still on the rails, I promise." I cough to cover up the threat of tears.

Bea talks to her mom every day, and the whole family pops in for a video chat at least once a week. My lack of family has always struck her as a great sadness, a heartbreak I know she carries for me all the time.

"Anyway, I think I'm giving up on men for a while," I lie. I'll never give up on love, it's the only thing that thrills me as much as my art.

"Sure you are," Bea laughs, but lets me have my game.

"And in my spinster state, I've decided you need a date. My gift to you. Want me to set you up with Wayne? He still captures more *accidental* footage of you than anyone else."

Bea shudders and crosses her arms in front of herself. She never dates, never. "Will I get to go back to giving up on romance in twenty-four hours when you forget your vow of celibacy?"

I snort with laughter.

Bea puts her arm around me and I lean onto her shorter shoulder. "We okay again? I miss being okay. Feels like it's been a long time."

"Yeah, we're good. Better than. We've got each other and we've got *21 Things*. And something new, actually." I bring up the paper-clipped stack of papers from my side. "I know every idea for post–*21 Things* has been rejected thus far, but I think this is the one."

"Ideas are good," Bea prevaricates and reads the title page. "What's *K-Town*?"

"It's what all the military people there call Kaiserslautern and the surrounding posts and bases."

"So, military . . . drama? Judging by the number of pages? In Europe?"

"Full-hour comedy with a dash of drama. Dramedy, though I will deny ever saying that word. Edgy. Real people, real lives."

"This sounds like an excuse for you to watch hot men in uniform. Can I nix any actors you've fangirled? Maybe I should do casting."

"Stop. Ian was good for the show. But, yes, you can have casting privileges if you like the pilot script."

Bea chews that spot on her lip, the one that bleeds sometimes. "Kat, I don't have the talent for anything beyond *21 Things*. This was magic."

"Of course you have the talent! What are you talking about? You make money drip out of advertiser pockets!"

"I'll do what I can. You create. Tell me where you want it. If Anna wins—"

"LA. An American network. It's going to be possible. Because we are going to get nominated and we're going to awards shows and we're going to have *it-quality buzz*. And then—National Network. National is where this show belongs."

Bea nods and bites her lip hard. I'm not surprised to see a slight red stain on her teeth. "Let's think on it. We might have something else. Something I've been too in denial to even touch."

Bea crosses back to her desk and opens a drawer. "Remember gushing all over Josh Dewson a while ago? It was at one of our first industry events. You spitballed at the table about how you wished you could time travel back to *Les Mis* and tell them all to shut the eff up? You were pretty drunk by that point."

"Yeah, I remember. Mostly how very embarrassed I was the next day."

"Well, you got your wish." Bea pulls out a manila envelope and holds it out to me. "One time travel back to the French Revolution–era courtesy of Josh Dewson. It's all concept at this point, but it's solid and he has funding."

"You're kidding me."

"He wants us. You, most likely."

"How long have you had this? Oh my god, Bea. Josh Dewson is a god in this business."

"Told you I've been in denial. But I talked to him last week. Problem is, he wants to film this spring and write as he goes. And it's big. Omega

Network, filming in Vancouver. So we have to think about it. I know *21 Things* won't last forever, but adding two shows right now?"

I flip through the pages of Josh's pitch. "This is brilliant. He got all of this from my drunken *Les Mis* hate?"

"So he says. I don't love the script pieces. Too formulaic. But I'm hoping he just sent this out for funding and has better ideas for actual production. He says he's ready to cast in January and film in February or March. Just wants us on board."

"He could have just taken it, the idea, and run with it. But he didn't. Oh, I have chills." Every dream bursts out of me, big and real and alive. "This is our leap. Our big opportunity. We diversify. We are on our way, Bea. On. Our. Way."

"Let's see what we actually land first. The military thing would have to be ready for pilot season." Bea dives back into her computer. "We'll need meetings in LA. And I need John on publicity. Could you have Nic find him? I need an update on our awards buzz and to see what he thinks of our options."

She's headed into terrifying multitasking territory so I leave her to it. Outside her office, I twirl once. It's here. Our moment. And I believe. In art, awards, the future, in everything.

I believe.

♦ ♦ ♦

Bea

Bea ran her eyes over her new budget projections, waiting for her brain to identify the out-of-order expense among the long list. The two weeks since Kat had announced the diversification plan had all but killed her. Kat wanted Los Angeles, where sharks circled up to eat young, female blood and then spit the remainder back onshore.

Bea called Meg every day for advice, at a loss as to how to move this plan forward. You didn't just call up major networks to ask for a pitch meeting. There were a million steps between idea and pitch, and Bea didn't know the first three. This morning, she'd met with John to discuss PR plans to heighten their visibility and move pitch meeting likelihood from impossible to improbable. Pretty much everything hinged on whether they scored a Golden Globe nomination at the announcement this afternoon.

Halfway through the day, the door flew open to reveal a disheveled and breathless Kat. "It's almost time. Stop what you're doing and open the website."

Bea shifted focus from revenue spreadsheets to Kat, whose hair sat on edge. She'd obviously run her hands through it a dozen times in anxious anticipation.

Kat paced in front of the desk and checked her phone. "I set five alarms and it's almost time and we have to watch. But what if it's bad luck to watch?"

"It's not bad luck. Everyone watches. People who say they don't are liars. So relax. If it's meant to be, it happens. If not, we keep working."

Bea closed her spreadsheet. Nothing to do but endure Kat's anxiety and subsequent superstitions. That was her role, to do the things Kat couldn't do well, like wait patiently or play the schmooze game with the men with big pockets. Kat was fine with artist types, but when the talk turned to money and what makes money, Kat broke out in angry hives.

Kat wore her lucky Star Trek tee, the one she'd worn the day she got the letter from Meg confirming her internship and the one she'd been wearing when Meg called to say *21 Things* got the green light for production. She probably had on the same underwear and socks from those days, too. Kat had superstitions for everything, as any good artist must.

Kat played with the Orion perpetual motion machine that spun a tiny cosmos on Bea's desk. The gift from Kat twirled as an endless reminder that she was a small piece of a much larger plan. Kat reversed the spin, then watched as it righted itself. Everything back in order. Always. No matter how many times she flicked a tiny planet, the orbits always realigned.

Kat sighed at her third attempt to disrupt the galaxy. "John insists our buzz is good, but I swear I don't even know what that *means* anymore."

John spoke up from the doorway. "It means our buzz is good, and the Hollywood Foreign Press Association set visit last month went very well. Fingers crossed as to how that turns out." Kat jumped. Somehow, she'd not noticed him. He took a seat in one of the large leather box chairs opposite the desk.

Bea envied John's cool unflappable manner. He used little space, contained each emotion. He'd react the same no matter the outcome to this crazy plan. He had made this happen somehow, transitioned from *no, Kat, not this soon* to quietly confident.

A fine, honorable line separated courting the HFPA and outright bribery. Bea wasn't sure which John had employed, but she'd followed all of John's instructions to the letter. Every bit of press had been carefully managed with Kat out in front to charm. Bea stayed in the back to make the deals. And each actor paraded about at the right events and said the perfect things.

John rested his chin on steepled fingers while Kat changed position every few minutes. They waited for the now-blank live feed to roar to life on Bea's computer.

"Still not on, seriously?" Kat gestured at the screen. She checked her phone again.

John's fingers flew across the face of his phone. "Nothing trending yet. No mentions anywhere."

Bea opened a mobile app for a local affiliate in Los Angeles. "Nothing's started yet. The live TV feed still shows the weather and traffic. LA is obsessed with the weather and traffic. Every ten minutes, there's an update about how much hasn't changed in ten minutes. Or three hours. Weather still good. Traffic still bad."

John sat back and slid his phone under his leg. "Globes behind the scenes tweeted the nominations are on deck. It's time."

The door to Bea's office pushed open. "May I intrude?" Meg stepped in.

"Oh my god. Yes, yes!" Kat rushed to embrace Meg. "Our good luck charm has arrived."

Meg smiled at everyone. "Is this really happening, John? You're that confident?"

John stood and gave Meg his seat. "Every time I talk to a member of HFPA, the show comes up of its own accord. The buzz is right."

"We've had a lot of buzz over the years for too few nominations."

John tapped his fingers against the desk. "I'm hoping today is the day." The Globes were a game; it was all a game. Place the pieces and watch the strategy unfold.

The computer buzzed as the screen switched to the live feed. An older, accented reporter introduced the proceedings, then gave the first announcements of nominations to this year's up and coming ingénue, Siena Russo, mega chest and mega star on the rise. She was the *femme fatale* of choice in any franchise these days.

"I can't watch," Kat muttered.

Oxygen seemed to disappear from the room, seconds passed like minutes. Each name read out sounded like a record played at the wrong speed.

Meg squeezed Kat's hand. "You've put in the work. The rewards will come."

"From your mouth," Kat breathed.

"Best Performance by an Actress in a Television Series Musical or Comedy . . ." Anna's category.

"Oh my god, oh my god . . ."

The names read off. The usual suspects.

And then Anna.

Kat squealed and hauled Bea up from her chair, to squeal in her face.

"Golden Globes, Golden Globes, I told you, I told you," Kat sing-songed over the subsequent nominations.

"Shh, girls. Anna was the most assured. Let's not miss the rest." John moved forward in his seat. Meg grasped his hand.

Ben's nomination followed quickly after Anna's. Kat's squeal turned into a high-pitched, birdlike squawk.

Maybe they should have had the whole cast in and made an event of this. But the whole gamble had been so uncertain. Bea had wanted everyone to have their private spaces if it all went wrong. She'd not really thought about what she'd want if it all went right.

Best Comedy Series appeared on the ticker tape. Bea bit hard on her lip, enjoyed the burst of pain for the way it centered her and stopped her racing heart.

A scream outside broke the news. Shouts along the hallway and then Meg clapped her hands as *21 Things* scrolled across the screen. John's hand slammed down on the desk with a huge "aha!"

And Kat? Well, she did the Kat thing. She spun Bea around like an off-center top while the office filled up with the entire cast. Ben popped champagne.

"To *21 Things*!" Kat yelled when a glass was in hand.

Bea put down the glass pressed on her. She'd dump it later. She hit play on Kat's favorite celebration playlist for a three-minute dance party. John bowed at Meg and they danced along with everyone else.

Bea hit stop when the song ended. Like it or not, those nominations tripled her workload. She didn't know where to start. Not like she could call a helpline and ask for *the most important person in Burbank* for a meet and greet.

John shooed everyone from Bea's office. "Back to work, everyone. Voting happens as much based on potential as actual content. I want good things in the press." The cast and crew filed out, still jittery and happy at the news.

John tapped on his phone. "And now the press releases are off, including the internal memo. So get your last moments out, Kat. The official remarks start in thirty seconds."

"We're going to Los Angeles. We're gonna wear fancy dresses." Kat returned to giddiness.

"Fifteen seconds, Kat." John's proud grin was wide and excited. His thoughts would be on Marian, his late wife who had befriended an Air Force brat and made John promise, on her last day on earth, to help Kat achieve her dreams in this crazy business.

Kat danced like a preteen watching her first boy band concert. "I cannot be chill in fifteen seconds. I don't think I'll be chill for *years*."

John looked at Bea, his message clear: *You do what Kat can't.* That was Bea's purpose. So she stood and collected herself in time for the first knock.

"Come in, please," Bea called out.

Kat clamped a hand over her mouth and, well—tried to act contained.

Royce Rudkins stuck his ruddy face into the office. "Meg. John. Got the email. Good news, good news. Always knew this little show could do great things."

Royce shook all the hands. Kat's thanks was tinged with sarcasm, but she made it through without giggling.

"We couldn't have done this without you, Royce. We'll count on your influence to see us through the next phase." Bea grinned at Royce and he smiled back.

"Of course. Making some phone calls today. And John, I'll expect a memo. Let me know how to spend my time."

Then Royce was gone. Bea turned to Kat. "Ok. Now you can let whatever you're thinking out before I send you to set. I've got a full afternoon of suits planned."

"Network support? That's such a joke. Except you, Meg. You've made everything possible. Thank you so much." Kat stopped bouncing for a sincere moment.

Meg hugged her again. "You'll be wonderful and charming and adored, sweetie. You always are." Meg looped an arm around Kat's waist. John walked along behind them. They moved as one down the hall. Meg whispered the day's lesson. John nodded in approval.

Bea slid back into her chair. She queued up the show's website and watched the banner change. *Nominated for three Golden Globes.*

But somehow, she couldn't really feel the joy. She wasn't the one carefully mentored. She wasn't the artist. She was an imposter. And one day soon, everyone in Hollywood would know.

CHAPTER 6

Ich kann's nicht fassen, nicht glauben,
Es hat ein Traum mich berückt;

I can't grasp it, nor believe it,
a dream has bewitched me

—Robert Schumann, Frauenliebe und -leben

Kat

The slow crawl up Santa Monica Boulevard separates me foot by tortuous foot from sanity. I'm batty, bonkers, nuts—up on my knees on the seat, my big poofy skirt spread wide around me with my arms raised to let cold air get to my hyperactive sweat glands. The air conditioning vents blow on my armpits with hardly a hint of cooling power.

"What are you doing?" Bea laughs.

"I can't be sweaty on the red carpet! You heard the stylist."

"It's only sixty degrees outside. You won't sweat, especially not in that blouse." Bea sits incredibly upright in her curve-hugging black lace gown while Ben sprawls next to me, risking wrinkles to his tux.

"Sleeveless doesn't mean sweat-proof," I protest.

Ben laughs off my concern and pokes at my ribs. He's so relaxed he yawned a minute ago, a semi-pro at these events thanks to his past big-ticket, small-role Hollywood movie career. Sometimes I wonder why Ben isn't a bigger star, maybe this *laissez-faire* attitude is exactly why.

"Ben! Sit up. We have to look perfect."

Bea hushes me without a look, her eyes on her phone. "Kat, dial it down. All the way down." She resumes the rhythmic tapping as she composes a message. Working. Really, Bea? Now? Bea talks a good game, but she's biting that spot on her lip again. Just as nervous as me. Though, honestly, I've cracked. Headed straight past the Beverly Hills Hilton and on to Crazy Town.

"Cool your jets, Kat." Ben does a decent surfer-dude impression.

That's my date. The lounging surfer dude. Curse the Globes and their miserly provision of tickets. Only ten tickets for our whole production. Jamie got a plus-one because he's married, and the rest came stag.

I had amazing dreams of walking as a group down the red carpet, but when I talked to the cast—crickets. No one wanted to come. Ben was the only member of the cast willing to walk the red carpet of the Golden Globes.

Bea is more press-shy than Punxsutawney Phil 364 days of the year. She's terrified of the worst dressed list, the worst anything list. The idea of the red carpet sent her into a tailspin not even I could pull her out of, and she dug her heels in like a donkey peering over the side of the Grand Canyon. Hell no. She will not go. I begged, pleaded, argued. But no. Once Bea's stubborn streak kicks in, you could die on a starvation strike and she'd shrug off your cause.

And it's ridiculous because she looks hot. Like, men-leave-their-wives kind of hot.

Full-body henna peeks out from under expensive black lace as sheer as Bea's modesty will permit. Her hair is piled on her head in this flirtatious bed head bun with wispy tendrils caressing her neck. She's sleek and sexy—a tame Lady Godiva with wildness held in by a corset.

But Lady Godiva will not ride.

If I had curves like Bea, I would *so* ride.

So here I am, the producer, about to hit the red carpet with one of my actors while the rest of our group slinks in the back door. Entirely unacceptable, but I was overruled.

"My date is obsessed with her armpits," Ben drawls. "Is that what smells in here?"

Bea smugly grins. "You're evil. To your bones. She'll be sniffing next."

I force myself not to sniff. My stylist said to stick, then spray, then stick. I can't remember the last stick.

"There's a definite odor." Ben sniffs. I smell red carpet doom. I angle my suspect armpits closer to the air.

"Bea, do you have extra deodorant? You have to have everything in that bag."

"Ignore Ben. Who knows what all has happened in this limo. Any smell isn't you."

Ben laughs at me as he rolls onto his back. There must be dozens of wrinkles in his tux. I throw my reticule at his mocking face, but he snags it mid-air.

"Oh, you! Leave me alone." I laugh with him, even as I pretend to pout by crossing my arms over my chest.

He tosses my reticule back at me. The small collection of contents jingles as it falls through my hands to the floor. I pick it up and finger the items inside. I've no idea what is supposed to be in a reticule, but I'm guessing smarter people include deodorant. Mine has lip gloss, my hotel key card, ID, a tampon in case stress throws off my cycle, the paper star with my name from my very first opera dressing room—for luck—and hairpins. For no real reason as there are no pins in my hair. The word was on a list in the makeup room so I put hairpins in my reticule.

Ben sits up and scoots beside me. "Seriously, Kat, you need to chill. It'll be more fun."

"Maybe." My stomach growls, reminding me about the silly *no food on live TV* rule. "We're going to miss dinner. All these stupid limos are so slow."

The long, long chain of fancy black cars winds toward the entrance of the red carpet. A chain of zero perceptible movement. We're going to arrive late and be stuck at a table with no food for hours and hours while everyone but us takes home a beautiful, golden, five-pound trophy. I huff and bang the window.

Ben rubs my shoulders with giant, painful circles, not the least bit relaxing. "It's only 3:26 p.m. I can get us through the gauntlet and into our second course before the plates are cleared."

"Punctuality is not one of your strong suits," Bea says.

"She's right. I'm going to starve tonight."

"There will be lots of champagne after the food."

"Drunk instead of starved. Such an improvement." Sarcastic Bea. I don't need sarcastic Bea tonight.

The drop-off zone appears with reporters and gawkers everywhere. My ring-laden fingers discourage me from running my fingers through the artful disarray of curls that is my hair, formed over an hour with a curling iron pressed to my head. Pure torture. All while watching "pre-red-carpet" coverage on television. I know the odds-on favorites for every category. We aren't any of those special people.

And Ian is here. Publicity for his latest action film—and maybe destiny? I'm as nervous about seeing Ian as I am about losing Best Comedy Series to one of those politically edgy, streaming comedies that are all the rage. I fan my armpits and pretend I can do anything but hyperventilate as the limo slows.

A giant golden sign announces where we are. My pulse trips over itself in anticipation. I hope I remembered that second swipe.

♦ ♦ ♦

Bea

Anna wore Givenchy. A divine, flowing white dress that billowed like clouds around her tiny body. She floated toward the stage—gorgeous, ethereal. The *21 Things* table stayed on their feet and applauded while Anna charmed everyone with natural humor.

"Crikey. I don't think I was supposed to win this. Should I check the envelope?"

Laughter sounded amidst the noise of the ballroom. Anna flushed and grinned as she stammered her list of names, a newborn star emitting its first glimmer in the overpopulated night sky.

Ben raised a glass as she disappeared from the stage. "Here's to our girl."

Kat clinked her glass only after Quinn jostled her. Her eyes were wild, on top of the world, but her look was dreamy and not on Anna. Or the table.

Kat craned her neck to get a better look at a recently-unmarried Ian seated three enormous tables ahead of them.

Ian.

No matter what Kat claimed, her plans kept winding back to Ian Graham.

"Well, there it is, folks. Kat only has eyes for Ian. All the way back, everybody." Ben lifted his champagne and chugged it.

"Shut your face, Ben," Kat snarked, but downed her own glass. She giggled as she spilled a bit on her chin. Tipsy Kat. Bea had lost track of how many bottles had passed around the table.

"I've forgotten the rules already, Ben. When do we eat the chocolates we snuck earlier?" Quinn asked, nearly as tipsy as Kat.

"Chocolates are reserved for winking at Ian." Ben clasped his hands and play-acted mad-winking as though a large horsefly had landed in his eye. Everyone laughed so loud that Bea missed another award announcement.

They were irresponsible children, but they were hers. At least they had all stayed at the Beverly Hills Hilton. A drunken stumble would carry them back to their rooms. No need for Bea to manage this many designated drinkers' rides home.

"Could you all be quiet? We'd like to hear some of the most amazing night of our lives. I'll likely never get here again." Jamie leaned across the table.

"Whoop! Drink up again," Ben shouted.

Bea sighed. The Globes were a serious sham of an event, more fun than pomp and circumstance. Old friends milled about chatting. Half the tables were empty, the other half were filled with laughing, drunk Hollywood royalty.

Ben seemed determined to join the latter. She'd already caught him with cocaine. He was jazzed, but manageable. More alcohol, though, could send him straight to impossible. Or to heroin. Either one would be a bad outcome to this night of nights.

"I think we've had enough of this game," Bea said, pleasantly but with a point. "Let's not be the drunkest table in the ballroom."

"Excellent point, Bea." Kat's attention flitted back to the table for a moment. "We still have our category coming up. Can't have you falling off the stage, Ben."

"I'd be following your fine example, boss-lady. How do you manage to fall over Ian at this distance, anyway?" Ben elbowed Kat.

"I'm only looking at him. He's right in my line of sight." Kat demonstrated the angle.

"Because you switched seats. Abandoned Ben and everything," Quinn said.

"And you can still only see him if you lean to your right, squint, and peer through at least four people." Bea couldn't resist a scientific fact.

Jamie's wife, Adhira, leaned in. "Since we're not to hear, I'd like some chocolate. Kat has to wink at him, is that the deal?"

Quinn leaned forward. "And we get the whole tray if he winks back."

Adhira nodded. She stood and smoothed her purple sari back into perfect form. "I can do this. I'm going in." She tucked a strand of long, glossy, black hair behind her ear and turned toward Ian's table. Jamie grabbed at her, but she walked straight toward the front tables as a commercial break counted down on stage.

Adhira was pure guts. Bea adored her, maybe she'd hired Jamie on the pure sign of intelligence that had been demonstrated in his choice of wife.

Ben whistled low. "Damn, Jamie. She just tapped Julia Roberts on the shoulder and asked her to step aside. She's my favorite person ever."

"This is better than Anna winning. That woman is fearless." Quinn leaned further to the left to watch Adhira wind through a frightening array of A-listers.

"There's chocolate?" Kat, the ADHD toddler, returned to reality for a moment. "Why is Adhira with Ian?" Gone again, faded back into Ian's world.

Adhira tapped Ian on the arm—Ian shrugged a dismissal until Adhira pointed at Kat. Broad, deep smile lines formed in his face. Adhira leaned in to whisper and then Ian laughed. He looked at Kat and winked, slow and full of exaggeration, intended for the camera to catch. Adhira leaned down to say something else to him, her delicate hand still on his arm, and he laughed again. Then he pointed to the empty seat next to him.

"I really love my wife," Jamie said as he bit into one of the chocolates Ben placed on the table.

"Oh, sweet, sweet chocolate." Quinn bit down with a blissful sigh. "Ben, I love and hate you right now—bringing contraband chocolates, denying them until sweet Adhira does something insane."

"Sweet Adhira? Jamie, I think you've lost her to the A-listers," Ben said.

Adhira sat at Ian's table, chatting amiably and reaching her small hand out to every famous face.

Jamie shrugged and ate another chocolate. "She always comes back. Tells me she'd never want to train another man."

Bea eyed the chocolates, too self-conscious to eat. She'd been sewn into her dress after being squeezed into a full corset and shapewear worthy of a congressional hearing on torture practices. Her stomach wouldn't allow a sip of water.

Kat reached for the biggest chocolate in the box. "Ooh! Thanks, Ben!" Elegant and able to eat—the gift of a good metabolism and small bone structure.

Adhira wound her way back as the lights flickered to pointlessly inform the crowd that filming would resume. This show was a circus, the only people paying attention to the awards were those that won and those watching at home. No wonder Christine Lahti ended up in the bathroom at the wrong time.

Ian and Kat were having a visual conversation she didn't want to hear, but then Ian tipped his head toward the stage.

Kat snapped to attention. It was time for the pipe dream Bea couldn't even believe was this close to being true. Kat reached out and squeezed Bea's hand. Pain obscured the ongoing ache from the whale bone sticking into her kidneys.

And then they won.

21 Things was announced as this year's best comedy series. Somehow—miraculously, unbelievably—Kat had seen it, made it happen.

Kat tugged her arm and she moved amidst the sea of her ragtag people, their whole group performed an excited, *en masse* stumble to the stage. "Oh, Bea, next stop—the Emmys. I know it. I feel it."

Bea grimaced a little, not enough for viewers to see. All aboard the nonstop, round-the-world, Kat-success express, the only train with no terminal stop. Already, the Golden Globe station faded into the background.

A flash went off in Bea's face. She wished for floppy bangs and a lopsided grin, a moment of shared humor amidst pretense. Instead, the photographer looked past her, as everyone else did. Bea let Kat take the mic for a heartfelt oration.

Bea would do the clean up. She'd speak all the industry names no one knew over top of music no one could hear as some precious Hollywood daughter ushered them off stage toward row after row of eager press who didn't give a crap what she had to say about anything.

♦ ♦ ♦

Kat

The weight of a golden statue in my hands is a fantasy come true, a visualization exercise now realized.

Tonight is for spinning dreams into reality. Do I say that in the press room? Possibly. I feel invincible. This sparkly, effervescent glow permeates every interaction. I laugh. The interviewers laugh. I'm as golden as my trophy.

Bea and I follow an usher back out to the ballroom floor, packed tight with tables and glittering people, past half a dozen hidden hallways. Each moment passes in the simultaneous yet contradictory feelings of time pricked down to its tiniest details, every second a celebration, and the hazy whirlwind of a dream that passes too quickly.

Every everything is possible tonight.

So when I see *him* half-obscured by a potted palm, his broad back clad in a black wool tuxedo jacket pulled perfectly across sinewy shoulders, I know he's for me. My next dream unfolds here.

Ian turns when I call his name. His hand rubs the back of his neck. His head tilts down, but his eyes look up at me. All those deep smile lines are for me. Because he likes me.

The thick taffeta skirt shuffles around me as I walk faster. Ian moistens his lips. Champagne and victory heat my skin. In Ian's space, I slide a hand inside his jacket. Ian in a tux is a delicious dichotomy—luxury and raw masculinity, roughness dressed up in civilized finery.

Ian wraps an arm around my waist to crunch me into acquiescence. The finely drawn breath of space before he kisses me so rich with detail and unforgettable sensation—musk and juniper cologne blended with wine and cigarette breath, the weight of my trophy in my free hand, the tickle of his hair along my brow line as his head descends to mine.

"I won," I whisper against his lips.

"That ye have, lass," he drawls, and my whole lower body quivers. His hand presses into the small of my back. We stop only for air, and then only barely. Maybe we're invisible behind this plant and maybe everyone can see us, and I don't care either way. Because he leads me, hand in hand, past every camera on the way to his table. He makes me Ian Graham's date.

For the rest of the show, I live in a freewheeling stage of public drunkenness, possibly televised—past tipsy or buzzed, past when you've lost count of how many shots or drinks you've downed, but before sloppy or stumbling or stupid—it's glorious fun, a revelatory revel.

Add the contact high from Ian—literal, prolonged contact with intent—and I am free floating through the most amazing new reality. A world where I drink golden champagne with Ian Graham, and he teaches me silly Irish drinking songs.

"Well it's all for me grog, me jolly, jolly grog, it's all for me beer and tobacco," I sing my favorite refrain and delight in Ian's laugh as he pulls me closer to his side.

He kisses my neck behind my ear—whoa, definite erogenous zone there—a touch that curls deep in my stomach as he sings the next line, "And where be my wench, me noggin' noggin' wench."

"She be right here, ye old bastard," I giggle at my made up lyrics. It's just us, me and Ian, as the crowded ballroom slowly empties.

"Aye, so she be. Give us a kiss then, wench?"

"Here? With all these people?" One of my hands finds the line on his body where that deadly sexy tattoo lies.

"Only live once, lass," Ian grins at me.

"Cats have nine lives, haven't you heard? And I claim yours, mortal." One of his hands covers mine where it rests. I'm winning. I hold all the cards. Because Ian wants me, and that isn't just winning—it's won.

So I take my reward. I love the dance of a kiss, the give and take, the way bodies get involved in a thing that starts as only lips. A reality more explosive and addictive than the fantasy I've been high on for fifteen years. I'm going to die of sensory overload as wants and needs twist up together and I'm twined around Ian like ivy, no intention of letting go before I've had all of him.

"Gonna take you to a party, birdy," he says during a pause. My heart skip-starts, jumps. Another fantasy, another win—I'm in. I am Ian's.

CHAPTER 7

Seit ich ihn gesehen,
Glaub' ich blind zu sein;

Since I saw him
I believe myself to be blind

—Robert Schumann, Frauenliebe und -leben

Bea

The tink and titter of the after-party had long ago faded into white noise. Bea and the cast sat amidst strewn jackets and abandoned shoes, worn down by all the excitement. Bea picked the pimentos out of the olives abandoned in martini glasses around the table and formed a pile on the white tablecloth.

Anna slumped forward, fully flat on the table. "My feet. So painful. The conversation worse. How many times do I say I'm surprised? What after that?"

"I'm brilliant and you should hire me?" Bea offered.

"Eh, no. You wrote me the perfect role. I should hand this to you."

"I've got one." Bea pointed at her trophy and then bowled an olive through her stack of pimentos. The red scattered.

Ben's hands covered her shoulders as he sat in a chair pulled close behind her. "Why the long face? Winners remorse, fearless leader?"

"Wanker stole my best friend remorse, more like." Bea scooped her pimentos back together.

"A wanker? I'm much too famous to be a mere wanker, aren't I?" Ben said in an unidentifiable accent as he dropped an arm over Quinn. She looked hot. Her gray sheath dress was almost no dress at all. Dress or no dress didn't matter: Quinn turned heads. She wasn't as talented as Anna, but her looks would keep doors wide open. Ben appreciated every ounce of her, more so in that dress as he openly leered at the gap in the top of the gown.

Quinn pushed Ben off. "Oh, that's not Ian at all. Not even a good Sean Connery."

Ben slouched in front of Quinn, a dead-on impression of Ian in thought. "And who are you? Edwin Drood in Piccadilly, was it? Or my waitress last week? Never mind. I'll bed you anyway. Get over here and let me lick your face."

Ben fell over Quinn in mimic of the oft-told awful snog. Bea held back a laugh as she bowled another set of pimentos.

Jamie reached around to grab Quinn out from under Ben. "Let her up, Ben. She should only have to live through Ian's pawing once."

"Oh, don't make me remember. Worst snog of my life. I could only forget it through hypnosis. My trigger word is wanker. I think of him and then *wanker* and then *poof!* the memory is gone." Quinn giggled and wiggled out from under Ben, but he wrapped both his arms around her. Kat insisted Ben wanted Quinn in every way. Bea wasn't so sure. A toss, sure, but something serious? Quinn had better taste and Ben seemed to enjoy switching out his bedmates.

"And who are you?" Ben said to Jamie. "Wait. No. Don't bother me with a name. Forgettable. I'll just call you Forgettable."

Adhira wagged a finger at Jamie. "Honestly, if I'd known how Ian treated you all, I'd never have spoken to him. Not even chocolate is worth inflating that head."

"Any larger and it would pop." Anna popped a pretend balloon with her hands.

"Anna, honey, he'd let you pop any of his inflated heads." Quinn licked her lips and grinned at Anna. If Bea had to bet on a *21 Things* hookup, it would've been Quinn and Anna. Their chemistry exploded like hydrogen and oxygen every time they got to joking.

Anna bumped Quinn with her hip. "I've low standards for men, but I'm not so desperate as to give Ian head, thank you very much."

"I can't figure out what Kat is thinking. To blow us all off at the Globes for that . . . that . . ." Adhira huffed and threw her hands in the sky. "She should remember that saying—Jamie, how does it go?—Hos over bros, no?"

Jamie laughed, his arms around his wife. "Adhira, love, no. I've explained this idiom several times. Bros over hos."

"Well, your version is idiotic. I like mine better."

Ben chuckled. "Kat is not going to choose anything over Ian's hose. Not ever." Everyone else laughed at Ben's off-color joke, but Bea grimaced. Kat was too entranced by the fame that shed like flakes from Ian Graham.

Bea scooped her mess into a cup. She needed to leave before things got worse and she ended up crying into the tablecloth. Kat wanted Ian and his fame-dandruff. "I can't kick my funk so I'm going to call it a night. Stay and enjoy the party."

Nicola arrived, a new fancy-colored, glowing drink in her hand. "No! You're not going to spend this night alone in a hotel room! Not on the biggest night of any of our lives. If we were younger and more famous, we could get into trouble at Chateau Marmont or—"

"What is there to do in LA when you're old and not-quite-famous?" Ben asked.

The group exchanged confused looks. Nic laughed first, which started everyone tittering. "Some famous people we are. Can't think of a single bit of fun. Come now, someone has to have a Hollywood dream."

Jamie spoke up. "The sign. I want to touch the Hollywood sign. Probably my only chance." Adhira smiled at him and nodded.

Bea considered her group of not-famous faces. These people made this whole thing worthwhile. Every difficult moment was for them, and they were worth any sacrifice. They deserved a night of dreams. "I've always wanted to go up there, too. I've only seen it from the freeway when we came for Kat's dad's funeral."

"The lady wishes to see the sign," Ben said, his voice tinged with the mischief that twinkled in his eyes. "Suit up, super friends. Car leaves in fifteen."

The cast dashed off in various directions to their respective hotel rooms. In her own room, Bea dug jeans and a t-shirt out of her luggage. She had no idea how to get out of the whale bone corset without Kat, so that stayed in place after the dress came off in a heartbreaking rip of seams. She'd have to hike in immobile, painful posture. She left her hair piled on her head as she carefully pulled a hooded sweatshirt over her head. Then tennis shoes and a touch of gloss finalized the look.

Ben knocked her door. "The sign waits for no one."

Bea pushed through the door and raced down the hall. "And what care I for an impatient sign?" Ben chased after her, laughing.

A clown car filled with almost-famous faces waited on the curb. "There you are. I was about to call it, leave without you," Anna said from inside.

Bea slid demurely into the cab. Ben pushed in and shoved everyone aside. Voices raised in pain and complaint.

"Whatever happened to the limos from earlier?" Adhira shared Jamie's lap with Anna.

"Once you win, you pay your own fare," Quinn quipped from somewhere beneath the mass of bodies. "And I will kill whomever forgot to brush after eating the onion pearls."

"Sorry, Quinnie. Does that mean we're not snogging mountainside?" Ben blew a long breath into the space Bea assumed contained Quinn. Quinn moaned.

Ben laid down across every lap. Bea leaned over him to address the cabbie. "Please, take us quickly to any trail that might lead to a view of the Hollywood sign."

The cab rumbled up to the parking lot of the Griffith Observatory. "Good viewing along the sidewalk. I doubt the trail is open."

"We'll take our chances, thank you." Bea handed the man double his fare because she'd always wanted to do that for someone. At least once in her life.

"The trail's over here," Anna shouted.

A fierce wind whipped tendrils of hair from Bea's coif. She shivered hard. Her thick sweatshirt felt like linen.

"Oh what an unfortunate *fuck*," Quinn said as she stared at the *No Trespassing* sign.

Bea grimaced. Her teeth chattered against the icy wind that shrunk her Spanx. An end to this adventure might not be awful.

Ben peered through the fence. "Just a hundred dollar fine? I am climbing this fence."

Adhira pushed at Jamie who approached the fence in frank protestation. "Adhira, I don't do these things. I'll be the one gets caught."

As though waiting on Jamie's cue, red and blue flashing lights lit the sky. A flurry of curse words accompanied the sight.

The officer shone his flashlight on each face but held the bright glare on Anna, who brushed her hair back from her pretty face in nervous affectation.

The officer switched off his light. "*Anna Driscoll!* My wife's a huge fan! We had to pay for the BBC subscription just so she could see episodes when they aired in England. She called in hysterics over the win. What a night, right?"

Bea grinned, adopting the charm that usually saw her to victory. "We'd love to meet her, but we've a date with this sign. Can you help us get a closer look?"

"Sorry, y'all. Private property. But I can get you to a better view."

"We'll take it. Thanks, man." Ben clapped the officer on the back. The man beamed.

They piled into the orange and white truck. Bea rode in the back so that Quinn and Anna could warm their fat-free bodies in the cab. The wind enlivened her skin as when she'd rambled back roads in Idaho during childhood. She was struck with a sudden longing for home. She was closer than she'd been in a year, but still felt so far from the world she'd known and the people she loved.

The officer stopped the vehicle on the mountain side of the fence. Two wheels hung over a small ledge. "Closest you can legally get. Be careful. It's steep."

The sign loomed as large and bright as stardom when they disembarked the truck. Foil warming blankets passed from officer to cast. Jamie pulled

Adhira into his lap. Ben, Nic, Quinn, Bea, and Anna huddled together against the chill under a pointless piece of silken tin.

"Knew you'd come around to the orgy idea, Quinnie, but I thought there'd be fewer clothes and married people involved. Would also have preferred a nice, heated room." Quinn laughed from inside the circle of Ben's arms.

Anna sang a line from a classic track about friendship. Bea's throat closed up as she thought back almost a decade. Kat and her music friends would hike into the caves up Logan Canyon near Utah State University, Bea had been dragged along for who knew what reasons; she couldn't carry a tune. They'd light a fire and sing until everyone fell asleep in giant heaps of snuggled bodies. She'd always been the odd man out on those outings. Not much had changed, except she didn't even have Kat.

When they could bear the cold no more, the officer gave them a ride back to meet his wife at the trailhead. She squealed and cried as she met the major and minor players. Then the group posed beneath the distant sign. Red-nosed and half-glamorous, Bea and Anna held up two golden statues—an iconic photo to match an iconic night. But forever incomplete. Forever without Kat.

♦ ♦ ♦

Kat

Tonight, there's no midnight, no bedtime, no reasonable hours. Tonight is an endless epiphany. On Ian's arm, I meet, mingle, and banter with people whose names I've breathed in reverence and awe since my first Billy Crystal Oscars opening montage. I am a devotee of The Oscars, The Globes, The Emmys. And now I, the novice, the acolyte in the temple of cinematic art—I have been allowed into the inner sanctum.

And somehow—I don't know how—I'm not falling flat on my face.

I think it's because Ian is beside me. His hand on the small of my back initiates me to heaven as we make a lazy circuit around the party, through several rooms scattered with couches and chairs, around a pool glowing with floating tealights—and someone in a slinky silver gown rising out of the water like Venus. In the furthest room are the largest seating arrangements, and the most amazing artists yet.

An urge to find a piece of paper to write down everyone I meet in case I forget a single moment of this dream rushes over me. These are the people. *The* New Zealand artists creating worlds bigger and more fantastical and grittier in detail than anyone before them. I've watched the movies innumerable times, and not just for Ian and his exquisite death scene. Hands reach for mine as introductions are made and the moment feels as brilliant as when they thrust gold in my hand hours earlier. The hours pass in neverending adoration. Me for them—and them for me.

The night ends when the power players ebb back into the ethers of my fantasies. Except for Ian. He stays. Real and solid and mine.

"And how was that for a night?" Ian pulls me next to him on the side bank in the limo. I have a glass of champagne in one hand. My other hand slides up his thigh.

"Most amazing night ever." The LA streets are silent in the post-party, pre-commuter pause. I'm drunk. More than slightly, possibly very drunk. Too drunk for foreplay.

The hours of maddening, teasing touches and verbal and social seduction culminate with my eager backward arch. Ian follows, accepts. I relax into sensation, let go of thought, as Ian runs a hand from my ankle up to my thigh. I'm bare now. Full access.

"Aye, that's m'gel." Ian's brogue and my answering laugh are thick with desire and alcohol. His belt buckle and the prickle of his beard send shivers between points of contact—neck and thigh. I want, I want, I want. And Ian gives.

My head issues a stray warning: I'm not made for casual sex, never have been. My heart gets in the way. Nothing here is casual, not for me. A part of me holds onto him as my first love, an instigator in my first feelings of sexuality. He is my first fantasy, my first real lust, my first—oh, stop it, Kat. Stop thinking so much.

Because he's touching me, deeper, just as I've imagined. Commanding more space, insisting on more. Time stretches and contracts around a dizzying, disorienting queue of sensation and emotion. Impressively passionate. Skilled. Ian's touch is everything his eyes have ever promised. And then *Ian* is everything, moving inside me—unbelievably good, that moment of possession. Fevered motion and breath.

I reach for the skin where Ian's illicit tattoo sits—*fuck off*—so divinely sexy. But the thought of it brings me back down from the stratosphere to my actual location. Sex in a limo. I am not *sex in a limo,* but here I am, having crazy, mad, passionate sex in a limo. With Ian.

So maybe this *is* me. Because I don't want it to end.

But he finishes too soon. While we're still driving and I'm nowhere near done. He laughs into my neck and his fingers are back at work, pressing, giving, until I'm there—not in pieces for days, but enough to leave me both satisfied and wanting more.

He's definitely more aware of our surroundings, where we are, because as quickly as I was undone he's put us back together. The limo door opens on Ian's hotel. He looks normal, himself, no evidence of anything.

Ian crooks his head at me. "Coming up?"

But—I can't. "I have meetings. I need some rest."

Ian harrumphs and slides out of the limo without looking at me. The dismissal is a harsh crash into reality.

The door closes and then opens. "Who's the meeting?" Ian asks, his eyes more focused than I've seen in hours.

"National Network. I'm pitching a new series. And then we've got the legal stuff and major planning for an Omega series with Dewson." I have hours and hours of meetings ahead of me for the next two days. Bea will not be hung over. Or pleased that I am.

"You're an ambitious one, birdy. Reichman at National will like that. Tell him I love your ideas. He'll like that even more. Then tonight you can tell me how it all went."

He winks at me as the door closes. Ian taps the top of the car for the driver to proceed.

CHAPTER 8

Es leuchtet meine Liebe,
in ihrer dunkeln Pracht,
wie'n Märchen traurig und trübe,
erzählt in der Sommernacht.

My love, it shines
in its dark splendor,
like a fairy-tale, sad and bleak,
told on a summer night.

—Robert Schumann, Dichterliebe

Bea

Bea tapped her toes and worried at a hem while red digital numbers switched up on the giant clock in the reception area. Kat was late. No, not late, but not the fifteen minutes early that business etiquette dictated was *on time.*

Bea checked her phone—again—to see no message—again. She'd networked all of LA to get this meeting at National, moved heaven and earth aside, and wheedled her way through calling trees thicker than the Black Forest. She couldn't reschedule without guaranteeing no one in LA ever took another of her phone calls.

The red clock announced another minute had gone by. Where was Kat?

The gold turnstile spun at least a half-dozen more times before Kat appeared, a bagel clasped in her teeth as she tucked a white blouse into her pants. Black heels pounded sharply on the tile. Bea had left them in Kat's hotel room with a giant pink *wear me* sticky note attached. The city demanded heels, trendy ones, and full business attire. No sneakers.

Kat waved at Bea with her hand over her eyes to block the light, and then nearly tripped when her heel slid against smooth tile.

Kat was hung over.

Bea closed her eyes to offer a prayer for patience. Lectures went nowhere with Kat, and they couldn't afford a repeat of last fall's argument.

"So, you're alive," Bea said with a forced grin as Kat jabbed the up button.

"Oh, I had such a night. I met the whole New Zealand crew. How many times have I gone on about them, right? Amazing. They were amazing." Katrine pinned on the visitors badge. "You're going to die at the list of everyone I met."

"Let me guess, all the important people you could ever want or need." Sarcasm was overtaking her senses. Bea hit the 8 button and the doors slid closed.

"I met Iona!" Katrine went on. "And Jack and Nan! And Viggo!"

"Shut up." Bea tried to go Valley Girl, but sarcasm ruined the effect.

Floors four through seven slid by before Kat spoke again. "Is there something you need to say?"

Bea chewed her lip. The mucosa had formed scar tissue. Not even a nice, restful vacation would save that spot. It would forever slide between her teeth at moments of stress. But the bubbling sarcasm worried her more than the scar. Sarcasm ruined meetings.

She turned to face Kat, tried to keep her voice kind and reasonable. "Yes. I have something to say. Do you know who *wasn't* at those parties last night? Us. The people that made you famous enough that Ian would notice. You didn't take a one of us along on your fame journey, did you?"

"You weren't invited," Kat said with a little sniffle as the doors opened. Defensive Kat. Self-righteous Kat.

Kat strode down the hall. People in cubicles chatted or listened to headphones. They didn't notice Bea, no reason to notice. She and Kat were unknowns in the production capital of the world. They would be forgotten by tomorrow if Kat didn't rock this meeting.

Bea had said her piece and that would have to be enough. Kat wouldn't rock this meeting if Bea didn't back off. One more sentence and Bea would take the whole of judgment from the Crusades to the Westboro Baptist Church from Kat. And she had. More than once. Then Kat would be in her indignant place, more likely to convey rebellion than responsibility.

Bea rolled her shoulders and linked her hands behind her back, old dance stretches that calmed and readied her for performance. Kat followed her lead by humming a singing exercise. The future meant more than any moment in the past.

A young assistant at the reception desk dripped up-and-coming LA professional. The girl dizzied Bea with three eyerolls before she finished the *they're here* phone call. Then she turned to them with fawning adoration. "Marty and Jodi are ready for you in the Pitch Room. They can't wait to see you. There are organic fruit bars on your way in, and I'll bring coffee. Free trade, of course."

Bea didn't refuse the coffee. She was responsible for half the tea wasted in London, may as well throw away full cups of coffee in America.

The underweight assistant led them back to a board room. Giant screens covered the back wall. The chairs curved in front of floor-to-ceiling windows looking over the LA skyline. The round Empire Records building screamed back at them that they were at the very top of the entertainment world—where dreams came to live or die. Mostly to die.

Kat's fingers drummed along the side of her leg. Beneath the tapping, genius flowed. Those fingers tattooed against Bea's briefcase for a moment and Kat winked.

Good. Artist Kat was in residence.

Bea rolled the numbers about her head and withdrew bound notebooks filled with market projections so large she couldn't fathom the idea of that many people watching one show at exactly the same time. Had Kat not pulled off the impossible at the Globes, Bea would never dare speak the numbers aloud. BBC was a global brand, but it didn't come close to National in terms of immediate reach.

Marty and Jodi joked with each other on the far side of the room, relaxed and flirty. Jodi was under thirty, one of the new breed of hot, self-motivated young people. She wore a ruffled blouse open to her navel over black, leather leggings. Her legs crossed toward Marty, VP of programming, and she leaned forward. Sex was always for sale in LA, or at least the idea of sex.

Marty rose to greet them first. "Congrats on the win, ladies."

"Thank you. BBC has been amazingly supportive." Kat shook his hand. "Wait until we show you what we can do with National behind us."

Bea dropped her shoulders and leaned in, cleavage first, to extend a hand. Her smile widened and her hips swayed to accentuate the curve.

Marty grinned back, his eyebrows raised. "We're excited to see whatever you have for us."

Bea sat next to Marty. He'd be easier to charm. Jodi worked on creative—she was Kat's target. Bea would whisper figures to Marty who would then project them as his own. That's how business got done.

"So." Jodi said with finality. "Show us the ideas that win awards."

"With absolute pleasure." Kat gestured to the presentation screen. The Prezi blinked on and Kat rolled through the pitch in full creative geek mode. Bea flipped Marty's bound pitch book to the appropriate pages as Kat pitched her series. She perched beside the Prezi on the back of a wide arm chair, her heels in the seat and feet bare as she told a quippy tale full of snap and humor about a young Army nurse, her circle of friends, and an arch-rivalry with a long-lost brother played out in the sprawling community in Germany with the largest concentration of US military outside the states. The energy of the room circled around her as her voice modulated along with the emotion in the story.

Kat had created her own social media rant that ran like ticker-tape along the side to show how her fun tale fit into National's goals for market reach. National wanted one get and one get only: Millennial females, the next largest market sector currently crowding the Gen X and Y moms out of the marketplace forever.

> ALLI DELGADO IS NOT A TROPE.
> Woman of color playing a nurse, you think, though, right?
> Support staff BS.
> How is that not a trope, another tired-ass piece of how women are treated on television all the time?
> She's not. I'll tell you why.
> 1—She's an officer in the GD Army of the United States of America and she rules her universe.
> 2—This is a story about her as a person outside the work, outside the uniform. She is not just her snarky commentary on life or the Army. She is a real person.
> 3—Then, the dude, JD.
> On the surface, he's so typical leading man material, right? White. Officer in the Army. Super hot.
> And this is where *K-Town* is brilliantly subversive.
> It gives the audience a military hero they expect and then shines the light on his SISTER.
> He's a plot device.
> ULTIMATE FEMINIST WIN.

As the last rolled, Jodi laughed out loud. She elbowed Marty, who laughed back with her. Good. Bea had worried about this part, but she wasn't the artist and Kat believed National would *get it*. They'd been committed to breaking the boundaries of storytelling for years, each show edgier than the last, the first American network to conquer almost every taboo.

Kat interspersed bits of dialogue with savvy description. And she sold the sex. Lots of sex, without a single child in sight. Mothers were definitely yesterday's plot device, families completely passé. But it worked. Marty and Jodi slipped forward to the edge of their seats.

"So, what I'm hearing," Jodi said to Marty, "is *How I Met My Brother* with a splash of *Illicit*. Is that what you're hearing, Marty?"

"It is. And I'm old enough to remember when war dramas were all the rage. In its time, *Army Nurses* was the top primetime drama. A feminist reboot. Great idea."

Bea flipped Marty's book to the page on market reach. "The vision for this is truly global. We'll tell human stories of every shape and color and truth, on a personal level that audiences will dig into, relate to, laugh with, and love. We plan to bring the *21 Things* audience along and have a marketing plan devoted to making sure they know that National made it happen."

Bea turned the page to the projected advertiser revenue based on market reach. Marty ran a quick finger over the figures and then moved that finger to rub his lower lip.

The real tension arrived—waiting for a reaction, a final positive or an uncertain negative.

"Should we bring in Bob?" Marty looked at Jodi. Jodi nodded with enthusiasm and then tapped out a message on her cell phone.

Kat shot Bea a wide-eyed glance full of triumph and apprehension. Bob Reichman was the real shark; they were done playing safe at the reef.

Bob entered—a friendly looking, silver-haired man in a tailored sport coat and gray chinos. His eyes settled on Kat with keen interest.

"Mr Reichman—" Kat started.

"Call me Bob," he said, with the grin of a talk-show host. His hands reached for Kat, both of them. He tucked her hand in both of his and grinned wider, perfectly white teeth gleaming in the fluorescent light. "Good to have you here. Great showing yesterday at the Globes. So glad you thought of National for your next home."

"Our pleasure to be here. How could we not think of you?" Kat purred.

"Look at this woman. Charm for miles. So, show me this idea. Let me be dazzled."

Kat clapped her hands. "Alright, here we go."

The Prezi clicked back to the wide shot. Every minute or so, Bob heaped praise on Kat's plate like it was the free shrimp at a buffet. Exorbitant, artery-clogging praise covered in butter and coated in sugary cocktail sauce that dripped from his chin.

After ten minutes, with an illustration of the buxom and handsome silhouettes that would one day be the cast, Bob waved his hands. "I am sold. A thousand times sold. This is National's next big everything."

Bea hadn't said a word, not one word about marketing or advertiser blend or anything business related.

Bob perched on the arm of a chair. "There's only one thing bothering me. And that's your other project, Kat. I'm right that there's another project? For Omega? That's a problem. How are we guaranteed that full Kat focus—that creative pizzazz—all that charm—if you're split between three projects in three locations? I'm afraid that's a lot of risk for National to assume, isn't it, ladies?"

"*21 Things* won't film again until the summer, when *Void* and *K-Town* will be on hiatus," Kat assured him.

Bob raised his brows. "National will expect your full focus on this project. We won't put out half your best." A good play. He was forcing non-competition.

"Monkey & Me is fully capable of producing more than one quality project at a time." Kat looked at Bea in panic. She'd stepped into business speak, her least favorite thing. But Bea was no help. She had no idea how any of this would work. Kat seemed to believe in magical transportation techniques and time manipulation whenever they discussed the details.

Bea felt mostly useless on both projects, actually. She didn't understand sci-fi. And *K-Town* made Bea uncomfortable. The men as a plot device and sex tool angle alone had driven Bea to apologize to all her brothers and male friends. She didn't know why it always had to be one gender over the other, why they couldn't tell stories about a unified and equal world, why it always had to be antagonistic. But that discussion only led to more lectures about Bea's small-town morality and white privilege and all the reasons her opinions didn't matter.

"Bob," Kat smiled. She'd found her confidence again. "We came to National because you have a reputation for trusting the creatives. So, trust me. We have the vision, the bandwidth, the energy—for anything we choose—or that chooses us. And we can make them happen with all the pizzazz that won us gold last night."

"You're a charmer. That's for sure. But National will accept nothing less than singular focus. Feel free to bring this back when that's possible." Bob stood back up. Marty and Jodi fell in step behind him.

This was it. They'd failed.

"Wait." Kat spouted. "You've got it. You want my singular focus, it's here. With *K-Town*."

Passion. A two-edged sword for Kat. She'd fall on that sword rather than give up her pursuit. Bea stared at her, mute over the impossible promise.

Bob stopped. He turned to face her with that wide, friendly grin back in place. "Then I'll have Marty review those numbers. You'll get me a budget, marketing plan, all the boring stuff. And if you agree to be in the building when I walk by, then I'll be happy to welcome Monkey & Me to National Network. And, Kat, we do need some men to watch this—large canopy, remember—so leave a few balls intact along the way?"

This couldn't be happening. Kat had already promised Josh she'd be involved in every detail of *Void*. Josh loved Kat, was orgasmic over Kat. There were plans to start filming. How could they do that if Kat was full-time at National?

But Kat was shaking Bob's hand and looking like she'd won another gold statue.

♦ ♦ ♦

Kat

I am naked and happy. Giddy nakedness and sybaritic joy. All of my wins tingle along my skin as soft bars of early morning sun play across Ian's face as he sleeps. One of his hands follows my exposed hip as I settle against the sheets, propped up on an elbow—the better to watch him in this unguarded moment.

My fingers trace the shadows down his jaw, feel the flutter of his eyes as he begins to wake. I want this moment to stretch forever.

Because this is the instant that colors my future in the vivid shades of spring and leaves my past in dreary gray. My heart blooms this morning. For this man. For Ian.

I've fallen in love before. With music, with words, with Bobby Brener when I was sixteen, and a half-dozen boys since. But this is different. A rising. Every cell in my body aligns itself to Ian, who stands above me. He calls me up. I'm falling in love, but in doing so, I'm being pulled up.

Up to Ian's world.

Ian's hand moves from my hip to ribs, and I giggle. Our entire last encounter involved the very adult art of the tickle. His touch feathers and sparks sensitive nerves. I wiggle forward to rest my head on my hands on his chest. I look up at him, illicit innocence as that velvety sweet emotion—love—continues to unfurl from my heart space.

"What are you thinking, birdy?" Ian throws an arm behind his head. He raises a lazy eyebrow at me.

"I'm happy, that's all. What are you thinking?" His hand draws lazy circles in the small of my back. I know what he's thinking, what he has to be thinking. Destiny. An emotion this strong can't be felt in isolation.

His hands circle my thighs as we kiss. I'm crazy for more of him, every taste and texture of him. But my phone sounds a shrill alarm. Ian releases a thigh to swipe at the phone. The phone goes silent, but still I heed the summons to my mid-morning meeting.

"I have a business to run," I say, but I arch and open for him, all of me pliant to his touch. I think briefly, but very seriously, of playing hooky from today's meetings and spending the day in bed with Ian. Everything has gone brilliantly all week. Approved, approved, approved. Bea can do today's rat race, Bea who doesn't even want love. I want mine. I need a lazy day of naked bliss and softly spoken words. They'd be spoken today, those three precious syllables. They shift about us in the ether. I'm close to many things as Ian works my body, those words a small piece of the whole.

But the alarm sounds again, unhappy to have been ignored. The insanity of blowing off a whole day of creative meetings with Josh Dewson, even for love, destroys my delight. My company matters to me, too, as much as Ian.

"Ian, stop, I have to get up."

Ian rolls out of the bed. "Course you do. Business before pleasure, Katrine. Always." He huffs to the bathroom. I hear water and pipes—a shower. He's about to wash me off. Somehow, I'm supposed to feel like I did something wrong.

Fuck that. If this were reversed and he had a meeting instead of me, I guarantee his male business pursuits would have me alone in a bed and he wouldn't tolerate my frustrated stalk to the bathroom. So, fuck the sexism, Ian Graham.

Anger rolls through me—I throw over the covers and follow him to the bathroom.

"Ian, seriously. I can't put these things off. I'm finalizing two shows. I deserve a little support," I say through the glass door of the shower.

"O'course. I got things to do, too, Kat. Fun can't last forever." My entire heart deflates. My up becomes a rapid down. I sink, sink, sink lower than Katrine was before she dreamed of Ian Graham. How did this morning go this wrong so fast? No. No. I know what I felt, what I feel. And it wasn't fake. But I know the rules.

"Look, Ian. I like you. You like me. We have fun together. And we're going to have fun tonight, right? I'll wear all the right underthings."

The glass door swings open. Ian pulls me in before I can think to protest. Naked Ian short-circuits my brain.

"Why wait." He nips at my ear and pulls me flush against him under the spray of a half dozen luxurious jets of water. "I can have you right now, birdy."

I give in. I want him too much not to give into him when he demands it. And Ian—demands. We demand and encourage and play each other's bodies like the string section of an orchestra—every pitch from low to high, aching tension and pleasure. Lather and laughter follow. When it's done, Ian pushes me out of the shower with a grin. "See you at dinner tonight, birdy." Then he goes back under the water.

A date. A real one. Not room service and sex. The day can't pass fast enough.

CHAPTER 9

"It was a strong effort to the spirit of good, but it was ineffectual. Destiny was too potent, and her immutable laws had decreed my utter and terrible destruction."

—Mary Shelley, Frankenstein

Kat

Walking away from Ian sucks the energy out of me. I'm supposed to be excited about my work, but the further I walk away, the less I feel like me. I'm unhappy, deeply so, more so with each step further from Ian.

The Golden Globes happened on another planet. A fantasy that belongs on late-night fringe sci-fi—a million light years away and five whole days ago—not part of my regular life at all. If there weren't a golden statue sitting on my hotel room nightstand, I wouldn't believe any of it had ever happened.

My left hand performs runs from Chopin's Etude No. 12 in C Minor—*Revolutionary*—while I stare at the plush banality of a modern, American hotel lobby. *K-Town* and *21 Things* story arcs run through my head on parallel tracks.

I'm so damn bored with it all—it's all the same. Only Ian feels new. Different. Exciting.

I know what my left hand is telling me. A memory in musical form. An etude played by a wisp of a Korean girl at my third piano lesson in the United States. She prepared the piece for a piano competition. Her fingers flew across the keys. Her right hand attacked the high octaves. I preferred the intensity of Rachmaninoff, but the angst of the Chopin in the hands of a small, emotionless girl felt wrong. I could bend that song to my will. I could win.

My teacher shrugged off my desire for competition. "You're talented, Kat, but not competition ready. We'll work for a university scholarship. That's the plan."

But for a year, I pushed myself to conquer the Chopin. I convinced my dad to buy me a baby grand piano and I pounded the keys nonstop. Day after endless day, I engaged in a fantasy of myself and Chrissy—not her real name, her *American* name, she didn't even see me as an equal capable of pronouncing her name—in fierce battle on a stage.

The next year, I stood on stage with Chrissy. I held the first place trophy while she sniffled and dabbed at tears under her black-rimmed glasses.

I spent the $1,000 award money on *Priscilla,* my crap Jetta, and quit piano.

Quit.

While my dad still had who-knows-how-many payments left on a baby grand piano that cost more than the beat-up Bronco he drove back and forth to Edwards Air Force base every day, I quit. I wanted to focus on vocal performance.

I quit that, too, after I won everything I could win.

That's what my left hand reminds me about today. Don't be a quitter, Kat. A trophy and an amazing pitch to Bob Reichman weren't the end of this TV journey. The shows must go on. I add my right hand for the dramatic chords at the sweeping conclusion.

See. Kat's no quitter.

Quitting is in my past, and my future sparkles.

Bea waits on the sidewalk toward the metro—she's faster because I indulged Ian and then stopped for espresso—and it's like the old days—the best days—go-go-going, together, in all our quests. "Hey, early bird."

"Hey." Bea toasts me with her Diet Coke can. "If only sleep-deprived were a superpower, right?"

She jumps into work before we're even on the train. "We've got three video conferences with the Vancouver office back-to-back this afternoon. I'm not done 'til seven. And Nicola threatened to quit if we don't hire another assistant. I'm assuming Nicola stays with you in LA?"

"She is deep on *K-Town*." I want Nicola for her ability to keep me on track.

"It's fine. But I should hire in Vancouver. I'll appease Nic with cake and a temp."

Bea pulls multiple *Void* portfolios out of her bag when we sit down on orange seats next to a man who smells of urine and marijuana—LA metro lines are definitely not the commuter-friendly world of the Tube—new set designs, costume sketches, character sheets, and a timeline that looks like a Picasso. "Sign-offs and notes, please. Since we have some time."

The stack of papers begins today's portion of the never-ending approvals process. My initials scribble in the corner of most pages, though I make a few notes about color. Too much gray. Why are Imperial shows always so gray? Drives me crazy.

The *Void* timeline draws in my focus—the worst gaps have been fixed but there's still a weird causality loop in the middle. "It's still here, that loop. Josh never answered the question of whether he was doing it on purpose."

"You can duke it out this afternoon." Bea smiles—but it's not a real smile, doesn't even reach her eyes. "Here, focus. Next item on the list."

Bea hands me her iPod. The guy next to her mumbles, and Bea hands him a bottle of water. That always amazes me, the way she's aware of everything yet singularly focused at the same time.

"What am I listening to?" I ask as she grabs the man's wrist to check his pulse.

"First-cut score for *Void.* Josh said it was imperative it get full approval from the musical *artiste.* That's you. Obviously. What could I possibly know about the emotional evocation of musical tone as a mere dancer with ten years of training in various musical styles? Not a thing. Not. A. Thing." She drops her hand on the man's head, then nods once. She's decided he'll live.

Earbuds push music in my head, almost deep enough to drive thoughts of Ian away. I listen for half a minute and then rewind and listen again. "Why is this full orchestra? What happened to piano sonata Beethoven?"

Bea shrugs. "If you don't know, I don't know. I'm just the messenger lady with the money bag."

"Ugh. I told him. No freaking cellos. This isn't a teenaged vampire story."

"Swap vampire for revolutionary and you've got the pilot episode. Not an original word or character anywhere. I've sent the writing team notes. Or I hope I did. It's so overwhelming there. Always more names I don't know and job titles I have to look up in the industry manual. Hard to sound credible when I can't even get the who's-who right. And Josh is so quick to point out that I'm not the creative genius of this pair."

"You're underselling yourself. Drastically." I'm not going to let Josh waste Bea.

"Thanks, but it's fine. Just a big jump for a little fish. I found an awesome apartment. It looks out over English Bay and is just fifteen minutes from the backlot. When I get bored by my own uselessness, I'll be able to watch whales and hunt bears."

"Oh, be serious. He better start listening. Or we're out of *Void*."

"I'm sure he'll listen to anything you say."

Bea collects the papers with my signature back into her bag. There's a definite slump to her normally straight shoulders. It's my fault. I messed up two days ago when I contradicted Bea over a stupid color choice, not even important. And now Josh won't listen to her about a thing.

"I'm sorry about the scenery thing. I was—distracted." I had been, walked in after a call from Ian, all heightened color and tingling everything. "It's no excuse. I do trust you. Bea, we're partners."

"Thanks. Enough about me. How's *K-Town*?"

"An official office in Burbank soon, Marty tells me. And casting in less than two weeks." In the meantime, we're temporarily based out of Josh's offices in Century City. We emerge from the metro to walk toward the industrial complex that houses Faux Monster.

"Casting in two weeks? That's quick. They're serious about getting you ready for advertiser upfronts in May."

"I know. Six episodes by May. I expected a pilot. That was the dream. A pilot."

"Well, you got a lot more than that. You're officially an *it girl* in production."

"Crazy. The schedule is killing me. I didn't think that part through."

"Yeah. Tough to get a moment to think. But have you got time for a girls' night before I leave on Tuesday?" Bea asks without emotion, scanning the street for a safe passage, but I can't remember her ever asking for girls' night. It's my thing, my friend ritual that makes her roll her eyes even as she plays along.

But I don't have time. I have Ian. Relationship-type *progress* with Ian. A date tonight that will spin into a fantasy weekend. Then on Monday I'm supposed to scout locations up near Edwards. I'll be gone until midnight.

Bea glances at me, her eyes obscured by Coach sunglasses. She shrugs the shoulder not burdened by a bag large enough for a ficus and a floor lamp. "Don't worry about it, Kat. Maybe I'll leave early for Vancouver." She strolls into traffic, grazing a passing Prius. Her heels confidently carry her toward the large gray box where Josh Dewson awaits.

The Faux Monster entrance looms under a sign with a gory zombie chowing on a brain. Bea presses her cell phone to her ear, in communication with Nicola about the temp. Work. Always work. Bea waves at me without a backward glance. "Marathon time. I'm off to the PR side until the afternoon."

"See ya." My left hand performs runs along my thigh. I'm really doing this, really expanding my company, my brand. It's all real. Because I won't quit.

And fate has given me Ian, too. The thrill of the morning returns as I pass by the receptionist. Winning. I can't stop winning.

♦ ♦ ♦

Bea

Bea dropped her bag and crouched next to it at the first sound of a ringtone. Faux Monster was a giant cubicle-laden warehouse. This stairwell had become her refuge, the only spot of privacy in the building. She grabbed out notes from several meetings and her budget binder—now grown so as to double the weight of her bag.

Her fingers slipped around the cold metal of her gold iPhone. She'd take five minutes, just five, to answer this call, while perched on a hard concrete step. "Hey, Mom. Sorry I didn't call back yesterday."

Her mom's voice sang across the line. "Oh, no problem. That nice police officer I dispatched to make sure you weren't the next Black Dahlia was quite nice."

"Stop, mom. I'm sorry I'm missing check-ins and video calls lately. It's crazy here."

"Which is why I'm not letting you go to Vancouver without a stop at the house. Bea, it's time to put family first again. You have two nieces you've never met, honey, and another coming in May."

Bea chewed the scar. It didn't bleed anymore, that was nice. "Mom, I don't think I can make it right now—"

"Make it. If only for a few days. It's not a request anymore, Bea. You feel off course to me. A visit would put your mother's mind at ease. "

Bea's eyes watered. She stared at the light to stop the flow of tears. "Mom, I'll make time when I can. I'll figure something out." Another bit of pressure. Exactly what she didn't need.

Bea clipped down the stairs as fast as she could while checking her iPhone. Kat still hadn't approved the interview schedule for the *21 Things* DVD release. She shook the phone in frustration. Fine. She could fly by Kat's cubicle en route to her conference call. She had nothing better to do, right?

The bag hefted back onto her left shoulder, and the tendon squealed in protest. That old dance injury hated her new bag. Her organizational system was slowly killing her, but the idea of changing a system was scarier than monsters. Bea pushed through the orange metal door with its creaky bar. At least three people noted her entrance.

The cubicles nestled in creative groups. The writers huddled in the north end, nearest Josh. Production staff wandered about to the west, discussing casting. Marketing slouched over phones with bright computer screens showing database number-crunching in the east. And here, at the back, the camera and crew operators planned out location and shot sequences based on a battlefield mockup Josh had ordered up a few weeks ago. An entire production world was housed in a five-thousand square foot open space.

Josh had the only glassed-in office. He watched like a foreman from his perch. At least a half-dozen screens lit up with video calls and preproduction shots of locations and sets. The rest of the office was shrouded in shadow. Josh moved about somewhere unseen.

Bea's attention fixated on Kat's flirting voice as she approached Josh's office. "I've already told you—you can't make an anti-*Les-Mis* with a sweeping orchestra and mournful cellos. You may as well hear the people sing across all of Manhattan."

Josh's laugh wiggled out from under the electronic laughs on-screen. Bea inched toward the door.

"Kat, let the poor composer do his job."

"Well, tell him to do it with a piano." There were more laughs. Kat was in her element. She'd be perched on a desk with her fingers tapping out some old piano piece. "At least the sets aren't that horrid gray wood anymore. But the screenplay—no, I don't care about your army of seasoned writers, so shut it. Let Bea have a go at it. She'll do time travel right for once."

Bea should enter, but she hated to interrupt Kat supporting the idea that she wasn't a creative imbecile.

"She doesn't know sci-fi, Kat. Yesterday, she confused the Avengers with the Justice League—" Josh's criticism hurt. Deeply. Not that Bea didn't know her limitations.

"No, science fiction isn't her strength. But half of it is set in the French Revolution. Nobody in 1800s France knew or cared who Magneto fathered."

Embarrassment kept Bea rooted as Kat continued to *uh-huh* through more details that begged Kat's good opinion, but not Bea's. They'd moved on to casting. Kat murmured approvals to most everyone. Bea wrinkled her nose at Siena Russo's name. She was a goddess. Flawless head to foot, with a curve for any male desire. And a laugh—she laughed like the devil's whispers.

But she was another ego-driven star requesting a heavy paycheck. And, worse, she insisted they cast her boyfriend in a role ten years too old for him. Bea had objected to the casting vocally on a half-dozen occasions.

"So, they came in for screen tests. We love her, obviously—" the casting director said.

"But we adore him," one of the PAs said.

The screen lit up with Siena and her boyfriend, Edward Wolverton. Edward smiled at Siena, a grin that spread over his whole face while curly black hair caressed the laugh lines. Two dimples popped as he laughed at something unheard. Siena smiled back, small and seductive. He grabbed her perfect hourglass figure to spin her around in a music-less waltz.

"They put that on screen once and we've locked in every romantic in the country."

Yes, they were sexy and funny—and both high if those reddened eyes told the right story—but the roles were an older professor, sent by Napoleon to find a mythical cave, and his long-term lover. Eddie was young, too young. Siena was supposed to be maternal, but nothing maternal spilled out of her skin-tight dress. This was all about fanbase, hiring an overblown ego at a bloated rate to lock in viewers. Josh and Kat were so busy checking off boxes marked *guaranteed success* that Josh hadn't noticed the setup was flawed.

An alarm buzzed her iPhone against her hip.

Late, officially, for her conference call. Crap.

Bea poked her head around the door frame. "You need to approve the *21 Things* interviews," she said to Kat. Bea may as well be Kat's personal assistant. Actually, no. Nicola got way more respect than she did. She could be Nicola's assistant. Then they wouldn't have to wait on the temp agency.

"Oh, right. I forgot to hit send. There." Kat grinned at her as she tapped her phone screen.

Bea grasped the door jamb hard enough to send a sharp pang down her arm. Pain gave her courage, another dancer thing. "I vote a firm no on the casting. He's wrong for the part—mostly known for samurai movies and Shakespearean festivals—and the risk of casting a couple could ruin the sexual tension we need."

"Bea, that's crazy. They're perfect. And professionals. It'll be fine. We'd be stupid to pass someone up with thousands of guaranteed fans who looks that good on film. Plus, he played Duncan Idaho once, and I can't resist a *Dune* parallel."

It wasn't an unusual conversation for them, normal really, but the heads on screens and Josh's exhausted expression made the whole thing humiliating.

"Well, if it's what everyone wants," Bea murmured.

She rotated on her heel and walked briskly toward her cubicle with no expression on her face. In her mind, she returned to bright red pigtails, sun-kissed freckles, and her jean romper. She held her breath, stomped her feet, pouted, and cried. But in real life, she faded into frigidity.

Nicola tilted her head toward the phone as Bea stormed by her desk. "BBC marketing waiting impatiently on line 3."

♦ ♦ ♦

Kat

An alarm sounds on my phone as I leave Josh's office. *Something pretty*, the reminder reads. Heat licks low in my belly at the memory of Ian's rich brogue, making plans for us. "Tonight, birdy. Spago. Eight o'clock. Wear summat pretty."

A mental review of my closet brings me up short. The Globes ensemble counts for exactly half the things I've worn out with Ian. I'm a trainers, t-shirts, and one business pantsuit gal, which means I need to buy a dress in the next two hours. And for that, I have only one recourse—Bea.

Bea is banging the receiver on her phone down repeatedly when I cross the threshold of her cubicle.

"Whoa. What did the phone ever do?"

"Can I not have one conversation today that doesn't involve someone's ego? Just one." Bea blinks and sighs. "What can I do for you, Kat?"

"Um, I need some immediate shopping advice. For dinner. Tonight."

Bea blinks again. An entire primetime lineup of emotions plays across Bea's face, including a murder. "Ian?" she finally asks.

My own face telegraphs triumph and hope. "If you could just give me the name of a store? Someplace between here and the hotel."

"Where are you going?"

"Spago. The Internet can't decide if one should dress up or wear jeans. I'm so confused."

"Cocktail dress. Little black, probably. Nothing fussy." Bea places her hands on her desk and leans forward. I can't identify the emotion in her eyes, so I back up a step, in case she's fallen into a vat of radioactive slime in the past fifteen minutes. "If I find you a dress, can we go the next twenty-four hours without mentioning Ian's name?"

Bea props her elbows on the desk and cups her face in her hands. She looks sweet but green goo could still be oozing beneath her desk.

"Absolutely." She mentioned Ian first, by the way, I don't dare point out.

Bea picks up her phone. "Hey, Liesl. It's me. Could you put together a selection of dresses? Size 4—obviously not for me . . . Spago . . . Mm-hm. Kat will be there in forty-five minutes."

She scribbles out an address and hands me the paper.

"Thank you." I bow and retreat. Bea returns to attacking electronics, banging at the keyboard and the phone in her hand. It's love. Bea-style. And I'm off, grabbing my phone and bag from my desk, practically whistling on my way.

Three hours later, my date with destiny arrives and I'm in the perfect dress. It's possible I'm overdressed—or underdressed, depending on definitions—but I fell in love with this dress the moment I laid eyes on its shimmering whimsy, as if someone had brought the stars down to earth. The plunging neckline is more daring than anything I've ever worn, taped into place around my breasts. An asymmetrical hemline reveals almost all of my right leg. The rest of the fabric clings to and maximizes my minimal curves.

I'm dressed, but only technically. My stomach somersaults at the prospect of Ian's appreciation, hungry eyes hovering on all the right places.

I step out of the car high on expectation. The paps are gathered, eager to grab photos. We're going public. Ian has taken our relationship public. I hug myself as I float inside, eager to see tomorrow's papers. "Kat Porter, I'm meeting Ian Graham."

The maître d' consults the calendar laid out on his podium. "I'm sorry, there's no reservation. And Mr. Graham is not here."

"Then he'll be here soon."

"Of course, miss."

LA protocols are new to me—is late the norm? Bea tells me when and where to be at work, but she didn't give me a primer on the social aspects, not outside of what not to say on the Globes red carpet.

More than one camera flash goes off as the front doors of the restaurant open and close. Each time, Ian should appear, but it's never him. Every passing minute increases my general awkwardness and corresponding slump in my shoulders. He's not here. And I wore this dress . . .

It's well past eight when I call Ian's cell and get sent straight to voicemail.

No. This isn't, this can't—do people still stand people up in the digital age?

The maître d' terrifies me, but he's my only hope of an answer. "I'm sure Mr. Graham's assistant confirmed."

"Hm," the unctuous little man scans down lines of text, as if he were the keeper of state secrets, not dinner reservations. "There was a call this afternoon to cancel the reservation."

"Thank you." A thunderstorm threatens to burst from my eyes. Misunderstanding, this has to be a simple misunderstanding.

Ian's cell phone sends me straight to voicemail, again.

An app summons a car while I fight to maintain my composure. This—this isn't right. Not after the week we've had, after all we've shared, after I bought a far-too-expensive designer dress for this date. This has been my week of winning. I'm on a streak. I'm this close to mutual declarations of love—to every dream ever coming true.

The Internet confirms my night is the thing of nightmares. Ian Graham departed LAX for England this morning, according to one casual sighting and an official TMZ picture and caption.

This morning.

My car arrives and I brave the gauntlet of paparazzi out front. Maybe I'll be lucky, maybe nobody will notice me or care who I am. Without Ian, I'm not anyone, really.

"Where to?" The driver asks.

"Beverly Hilton., but first, do you know a good store close by where I can get some ice cream and movies?"

"Yep, no problem. You alright?" The driver asks when we pull up to the superstore. He's older, a comforting, avuncular air about him.

"Yeah, I'm fine," I lie. "I'll be out in a few minutes."

Brightly-lit aisles covered in red branding highlight how out of place and most definitely underdressed I am. It takes longer than a few minutes—I stare at BluRay covers without seeing them, until I find the right title with its red robot eyes cover art. If I were home, in London, I would just pull it off my shelf. Here, I have to buy it. I should get a digital copy, but I find the physical copy comforting.

Ice cream—cookie dough, cherry, chocolate, and bourbon praline—picked out of the freezer, I head to the express checkout. A short, round, Latina woman with bedazzled nails rings me up and looks at me with a knowing sort of sympathy.

I'm living a regular LA love story. That's what I've lived these past days. Fleeting and without consequence, a matter of propinquity and easy desire. Sex, actually. Call it what it was. It was sex. I was nothing to Ian Graham except an easy piece of ass. So easy.

The car takes me back to the hotel and I tip the driver too generously, maybe, but he's saved my dignity by carrying me away from the scene of the crime.

The lights in the hotel feel too bright. I wish it were dark, everywhere. Maybe then I could hide. I'm afraid the paps will put two and two together and tomorrow there will be a nasty TMZ piece about Kat Porter and Ian Graham's LA fling.

Except, I'm probably not that important. Ian sleeps with lots of women. The tabloids only report when he puts a ring on it or sleeps with someone that someone else put a ring on.

A crazy, tearless wail explodes at the door of my own hotel room.

Bea's door seems to pulsate, to radiate everything I need. I knock, loud. She opens with an improbable baguette in her hand, her hair piled all crazy on her head, while hip hop sounds from the background.

This is my real world, my right world. Bea in an X-Files t-shirt and pajama pants, dancing while she works. Bea—my best and forever friend, my person of all persons.

"Hey, you. I wasn't expecting anyone. I was totally prepared to defend myself with a baguette."

"Chasing them away with carbs?"

"You know it." Bea's eyes drop to the plastic bag in my hand, surveys my dress.

I rub my hand over my watering nose and then offer my collection to Bea. "Can we eat ice cream and watch *Terminator 2*?" My own personal heartbreak recipe—sugar, fat, and Linda Hamilton kicking ass.

"Yeah, of course." Bea pulls me into a hug, tight and safe and loved. "Would you like me to hit him with my baguette?"

And that's when I finally cry.

CHAPTER 10

Das ist ein Flöten und Geigen,
Trompeten schmettern darein.

There is a fluting and fiddling,
and trumpets blasting in.

—Robert Schumann, Dichterliebe

Kat

I've spent a week putting away my stupid fling with Ian—less time than I would like—but all the time I have. The rest of my fantastic future, the parts I worked for and earned, those are here, now, and real.

The hotel gives way to an apartment—I'll miss the room service, as evidenced by a final bill that makes me grimace. Bea will have a fit when that expense hits her books.

The rental car is small and zippy, perfect for LA's web of freeways. I drive east and south to Riverside National Cemetery to visit my dad's grave before I settle into my new semi-permanent home. He labored to his last day to ensure my dreams were fulfilled. Years of a three-hour daily commute to Edwards Air Force Base so I could attend a performing arts high school in North Hollywood. He never retired—half to help fund my education, and half, I think, because he didn't know how to face an empty house. Even long gone, my mother's absence always weighed on him.

Coffee, a danish, and a small bag of cleaning supplies sit next to me as I scrub the headstone. Dirt and water marks come off the stone as I talk to my dad as though he's alive. I want him to know his sacrifices have value to me.

My heart stings anew at his loss, but as I leave the cemetery I feel lighter than I have in days, ready for my fresh start.

The apartment complex in Los Feliz is easy to find, with its neat historical touches of towers and courtyards. Nicola chose well—comfortable, and with easy access to the Burbank studios where the majority of my time will be spent. Parking is an ordeal, between the narrow streets crammed with cars and my rusty skills, but I avoid scratches and dents to the car.

Two monstrous suitcases plus my laptop/messenger bag burden my walk up the stairs. My she-woman fantasy of moving myself fades. I should've used the delivery service Nicola suggested.

A California blond in a blue muscle tee jumps over a patio railing. "Hey, don't do that. We need a chance to look useful."

I run a hand through my brand-new, post-fling pixie cut. "Normally I can manage, but is this place nothing but stairs?"

An even cuter California boy jumps over the railing to join Muscle Tee. "Whoa. A Brit? We don't got one o' those, do we guv'nor?" He feigns an accent. An accent. I haven't thought of myself as having one before this moment.

"Yes, I'm straight in from the Motherland."

Muscle Tee crowds back into the conversation. "Awesome. I'm writing about a guy from England. I'll have to check my dialogue with you sometime."

The cute one is definitely cute. He winks at me. "Dialogue. Right. That's not what he plans to check."

The guys lean against the door and banter while I fidget with the door code.

"So, what's your name, English-lady? And what brings you to Hollywood?" Muscle Tee crosses his arms and smiles at me.

"Kat Porter. And I'm here to make a TV show."

"Actress?" The cute one looks me up and down. I want to guffaw.

"No. Executive Producer. Thanks for your help." I punch in the door code and hear the lock release.

A collective gawk changes the tone to deference. My luggage comes in amidst requests for portfolio views and feedback. Then the handsome boys are gone.

I crash on the wide leather sofa and call Bea, but she doesn't answer. "Hey, I'm official, apartment and all. Call me. Are you even alive up there in the frozen north?"

K-Town is real now. We've got funding, a crew, a director, and a casting agency. But I don't have a cast, a frame of film, or even a timeslot. For that, I need a killer pilot to impress the suits at the upfronts in May. My fingernails clasp in my teeth with elbows propped on my knees as I contemplate my to-do list, but then I fall asleep with no real plan.

On my next day back at National, a badge waits at the security desk. I'm official. I tap the small white rectangle with my name and the round National Network Studios logo. I need to scream in excitement. Instead, I nod politely at other people on the elevator. I'm wearing one of two pantsuits I own—the silver-gray one, with a white open-collared blouse and chunky jewelry—because it's what Bea told me to wear on the first day. So far I fit in, at least sartorially.

Nicola meets me outside our small suite of offices—still bigger than what we had had at BBC—and hands me a latte. "There are people here." She tilts her head slightly toward the inner office.

"What do you mean by *people*? I'm early. Aren't I?"

"Yes. They've come to greet a legend in the making."

"What?" I cover my attack of nerves with a cough.

"Knock 'em dead!" Nicola whispers and opens the door to where people are waiting.

People is a repeat of pitch day—Marty, Jodi, and Bob, the man, himself.

"Kat! Wonderful to finally have you here." Marty shakes my hand vigorously. His eyes drop down to the meager cleavage revealed by the open vee of my blouse.

Jodi squeezes my arm. "I understand you have a solid couple days of casting sessions. Let me know if you want a second opinion."

"Hitting the ground running." I lift my shoulders to stop Marty's leer. Jodi has on another vee-to-midriff blouse. Maybe she avoids the leer by putting everything on open display. I may want to follow her example. Marty's eyes continue to delve.

"Welcome to the National Network family, officially. Thrilled to have your talent and vision part of our lineup." Bob leans slightly forward as he shakes my hand and maintains eye contact. He might have played me into tying myself to LA—okay, he totally played me—and he's definitely a shark, but I like him. He's got vision and good instincts. He approved *K-Town,* after all.

"Thank you, Mr. Reichman, it's a real—"

"Uh-uh," he shakes a finger at me. "Call me Bob. We're not so formal as the BBC." In all the ways that Royce Rudkins is icky and underwhelming, Bob exudes intelligence and natural magnetism.

"Thanks, Bob. We really appreciate the level of network support we've received so far. And we won't disappoint."

"Well, Ian's never been wrong. He tells me something is the real deal, I lay out the carpet and thank him for the tip." Bob nods at me. Marty and Jodi follow him like a little entourage right out of my office.

I'm left behind like a sad baby bird waiting on a worm. My mouth opens and closes as I squawk a farewell.

Ian?—

Ian said?—

About me? When?

What the hell does that mean?

"So-o-o?" Nicola asks when they've gone.

"What did you mean by *legend*?"

"People are talking about you. It's all good. The Globes win. Buzz about *K-Town*."

"All good, you sure?"

"Absolutely. A good eavesdrop is my favorite part of the job," Nicola says. Collecting Grade A gossip is one of Nicola's best talents. If there were something to worry about, she'd know it already.

"Okay, what's first? Give me the agenda."

"Signatures and emails while you finish your coffee, and then across the street for casting. Jeff, the director, and Philip, from the casting agency, are meeting you there. They're both great, especially Philip, so I expect things will go well. They've a long lineup of eager young things, though, so it'll be a full day."

The Ian comment floats in my head along with an echo of his words from the morning after the Globes. A strange medley plays in my head and heart. One part joyful, broad chords in C major—Ian cared! He called!—and one part E minor cacophony—I'm here because some famous man called a rich man and told him to give me a shot. My self-belief stumbles—am I an artist or a good lay? Which one provoked the phone call?

My already close-clipped nails disappear under endless chewing. All those years of piano mean I can't stand my nails long, but the clear, barely-there tips seem out of place with LA. I'm an imposter. Every bit of me. Just some stupid girl Ian Graham screwed on the Hollywood equivalent of prom night.

The cool metal door outside the studio lets me pause and count to ten. Doesn't matter why I'm here. *K-Town* has everything—a full budget, a crew, a sound stage, killer scripts written by an incredibly talented artist named Katrine Porter. All it needs is a cast. Maybe I slept my way here, but I still deserve this. It's my moment and I'm going to take it, dammit. Screw anyone who tries to say otherwise.

Five hours later, when we break for lunch, I'm back in my element. My words in actors' mouths have my head and heart singing in harmony again. It's been an ordeal—I didn't know there were this many unknown actors in the world.

Philip Carter, our casting director, is a pure delight and assures me we're *almost there*. He moves headshots around the table like a casting puzzle to be solved. He's read all three of my finished scripts, not just the pilot, and his depth of understanding shows as he ranks the candidates.

We break for lunch with only two definite castings. Lunch is catered from a cafeteria somewhere on the lot, including a bottle of wine. Oh, California, never change.

Flatbread covered in arugula, apple, aged cheddar, and a touch of honey slips past my tongue. Philip pours me a glass of Chardonnay.

"I'm having a culture shock moment. In England, we have tea with lunch."

"They usually pair these things pretty well. Give it a try. Though anything would work with this spread. Except maybe Romulan Ale."

Philip grins the most winning smile. He seems young for a casting director—mid-30s, not much older than me—and maybe too cheerful, but I have no complaints. I sip the wine obediently. "You're right, an excellent pairing. Just the right touch of oak to go with the apple."

"I'm glad to be right." He grins again, his brown eyes flashing bright against his dark brown skin. He has an easy, open humor that softens the seriously sculpted features of a modeling-career-worthy face. I wonder if he's flirting or if it's just that LA way of doing business in the currency of seduction. "If you enjoy wine, I'll have to get you invited to our wine pairing weekends."

"Nothing wrong with wine and food. Ever."

"I agree. The best pairing. Except perhaps geeks and science fiction novels. I noticed you have *Welcome to Night Vale* in your bag."

"Yeah, I aspire to have time to read it, but I'm either working or sleeping."

"Tsk, tsk. Haven't you heard of work-life balance?" Philip teases. Something inside me warms at his tone.

"Do you listen to the podcast? It's so delightfully—"

"Odd," Philip finishes my sentence. "Love it, never miss it."

"Right? I always hear people talking about great literature I've never read. And my best friend can hold incredible conversations about Pulitzer-prize-winning this and that, but I always come back to the geek stuff."

"Understood—" Philip emphasizes each syllable. "—My parents filled my bookshelves with all the greats—Alex Haley, Maya Angelou, Langston

Hughes, Richard Wright—but what was under my bed? *Star Wars* extended universe and *Dune*. Have you read the new *Dune* series?"

"No. I'm scared. Are they worth it?"

"I won't ruin it by giving an opinion."

"Oh! That's not fair. We giant nerds have to have each other's backs."

"I can't deny it. Not even cool enough to score a geek designation. We'll discuss *Dune* prequels once you get to them. Maybe on a wine weekend."

"Sounds good." I catch myself biting my lip and nearly correct myself, but then I force all my usual *yes, I'm interested* airs. Bea would approve. Not even ten percent jackass, and definitely good for the heart.

♦ ♦ ♦

Bea

Bea slid her booted feet through the half-inch of slush that had fallen from the sky. Her toes stung as the icy chill of an unusually cold Vancouver February weaved its way through two pairs of wool socks. Nothing stopped the howling wind from curling around aching fingers shoved deep into pockets. The semi-frozen sludge slipped beneath her feet as she trudged the two blocks from train station to film studio.

A cold and unfriendly day that matched her mood.

She pushed through the door to the studio and stopped flat. New ten-foot posters of Eddie grinned down at her. Eddie flexed the taut muscle across his back and made his signature, giant tattoo of a Japanese symbol come alive.

Beyond the posters, the French cast milled about a fully-dressed set. How could they be in rehearsal without a script? Bea had forced Kat to call and nix all forward progress on the French revolution scenes after the read-through had been horrendous. The script needed to be revamped.

But somehow, the awful script was coming to life. A military-style, 19th-century tent stood under harsh white light, and, in the distance, the cave that would transport characters between time periods was being lit with large lamps. What were they rehearsing?

Bea jumped as a voice called out her name. Eddie stood not five feet away. "Feeling lost? I provide door-to-door direction services. Ten out of ten people find me more charming and helpful than Siri or Alexa."

It was the first time they'd spoken since an odd run of silly text messages that started after the women in styling asked Eddie if he considered himself more Ryan Gosling or Ryan Reynolds. Bea had no idea why he'd texted her for a response, but they'd gone on for over a day before he stopped responding.

An emotional orchestra tuned up inside Bea, belied by a serene smile. "The rumor around here is that I'm the official showrunner, but I didn't approve or organize this setup, so I'm contemplating drowning someone in a bathtub. You should probably walk the other way rather than get mixed up in this."

"Pity I spoke to you then. Now I'll have to be your accomplice. I'm an expert gravedigger among all my assets. But we should create a believable story." His English accent gave the words a smart, intriguing pulse while a good-natured smile played on his face. A gray sweater clung to a lean but well-muscled form. Smart and sexy. Smexy, as Kat would say. He had a great sense of humor, too, if Bea were intent on cataloguing his positive traits.

"I doubt a Shakespeare lover like you could resist a monologue," Bea teased.

Eddie leaned in closer, his arm perched on a mop handle. Eddie had the most amazing amber eyes. Film captured them as common brown, but they weren't. They glimmered like jewels lit from within, especially when he laughed. "Then we've a plan. I'll distract the authorities with riveting pentameters so you can sneak out of the country."

Bea grinned, caught his gaze, and then regretted it. She focused on the mop. "I don't remember swabbing among your list of duties."

"Actor concession. Gives me an excuse to make every day *Talk Like a Pirate Day.*"

And that did it. Her foul temper melted away. "I draw the line at pet parrots. They poop all over the cameras. Keep that in mind if your peg-leg fantasies go wild."

Eddie laughed out loud, and Bea understood what made his fangirls obsess over every detail of his life and body. Eddie made you *feel*. Kindness and humor were cards in his hand and he dealt them out generously until a person was stripped bare and thrilled at the loss.

Eddie rested his chin on the handle of that puzzling mop. "A lovely smile like that will help you conquer whatever had you murderous. Don't let them push you around. The industry is used to beautiful women wielding power. Women with other skill sets make them nervous."

Eddie returned to cleaning up spilled coffee and then tossed an empty cup with his name on it in the trash.

Bea's thoughts had all run away, and she couldn't call them back. She had a crush. A stupid, awful, make-you-giggle crush. Kat loved that giggly, fangirly, obsessed emotion; To Bea, it felt like losing a limb in severe trauma: disorienting, disengaging, and foolhardy. She'd had only one crush, in high school, and then she'd crushed those silly and suffocating emotions.

Yet they'd returned, unwarranted and unwanted. A crush on Eddie, who apparently didn't put her in the beautiful category. That stung more than a little.

Josh emerged from his office, hurrying off to somewhere not on his calendar. Bea walked to where Josh and the director conferred over a map. She wandered wordlessly behind them as they discussed snowfall and the upcoming battlefield sequence. She crawled into the back seat of the black SUV without asking permission.

"Oh, hi, Bea," Josh said when he noticed her.

"Morning, Josh. Where we headed?"

"Scouting for snow locations. Sure you want to come? Gonna be cold."

"I'm absolutely certain I want to come. I grew up in Idaho. I know a lot about snow."

The car revved to life, and the men resumed their chatter. Bea made phone calls in the back. She had no idea what she was doing, but she was going to do it with confidence.

Six hours later, Bea kicked at the wispy flakes beneath her feet. There really had been no reason on God's green earth that she needed to give her opinion on snow depth. She barely listened to the riveting conversation about snow machines versus powder flakes versus CGI. Though, CGI was ridiculous. "CGI? Really? I'd rather color the film by hand than waste money on a digitized snowscape."

Josh nodded after a wry laugh. "Well, we can't have Bea spend all the Monkey & Me money on white crayons. How about we blow the snow Tuesday at midnight? It should stay stable the whole day. But then we need a script, Bea. Just nod and say I can film the pilot the way it stands. Kat won't give me money until you approve."

Bea sighed and kicked at snow again. "I hate the pilot. It's boring."

"No one likes a pilot episode. But we need something to air in June."

"We all like the battle. And the library—I like all the stuff with the girls in the Brooklyn library. But the French cast—just—give me the weekend. If I don't produce anything I like better by Monday, we film the pilot the way it is." Bea yawned. How long had it been since she took a break? Or slept a whole night? Her stomach growled.

Josh conceded. "Okay. But on Monday, you run the show as currently written. Agreed?"

They all nodded. One weekend. To get inspired about a show featuring a group of French revolutionaries time travelling to modern-day Brooklyn in an effort to save Napoleon's hide. Maybe Kat could conference in, not that she had or showed any interest in doing so, but maybe if Bea sounded desperate.

Roger peered at her over his clipboard where he blocked out prop placements in the library. "Hey, Bea, could we go over sponsor wish lists one more time?"

"Tonight? I'm wiped. Do you ever go home? Doesn't your wife need to see you occasionally?"

"She's understanding."

Josh yawned, too. "Sure. That's what we all say. Then one day, you're on your own again. Yeah, let's call it. We've had the same conversations all day. We need to get out of here and find our creativity again."

Bea mulled over Josh's words the whole ride back to the studio. She rarely spoke to Nicola or Matthias anymore. Gabe or her dad? Never. But that was how this business worked, right? No one went home. The families waited.

Or didn't exist at all.

Probably the part of this business Bea did best. There was nothing to hold her back and no one waiting at home.

The black SUV pulled into the parking lot. Roger and Josh dispersed to their respective vehicles. Bea walked into the fading light toward the train station.

At the end of the parking lot, Eddie and Siena gestured angrily at each other with hands slicing the air like double-edged swords. Eddie's wet, black hair was frozen in sharp angles like dark knives poised to slice his skin. His eyebrows slanted down over eyes narrowed into obsidian orbs and his laugh lines combined into a singular scowl. Not handsome anymore. Bea tried not to be seen as she hurried past the unhappy couple.

Eddie brushed past her a moment later. He turned up an empty street and started to run. Then he disappeared at the other end. Moments later, Siena's green Fiat squealed and slid around the corner in his general direction.

Eddie and Siena were an odd couple. His happiness was at odds with her wild temper. But couples never made sense to Bea; she could never explain what pulled them together or what kept them from flying apart.

Bea abandoned her ideas of the train and hailed a cab. She deflected attempts at conversation, lost in lonely thought. Inside the lobby of her building, she shook the ice from her hair and body in front of a large mirror. Oh, why had she worn jeans and a bulky sweater today? She looked like a disheveled ginger yeti amassing fat stores for winter hibernation. No wonder Eddie thought her unattractive.

With a shout of frustration, she stomped her feet and let the last remaining sludge spray her jeans and sully the carpet. No. It didn't matter. She was lonely, that was it. For the first time in her life, she didn't have a friend or family member at her doorstep. As soon as she made some friends, this feeling would pass.

She climbed the three flights of stairs to her apartment and then stepped out of her clothes on the way to her bed. She sprawled across her bed and pulled her pilled, hand-quilted blanket across her back. Her cell phone glowed beneath the quilt. Then it quivered. Matthias's most sardonic expression jumped around with the screen.

She hit the green button.

"I hate Kat," she said before he said hello.

"If only that were true, *gattina,* then I could say a dozen things you wouldn't like. Enjoying Vancouver?"

"Not a bit. I've accomplished nothing. I'm permanently cold. And Edward Wolverton called me ugly."

"Was he sober enough to see straight?"

"Stop. No, don't stop. I need every ounce of mean you've got today. I'm supposed to fix this whole stupid plot by Monday and I don't know where to start. I curse Kat, curse my own ambition, and hate that I left London for this mess."

"You're missed, too. Open your email."

Bea opened up the account on her phone and clicked on the email from Matthias. "Because you insisted . . . ," he'd written.

Bea scanned the lower portion, and then sat up. "Oh! You won! That's so great. The photo deserved attention." Bea clicked on the photo of the mother in her burqa with her children in the days after the bombing.

"You have to be here for the exhibition. I've sent the dates. No excuses."

"Wow. And that's as much money as you got for that nude picture of Deebs last year at his twenty-first birthday party. Who says photojournalism doesn't pay?"

"Once in a lifetime, you'll be right. But here's the photo that will pay more."

Her phone chimed a text. Bea opened it and shuddered. "Oh, gross. Deebs. Fame has not been good for you. Can you actually sell that photo?"

"Dumb kid hired us to be on-site since his next album is due next week, then got into a fight with a transgender prostitute. Dozens of us there, but I got the best shot. That's a three-thousand-dollar bit of photojournalism."

"Is there seriously no one in his life to pull him back from the edge? No one?"

"That's his dad holding the woman's arms."

"Asked and answered."

Bea and Matthias degraded into gossip and old arguments about responsibility versus privacy. As usual, Matthias's insistence that things done in public are public knowledge held weight, but she stopped him short of moving the conversation to Eddie and Siena for no good reason beyond misplaced loyalty. On *21 Things*, she safeguarded her actors' privacy for the benefit of everyone. Here, the worse the publicity, the more gleeful the producer response. It was one of a million things she didn't understand.

At the end of the conversation, she laid back and let the quilt fall over her head. Eddie's face came too easily, both the happy no-worries version and the ugly anger she'd seen in the parking lot. He had a face that told a dozen stories.

As Eddie's face toggled between expressions, a story emerged. A man driven to Napoleon's army by a life of poverty, a madman hidden by military genius and a romantic's heart. A scene played out in her mind.

Bea sat up and reached for her laptop. She had Dom, and, if she had Dom, she'd find the rest of the characters. Her fingers flew across the keyboard while her own grin reflected on the screen.

CHAPTER 11

"But success shall crown my endeavours. Wherefore not? Thus far I have gone, tracing a secure way over the pathless seas, the very stars themselves being witnesses and testimonies of my triumph. Why not still proceed over the untamed yet obedient element? What can stop the determined heart and resolved will of man?"

—Mary Shelley, Frankenstein

Bea

On Monday, Bea knocked on Josh's trailer door. Excitement and fear made her hands tremble. She slid in and closed the door when he answered.

"I need one camera, Roger, and the French cast for a morning. Won't cost enough to even bubble the budget. But I want you to see it, not only read it. If I don't sell you on it, then you win. I'll tell Kat to sign off on creative and I'll chase advertisers without complaint."

"Did Kat sign off finally?"

"No," Bea said, definitively. "This is mine."

Josh's mouth pressed into a line, then he quirked a grin. "Brave move. So, okay. One camera and two hours of Roger's time. That's what you've got."

The days passed as slowly as the moments before the end of a school term. Bea planned every detail of the shoot. She consulted with military and history experts until everything was where she wanted it to be. She only got one chance to prove her point, so she double- and triple-checked.

"Are you pleased?" Eddie asked behind her when the day of filming arrived. He leaned against a tent pole with his arms crossed.

Bea had steeled herself for seeing Eddie as Dom, but his voice and body on set made it all real—all too real—especially the way he made her head go fuzzy. But she needed to talk to him and not think about her precious feelings. Siena had screamed at her for ten minutes over using Eddie's *most sacred symbol* as a plot device. Bea hadn't thought that through and Eddie deserved a chance to say no.

"Are you okay with using your tattoo? We could cover it and create something less personal."

"It's on my back. Be silly not to use it. I'd rather not start every day in six hours of makeup, but thank you for respecting what my tattoo means to me."

"Of course. What does it mean to you? But if that's too personal—"

Eddie's face settled into less of a grin. "It's the *sen shin*—an idea without translation. In martial arts, it's the idea that you live your life with perfect integrity. Complete commitment, passion, and honesty in everything you do. After I achieved master status in my gap year, it's the symbol I chose to guide my life."

Bea let the words hang. Nothing else to say, really. And every time they talked she lost a little more control of what she felt for him.

Eddie looked away. He ran a hand through his hair and shook his head, ever so slightly. He'd been oddly serious since the read-through. This particular gesture had been increasing whenever he spoke with her. Bea had no idea what it meant or why.

Eddie glanced sideways at her. "But I hate that symbol whenever I have a scene like this one. Complete commitment to a monster is rough on the brain. Method acting works well when you play the hero. A bit painful when you're the villain."

"Yeah. I can understand that. Thank you for doing this. I'll leave you to prep." Bea turned and finished checking the items on the table. Everything was as she'd ordered.

Siena hurried on set in her robe, a small woman capable of filling every ounce of space. She crowded Bea aside without ever touching her. Eddie's grin lit up, and he crossed over to wrap his arms around her waist and whisper something that made her laugh. Bea brushed aside the flash of jealousy. Apparently, she'd crush on Eddie for the rest of forever.

Bea took a seat in the blackness behind Roger. The lights dimmed and brightened in turn as the scene was called. Then they settled on the softest possible setting to create a tent lit by candlelight.

Siena dropped her robe. Not an inch of imperfection. Bea must hate herself to have written Siena in the nude. Or maybe she needed reminding of what Eddie saw in the shower every morning.

The clapper fell, not even labeled since this scene would never officially exist if the experiment failed.

The scene opened with Eddie and Siena playing with an orphaned baby found near the most recent battlefield. Siena cooed at an infant who grinned and babbled in response, seemingly enthralled by Siena's breathtaking beauty. The baby responded as females generally did to Eddie. Little Hannah reached up and smiled at him. Eddie counted the beats perfectly before breaking gaze with the baby to lean toward Siena.

The scene was entirely in French. The tone was easy and lovely and as filled with sex as ever French was or could be. Bea knew the English words from pre-translation, but she watched her translator from the corner of her eye to ensure what was spoken matched what she wanted.

Siena positioned herself on the bed, open and seductive and almost crude. Her arms reached for her lover. Eddie placed one knee on the bed. The camera tightened on Eddie's back as Siena pushed off the open jacket. The tattoo and muscle came into full view as he descended on top of her. Siena had thought well through this moment. Her nails started center and raked outward across the tattoo, accenting the entire span of black with red lines. They'd grab that shot for promos.

The kisses and caresses seemed to go on forever. And then there was sex. One hundred and twenty seconds of barely-legal-on-American-TV sex play.

As the couple broke the embrace, Roger made a *roll-on* sign with his fingers to let the whole sequence play as a single take. Siena slipped under the covers, shaping the sheets to accentuate her curves, and then feigned sleep.

Eddie stood and moved to the front of the tent. The camera moved into place.

Bea shifted forward, trying to catch every nuance. Perfect, it had to be perfect.

An officer entered as soon as Eddie finished dressing. There was an exchange of dialogue that established the mission. Then the man glanced toward the almost-bare chest of Siena but returned his eyes immediately with a hint of embarrassment.

A super-quick flick from Eddie sent the actor's glass flying from his hand.

"Hey! What there?" The same hand suddenly clasped the man's throat.

"Hush. You'll wake my love." Eddie said as he appeared to squeeze harder. Bea worried the next moment may not work, but Eddie shifted as needed. Gleeful excitement overwrote the natural friendliness. Good. Eddie hesitated to the right count and then his other hand joined the first, and his mouth turned up in a grisly, self-satisfied grin. On cue, a small line of fake blood emerged from the victim's nose. The body slumped to the floor.

Bea's stomach leaped forward in a thrill of excitement. Yes. Yes, yes, yes. Exactly how she'd envisioned it. Disturbing yet compelling. No one on the set dared to blink.

The scene ended as Eddie fit his body to the curve of Siena's. He bit her shoulder and ran his hand along the curve of her hip.

A silence—awe—had settled over cast and crew.

Roger called the scene in a whisper. The moment of respect continued until Eddie and Siena moved. Hushed approval exploded into a round of applause.

Then Josh spoke from behind Bea. "No need to spend money on the focus groups. Writers meet at ten sharp tomorrow. Take this where it needs to go."

Bea released the chair with a flood of happy everything. She'd done it. She'd written something and put it on screen without anyone's help. And it was good.

So, so good.

She walked across to the craft services table, and grabbed a cup of ice to press to her forehead. An almost-black darkness surrounded the set where only Eddie remained in light. He pulled on his military jacket in preparation of the second take. His hands shook a bit after all he'd poured into that first take.

Still, Bea wanted a little more.

She walked up next to him, close enough that only he could hear. "Martial arts master, right? You can move faster than you just did. Don't worry about the camera; we can play with it on editing. Move as fast as you can."

Eddie didn't look at her. His jaw remain locked in the harsh lines of killer Dom.

Bea chewed her lip twice before speaking again. "You sure you can roll this back for us? Do you need a break?"

Eddie shook his head as he buttoned up his coat. "You bring in that baby and I'll be right as rain."

On the next take, Eddie moved so quickly to grab the actor's throat that the man gagged on his line. Eddie's eyes carried a deep, scarring hatred that turned his amber eyes black in the soft light. Perfect. Bea gave Roger and Eddie a thumbs up while magic tingled in her gut.

This would be television too good to miss.

♦ ♦ ♦

Kat

Philip's hands completely cover mine. The loud, backlit DJ pumping girl rock remixes fades out of focus. I can't see the lights running around the fancy glass bar or hear the general noise anymore. Only Philip exists. His smile and smell and person obscure the potent atmosphere. He's my favorite drug and I drink him while we wait. My fist curls into his palm. He wraps both hands around mine and then strokes my thumb with his. His eyes crinkle at the corners. A little purr buzzes the back of my throat as he looks at me.

Philip releases my hand to caress my cheek. I move in for a kiss but then I'm jostled from behind. Philip's thumb glances off my nose and digs into the space just below my eyebrow. My yelp turns to a laugh when Philip's face falls, aghast at my near-injury.

Theo, newly-hired male star of *K-Town,* apologizes for knocking me but then takes off teasing. "When you two fucked last weekend I thought I wouldn't have to put up with the mooning anymore. I've brought friends. Don't embarrass me."

My trainers connect with Theo's shin—a warning shot. "Oh, you're just jealous because my boyfriend's hot."

"Not true," Theo pouts.

"Those were your exact words yesterday." I stick my tongue out, being bratty.

Boyfriend.

The word comes easier than I thought it would after my heartbreak over Ian. Everything with Philip is easy. We went to dinner the night we finalized casting and every night after.

Theo snaps in my face. I'm disoriented for a moment—it's hard to look away from Philip even after spending a whole weekend in bed with him. "Kat! You are definitely paying the tab. God, you two shouldn't be in public yet."

Philip gazes deep into my eyes and rubs one of his large fingers along his lower lip. My lower body squirms in response. I don't want to be here, either, but I've had the most incredible artistic epiphany. And Theo is going to love it.

Philip slides me back against his chest. Those incredible hands spread across my abdomen, covering my whole belly. His thumbs touch the underside of my bra and his pinkies rest at the line of my underwear.

Sex. All I can think about is sex.

But sex with Philip isn't the only sex on my brain. I've also been thinking about Theo's character and sex. Yesterday, Theo grinned at his costar, Masden, and I melted into a delicious writing fantasy. That's why we're here tonight.

Masden appears across the bar and I wave hello. Theo follows my wave. He looks back at me with eyebrows quirked, his gorgeous green eyes full of humor. "Ooh, a secret conclave with the producer in the dead of night."

Theo silences after I kick him again, harder. No info until everyone is together.

I signal for a round of gin and tonics that glow blue under the trendy black lights. Theo and Masden clink glasses before sliding the drinks back in unison. Both have chiseled cheekbones and high brows, but Masden is large and burly while Theo is lanky. Together, they're beautiful with a natural, comfortable chemistry that's stimulated my whole line of thinking.

A few typed pages that I threw on paper this morning emerge from my bag. "I've had an idea, guys. I want to sell it to the writers tomorrow morning, but I want you to see it first. Let me know what you think." Their eyes graze the pages and Theo's grin grows so wide, so happy, I feel like Santa Claus.

We drink until we're all stupid, then Philip drags me home for more of that great sex. I'm as high as I can be when I walk into the writers' room the next morning.

I love writing, adore every moment of the creative process. Bea and I drafted *21 Things* in what was the best year of my life. We scribbled in cafés and talked about writing all day and most nights. Our apartments transformed into giant storyboards as we plotted out every detail.

The writers' room at National is almost orgasmic for me. There are *eight* writers on staff for *K-Town*. I'm the EP, so my storyline decisions matter, but then it all collapses into bickering over lines and characters and cause-effect discussion—good sex accompanied by classic rock 'n' roll. I've got staff to handle everything here at National and I let them. I live here, in the writers' room.

In my element.

I really am a creative genius. I've always said so, but now everyone knows. This is my world, bitches, watch me own it.

But today, I don't own it. I'm completely unprepared for—and a little incapable of handling—the totally different experience that greets me in the gold and mahogany room that's usually my happy-bunny place here in Los Angeles.

There's an undercurrent of the bad type and zero buzz of excitement as I turn the new pages over for the usual artistic feeding frenzy. Silent faces exchange uncomfortable glances. Pencils tap against paper in the awkward void.

"You're sure? Really sure?" The head writer looks at me over his reading glasses. He's the only older face in the room, a veteran writer whose truncated resumé still includes episodes on almost every National Network show since the dawn of time.

"Of course I'm sure." I can't keep the youth out of my own voice. My retort is too strident. But, really? Of course I'm sure. I wrote the pages. I put them on the table. I'm completely sure.

The undercurrent turns to murmuring but no one touches the pages.

"What's the problem?"

"Problem?" An unexpected bellow from the back of the room. One of the young and cocky, though this kid wrote his first accepted script as part of a high school English class. His writing chops chomp mine, despite his age. "This changes the entire *show*. Did you clear this with the higher-ups? I hope you did. They're getting a drama now, and I'm pretty sure they bought a comedy. With a Latina lead, not a white male."

The undercurrent changes to cursing. I put my hands on my hips and stare everyone down. E-fuckin'-P, so listen to the lies I'm about to tell. "Yes, I have VP of Programming's okay. And it's co-leads now. Nothing wrong with that. More white men, a mandate from Bob—"

I'm cut off by belly-laughing from half the writers. My hackles rise so high I'm shocked I don't *caw* and take flight. "Get to work. We don't have long to prepare this for shooting."

My serious voice gets their attention. There are shrugs, head shakes, and a few eye rolls, but everyone settles into work mode. It's not happy work, but they polish the new scene until it shines. The storyboards shift, pieces erased or moved—a new vision coming to life. My enthusiasm creeps back to the heights. I leave with a mostly ready scene to show the higher-ups. Marty loves me, so I'm not worried. He'll support my decision. If he doesn't, I'll use Ian the way he used me. It's the Hollywood way.

Theo shouts for me when I pass by the room where the director holds a read-through. I stick my head in the door and wave at everyone.

"There she is. Our hero. The *artiste extraordinaire*!" Theo jumps from his seat and throws his arms around me.

"Theo! Did you tell everybody? You're not supposed to blab." I laugh and punch him in the arm again. Gods, I love actors.

"I couldn't contain myself. I get to kiss someone I'm attracted to on set. You're perfect, Katrine Porter. Have I told you that?" He grins and both dimples pop out on his cheeks. He's so perfectly male. He and Masden will be the couple of the century.

"I should have taken you to the writers' room with me. They don't seem to have the same enthusiasm."

The director stares at me. I smile at him, but he leans back without returning it. "Changing a comedy to a drama and switching out your leads after a week on set? Reshooting the entire pilot? I imagine they were too busy revising their resumés to rejoice in your revolution."

Theo clucks at him. "Oh, stop. Don't be a suit. Not for one minute. Kat is going to change the world." Theo kisses me on the cheek and hugs me again.

"We've all heard it, Theo. Can we get back to the read-through? Any objection, Kat?"

Theo's arm falls away under the glare of the director. National Network is a dream, but I miss our flexible, friendly life across the pond. Definitely no tattoo show-off in this rehearsal. "No. None at all. Make my world come to life, everyone."

The read-through commences with the director's nod. Theo throws imaginary roses and kisses at me as I exit. I can't help but laugh, even as I note that the actress who plays the female lead sits with her arms crossed and glares at me through the whole exchange.

Calling Marty is next. "Hey, did you read it?"

"Kat, you can't be serious. This is a big change."

"I am. It's going to be amazing. You'll love it."

"Theo's called me twice to make sure I say yes."

"So, say yes and clear the way."

Marty stays silent long enough that I play through the entire first two stanzas of *Moonlight Serenade* on my desk and wonder if I should have done this in person to distract him with cleavage. Finally, he exhales loud enough to rattle my eardrums. "Promise me I won't regret this and I'll say yes."

My fingers switch to *Ode to Joy*. "Trust me, Marty. We'll have a male co-lead, audiences will love it even more. It's going to be fan-freaking-tastic."

Then I have it. The green light.

The next weeks pass in an absolute passion state. I eat, drink, and breathe my vision. My hands touch every piece—I split my time between the writers room and the set—if it weren't for Philip, I think I would sleep here, like I did my first weeks on *21 Things*.

A rare moment of quiet in my office finds me looking at my sister's Facebook page, and an even rarer moment of insanity finds me calling her to suggest we meet up and spend some time together while they're visiting Disneyland. It's what both my dad and Bea would want me to do, I reason. But insanity leads where it always does—straight to heartbreak. My sister, as usual, knows exactly how to crush my soul. My head collapses and doesn't rise again until a knock at the door summons my attention.

Theo's head pops in as I wipe tears off my face. "I come bearing mimosas."

"Whoa, Kat honey, what's going on?" Theo plunks champagne and orange juice down on my desk, and then sits on the edge to turn my chair to face him.

I sniffle and shake my head.

"Tell Theo everything. What are best friends for?"

"My stupid big sister," I start. I'm not sure where to go from there, though. Rachel has a gift for making me feel inadequate and silly, a skill she's been honing my whole life, and now her cold disapproval twists up my insides yet again. "I don't know why I try."

"I'll pour, you talk." Theo retrieves plastic cups from a cupboard. Friday morning mimosas have become one of our rituals.

"They're doing a family Disneyland trip and I thought—maybe we could try to not be enemies. It's the first time in years we've been on the same continent. But she doesn't want my bad influence ruining her kids."

"What is she smoking? You're amazing."

"The harshest of all drugs, *das Opium des Volkes*. She's the worst Christian zealot, like full-on hateful and everything. She homeschools and doesn't own a TV and thinks sex was invented by the devil, so everything about me falls under the *hellfire* column."

Twelve-year-old Rachel sanctified big sister arrogance through her religious fervor. All I ever needed was Dad and music, so I remain baffled as to what Rachel found among the Southern evangelical movement.

"It's so much worse when it's family, I know that from personal experience." Theo rubs my arm.

"What did your family do?"

"Kicked me out, disowned me. Big, Mormon family full of good line-toe-ers, boasting missions and temple weddings. And one disappointing gay kid at the tail end. I forced my dad's hand by daring to be myself. He's got enough other kids that he never seemed to miss me, and a couple of years bouncing around friends' houses taught me who I am and who I never wanted to be." Theo tries to smile around it, but the watery shimmer in his eyes betrays him.

I stand up and hug him. "You're amazing, he doesn't know what he's missed out on."

"Neither does your sister. So, fuck them. We don't need them. We've got each other and the most amazing new TV show about to hit everyone's must-watch list."

"A few tweaks away from greatness." Like a villain. My drama lacks a good someone-to-hate. My head reels a bit on an idea. "My sister would make an awesome bad guy."

The champagne has gone to my head, maybe. Either the confession or the alcohol makes me buzzed and bubbly.

"Now's your chance. Take my dad along for the ride. I've got plenty of stories."

My fingers itch now, the urge to transfer ideas from head to page almost overwhelming—more incredible changes. *K-Town* will change the world.

"Well, if they didn't want bad things said about them, they shouldn't have done bad things, right? We finally get to say what they won't hear otherwise. Shine the light of art and maybe do some good."

"To genius, and to you, Kat Porter," Theo toasts. We clink our red plastic cups and hug again. No more tears.

CHAPTER 12

Und wüßten sie mein Wehe,
die goldenen Sternelein,
sie kämen aus ihrer Höhe,
und sprächen Trost mir ein.

And if they knew my pain,
the golden little stars,
they would descend from their heights
and would comfort me.

—Robert Schumann, Dichterliebe

Bea

Bea hung up the phone and clicked through her spreadsheets. She'd given herself a week in the office to catch up on the business side of Monkey & Me. A million items kept slipping by the wayside as *Void* required more and more focus. At least she finally had an organization system that worked for her. She'd had the brilliant idea to hire a library science major as her personal assistant. Her binder system had been digitized and all old entries transferred into a database. Honestly, she was worth double what Bea was willing to pay her.

But despite her wonder-child's overall enthusiasm and efficiency, the *K-Town* numbers still weren't up to date. Bea hit the button that summoned her assistant.

Lizzie slid around the corner a moment later, her plastic glasses frames held tightly in her teeth. She took them out and placed them inside the kinks of her silvery-brown hair. "I called again, Bea. Twice. Nicola said she asked Kat why the holdup."

"I need numbers, Lizzie. My pretty spreadsheet has nasty holes."

"I know. I'll call her again. Anything else?"

"Yes. Dailies?"

"Josh said they'll be on-screen at one. You're supposed to bring snacks."

Bea glared over the top of her computer screen.

"I told him I'd be happy to borrow the cave and cancel feminism. But if that doesn't work, he should order up his own snacks since it's been fifty years since that was an appropriate order for a woman at work."

Bea grinned. Honestly, worth every penny. Best hire since Nicola. "Lizzie, I love you."

"You only love me for my database." Lizzie grinned and then tugged the glasses from her hair. "How often should I bug Nicola before I—you know—*bug* Nicola?"

"Every hour. At least. I hate these nasty holes. Tell her I made you do it."

The door slid closed. Bea walked to the window of her office in downtown Vancouver. Her hand stroked the stack of scripts she'd approved that morning. *Void* was humming, as *21 Things* had.

Lizzie came back an hour later with a large, iced soda. "I got ahold of Nicola. She says to bring you this and make sure you are in a safe place to scream when you open your email. Something about Kat being *maybe, a little, or more than a little,* over budget." Lizzie pretended at Nicola's Italian accent that only emerged under stress. Otherwise, Nicola spoke in the cadence of the American sitcoms she'd used to learn English.

Bea clicked her email. The spreadsheet opened on ugly red totals. "What the—what are you doing, Katrine?" Bea had noticed the huge expense requests over the past few weeks. They were large, above estimates, but Bea had assumed Kat was spending all the Monkey & Me money first. Now, it appeared she was spending *everyone's* money at an alarming rate. And for what? Reshoots? Double-time for writers? What was she doing over there?

An urgent message popped up on screen while she waded through the expenses. From Matthias, but locked. Bea entered *gattina* in the password field. The message opened on a link.

At the bottom of the email, Matthias had typed: *This goes live in an hour. Nothing I can do to help.*

Bea clicked the link to see screenshots of the Hollywood Gossip Network site. Photos of Katrine and *K-Town,* nothing too surprising. Bea had heard Kat's ideas for shifting Theo to a more prominent role to represent the LGBTQ community more visibly. He did look gorgeous next to his on-screen husband, and the kissing shots should please viewers.

Bea maximized the other screen shots for the story.

Don't quit your day job, K. Porter. The Hollywood darling pissed off every Southern granny at the GLAAD awards last night. The American Family Convention and three other Christian coalitions call for a boycott on 21 Things *and* K-Town *until K. Porter issues apology. Don't know about you, but we don't think that's coming anytime soon. She's pretty cozy in social media hell. We only hope she's got a Plan B, career-wise.*

Bea sat back, stunned. She clicked play on the video attached to the email. This rabbit hole better have magic mushrooms and a lovely allegory about growing up.

In the video, Kat laughed with Theo, arms locked around each other, at the GLAAD awards. Kat had caught red carpet fever. This was her third walk down a carpet in the six weeks since the Globes.

Hot Mic!! Hot Mic!! flashed over the segment as Kat and Theo moved off-screen. Transcribed words ran below video feed of two starlets talking about dresses and the welcome surge of LGBTQ love stories.

"Did you know REV News Network had a prayer circle for me?" Theo's voice was muted. Kat's mic was the active one. Rookie mistake. "Prayer failed yet again. I'm still gay."

"Love is love is love is love is love. Haven't they heard? I can't wait until *K-Town* starts to push buttons. People are people and should be free to do what they want. And who they want."

Then another voice or a garbled Theo—unknown per the ticker-tape—chimed in. "The more ridiculous we can make them all seem, the better. If it were up to me, we'd put Christianity out of business."

There was a rush of interference as Kat handed off the microphone, still live. She'd had no idea that the mic recorded every word.

The reporters from HGN arrived on screen, huddled around cubicles with coffee in hand.

"And then—did you see this?" The lead reporter in the clip pretended to call up the social media account from *K-Town*'s lead actress.

Sad tale of minority women in Hollywood. Yesterday, I was the lead. Today, I'm a missionary with a cross to burn. #fuckyouNational #fireme

The photo showed the actress in a nurse's uniform with a black book clutched to her chest. On her left hand, a silver ring marked with CTR glimmered.

The exact ring gleamed on the same finger on Bea's left hand. Her chest squeezed tight as the image hovered on the screen.

Bea didn't doubt the characterization matched the vitriol from the actress.

The reporters came back on-screen, laughing and exchanging jokes. Several made explosion signs. There were jokes about Kat's resumé burning in trash bins at every production house in America.

Bea let the screen go black. Kat had written Rachel, all her pain about Rachel. Twice, Bea had cut similar characterizations from *21 Things*. Kat saw Rachel's face over every symbol of Christianity and felt Rachel's abandonment as keenly as the day she'd left their father's funeral without so much as a farewell. But this time, she'd also written Bea and Bea's family. Maybe Bea didn't talk much about her faith to spare herself arguments with Kat—and heaven knew there'd been precious little time for worship—but she was still the same Mormon girl who'd preached the gospel for a year and a half on a Mormon mission to Guatemala.

For two minutes, Bea reeled with fear and shock and worry and an emotion so empty and ugly that Bea worried she'd be sick. Betrayal. Deep, gut-wrenching betrayal.

But as much as this was personal, it was business. And Kat's vendetta against organized religion could cost them.

Bea called the airport to arrange a flight and buzzed Lizzie.

"Lizzie, call Josh. Tell him there's a crisis in Los Angeles. I'll get one of my showrunning team to step into my shoes and oversee everything remotely from the office in LA."

Bea held the phone in front of her as she walked out the door. Nicola's face filled the screen.

"All press is good press, right?" Nic's voice shook.

"Let's hope so. I'll need meetings with everyone the minute I get into town."

♦ ♦ ♦

Kat

Philip hugs me tightly again, then tilts my head up to look at him. He has the warmest, brownest eyes and warmest arms that have cared for me since Bea called me from the plane to yell about everything from my runaway ego to apparent need for a full-time nanny. I cried. Bea made me cry.

Philip holds me in front of National Studios as tears threaten again. His eyes search mine. "I was saving this for later, but maybe now is the right moment. I love you, Kat. So, no matter what, I'm in your corner."

Some unseen fist grips my heart and I don't analyze a thing. You don't let a guy as good as Philip declare his love and not say it back. "I love you, too." I reach up and kiss him. "Though you're welcome to reconsider once I'm an eviscerated, homeless shell of a former producer wandering Burbank in a search for revenge."

"I'll bring you the good cardboard. Steal it right out of the bins at Best Buy. You won't feel a single raindrop during your homeless wanderings."

The moment lightened, Philip puts an arm around my shoulder and steers us toward the door. "But it won't be that bad. PR hiccups happen in this business."

"Yeah, Bea will fix it. And then she'll kill me. Maybe I won't need that cardboard after all, lucky you."

Philip kisses me once more. Then I make my death march to the third floor conference room. Bea's voice can be heard from halfway down the hall. She's a rational person, in general. Quiet. I've seen her go days without saying a thing, but when she wants attention, everything about her becomes large and loud.

Bea points to an empty chair as I step in the door. She's in front—in command—with a long list of numbers and sponsor lists. I'm the chastened child in the corner.

I might as well be dead for all the credence my voice gets in this *eight a.m. sharp* meeting. Bea and the suits talk numbers, endless numbers, and I listen. Fifteen affiliates have exercised their right not to air *K-Town* without even seeing a pilot.

A large map with virtual pins and dollars and numbers on the projection screen tells a grim tale, I can read that much. Money. Lots of it, even the network's base investment in my show, is at risk. What magic can Bea pull out of her big money-making hat?

Her hands are on her hips, head tilted to the side. She stares at the map. Every few seconds, her braid swishes in response to a rapid shake of her head as she makes and dismisses plans. Come on, Bea. Save my baby.

"What if we just pull the pieces that will ruffle feathers? Reverse the whole storyline? We've been uncomfortable about it from the start." Gray Suit goes full defcon three. The nuclear option. Everyone squirms. My blood starts to move past low-simmer, my default setting for any suited-up meeting.

Bea furiously shakes her head. Good. She's not nuclear.

But Pinstripe speaks. "The problem is that right now we have to choose who to incite. Now that they know the storyline existed at one point, we risk viewership no matter what we do." He points at New York and Los Angeles, the biggest numbers on the map.

Bea turns and faces us. She chews the inside of her lip before speaking. I'm surprised there's not blood running down her chin. "So, let's talk reality. We need top ratings in every active market to offset the Nielsen losses we can already count on. With the number of pro-military blogs blasting the show, we've lost the military contract before it was even a possibility. Every assumption we've made about this show so far is wrong."

Oh, hell. She's right. AFRTS was one of our big selling points in the initial pitch. Here's a show predestined for military network distribution and worldwide viewership. Liar, liar, pants on fire, Kat. I sink a little in my chair.

But I shouldn't have to. The storyline is solid.

"I won't change a thing," I say through clenched teeth. "Not for politics and not for money." The suits ignore me, of course. Politics and money are what they're about.

Bea pounces on my pout. "Not about a single storyline. It's about *K-Town*. We believe in the product, right? We're agreed on this?"

Bea's question about belief in the product hangs in the air like a guillotine. Slowly—too slowly—the suit-heads nod. The guillotine pulls back up. My baby's neck is safe for now.

"So, tell me how we do this." Bea pulls out a chair and sits down. Defeat. I've never seen Bea give up, but she doesn't have a plan. She sits and waits while the suits scribble on notepads and shift in their chairs. Then Gray Suit clears his throat and leans forward.

"What if there's another option? A compromise that lets us keep San Diego *and* New York if we spin it right." Gray Suit taps his pen against his white legal pad with no notes. "Reshoot the religion angle, avoid the hefty topics. Show that Kat doesn't have it out for conservative Christians."

Bea leans forward. She nods. Gray Suit keeps talking. The options for reshooting swirl around me like those little cartoon birds when a character gets whacked on the head.

I hate every suggestion, but I say nothing, absolutely nothing, as a master plan to change the DNA of one of my plotlines becomes consensus.

But then Pinstripe interrupts. "I don't know, guys. I think *K-Town* will survive a little spotlight on homophobia. It's a good shake-up moment for America."

"I like that," I say to Bea.

Her ears turn bright red, but her voice stays calm. "I don't like cancellation."

She has a point. I guess. Burning it all to the ground to make a point sounds more appealing, though.

Marty stops communicating via Morse code and forms a sentence. "We do need to get the girl back front and center. All I care is that she's back to at least sixty percent screen time and a hero."

Bea sits forward. She nods and makes number notes in the margins as she recalculates market share in her head. Gray Suit moves pins around. A big old game of Battleship with no respect to the care I took to place all the pieces in the first place.

Bea smiles. Everyone smiles.

"Excellent, looks like we have a plan."

She nudges me under the table. Oh, right. "Thank you, everyone." I force a smile.

The talking heads file out of the room and Bea and I are left alone.

"Well?" Bea turns to me fully. "That turned out, okay, I think."

"I guess. If artistic integrity has lost all meaning."

"Don't be petulant, Kat. Everyone in here just did their very best to make sure you get everything you want."

I try to rally. "Okay. Thank you. But I'm not jumping up and down over the fact that the plan is to destroy my story arc. The network supposedly believed in this."

"They believe in money. Money makes TV. Your hot mic cost them money."

"But it's ridiculous! Bowing to market pressures and the easiest common denominator, making easy entertainment instead of telling stories that matter. Verdi could foment revolution, but I'm not allowed to do anything remotely controversial."

Bea pauses. Her fist opens and closes on a purple pen. When she speaks, the words clip and spit as they climb over a very large emotion. "What was that rebellion, exactly? Who did you want at the battle line? Christians. Mormons. My family. Me?"

My cheeks sting though she hasn't raised a hand. But I meet her at the front. My daddy didn't raise me to back down in a fight.

"Geez, Bea. Sensitive much. You're not even all that religious anymore. It's my art under attack."

"How can your art be more personal than my family?"

"I never meant you."

"Clearly. No one ever means me." Bea's voice has gone flat, only sarcasm remains.

"I wrote the truth. I wrote Theo's family and Rachel. The truth of our lives. And you know it. You can't say I said things that aren't true."

Bea opens her mouth, then closes it with a head shake. Her professional smile returns. "I don't. Bad people can be found in any social group. But we should take responsibility for the messages we send, and think about the people we hurt with each message. We owe them something, too."

A bubble of frustration pops on a philosophy I can't support. "That's not art, Bea. That's not what art is."

"TV isn't art, Kat. It's a product. A product that needs to make money."

I remain silent. I don't need another lecture. I don't need business Bea, I need my creative partner and best friend, but I don't know where that person is. "I don't know. Maybe I just—maybe this isn't my business. Maybe I have no place in business."

"You seriously don't say that to me right now, Kat. Not after what it's taken to get *Void* off the ground. It's one scene. Just one. You've filmed almost forty-seven others that everyone raves about." Bea's mouth pulls tight and she wrinkles her nose. Pragmatic, get-over-it Bea.

"It's moot, though, isn't it? *K-Town* is dead, even if we get to finish filming."

"Most likely. Then Josh gets his grand wish of you working on *Void* and it all ends happily ever after. You still go on to bigger and greater things. So, can we dial down the ego panic?" The way she stares past me makes me wonder if she's lecturing me or herself.

When her eyes come back, the fire is gone. The irises shine like green moss on aspen bark. She gives me a one-armed hug. She's super-high-powered Bea but I can impose my heart-image of her over the made-up version in the window. Her loungewear appears and her neat braid becomes a messy ponytail hanging over her shoulder. She smiles at my reflection. I smile back.

"Do you want me to run the people side with Theo? He'll be mad as anything about losing his breakout role to a girl."

I turn full on and hug her. "Are you seriously willing? He's going to hate me."

"Of course. Difficult men are my specialty."

"It seems my specialty is finding difficult men for you to deal with," I half-laugh.

"That's become very true. So, you're about fifteen phone calls and one grumpy actor away from this whole thing going away. Bright side."

"Thank you. And you're right. I want to do this right."

"Exactly. And now that we're all happy, I promised Bob that I'd read all the scripts to see if there are any other tricky spots. Apparently, we get one apology per cycle. No more."

I roll my eyes. "Sure. Whatever Bob says. Can you believe the way he insists everyone call him Bob?"

"I can't stop saying it sarcastically. Thanks, Bob. You're the best, Bob."

I snort-laugh. And then I can't stop laughing.

Bea drops an arm around my waist. "Sure, Bob, we'd love to make beautiful TV together, Bob." She smiles enough to let me know all is forgiven.

"We're good? I'll get you all the other scripts. Nic got you all set up in the office?"

"I'm official. Nameplate and everything. And we're always good. Even if I did just stab a stake through your artistic core."

We part ways on our different missions. It should feel like the old days—divide and conquer—but it isn't quite the same. Bea's never stood against me before, never doubted my vision, and never refused to see the art behind the enterprise. Somewhere in Vancouver, Bea turned into a suit.

CHAPTER 13

"These wonderful narrations inspired me with strange feelings.
Was man, indeed, at once so powerful, so virtuous, and magnificent, yet so vicious and base?
He appeared at one time a mere scion of the evil principle and at another
as all that can be conceived of noble and godlike."

—Mary Shelley, Frankenstein

Bea

Void premiered on a Saturday in a grand Hollywood premiere event at *Le Chateau* in Hollywood Hills. The Getty Center shone down on them with white marble, heaven above the hell of America's busiest freeway. Getting here had been a nightmare. Almost two hours to make the twenty-mile journey from apartment to venue.

Bea and Josh had opted for full French fashion to highlight the roles of Dom and Claudette, including French cuisine and wait staff in tails. Bea worried over every detail, including her own look—a 1950s couture French cocktail dress in black and white with a ragged hemline, and black stilettos with a three-inch heel. Her red hair fell in long waves disrupted only by a single small, French braid that extended from ear to ear. Droopy bangs brushed her cheekbone below her right eye. Soft makeup. Pink lips. Head-to-toe Parisian chic.

At the entrance, Kat approached the venue at a near-run, dragging Philip—that handsome teddy bear—behind her. She was Hollywood now, with jagged-edged, layered hair colored a variety of lowlights and highlights. Her daringly-cut gossamer dress twinkled as though covered in the entire cosmos.

She was starry-eyed and sparkly—and, Bea hoped, a little happy. Gah, they could use some happy after the catastrophe of last Friday.

K-town died at upfronts. The toxic social media blitz brought too much culture war to a show about patriotism and youthful enthusiasm. Enough people wouldn't let the argument die that mainstream advertisers said *No, thanks*. The network retooled the series as a one-and-done summer limited event, devastating Kat.

Maybe Bea had gone wrong, pushed too hard for concession. Maybe she'd failed Kat.

No, not maybe. Probably.

Definitely.

Philip paused at the railing with Kat. It was a funny thing about Kat, that for her all her feminist bents and rantings, something in her leaned toward the idea of being someone's woman. Philip tugged on her waist, then he wrapped his arms around her from behind and whispered in her ear until a wide smile broke across Kat's face. She turned and gave Philip a lingering, love-filled kiss that ended on a laugh.

Philip had gifts no man had possessed where Kat was concerned. He calmed her, centered her, found a way inside when all Kat wanted to do was push away. He was the first boyfriend Bea couldn't find a thing wrong with—well, except for the full-throttle midnight sex, but that wasn't new with Kat. The pleasant change was that Bea didn't resent trying to engage in breakfast small talk with whatever Tarzanian yeller Kat entertained.

Bea wandered over to the railing, careful not to disrupt their moment. She waved at Josh, who stood below to greet arrivals. He mouthed, *Save me*. Bea shook her head no, and then smiled when Josh flashed a grimace-grin and turned back to the crowd.

Kat took notice of her as she grabbed a glass of champagne from a circulating tray. "Pressure's on, Bea. We need a Monkey & Me success."

There was a hint of bite to Kat's words. Or maybe Bea expected there to be one. She opted for the high road—small talk until Josh joined them at the railing.

"What are you doing up here?" Josh chided, trying to pry Bea from her comfortable perch. "Come and meet your first flock of adoring fans."

"Don't be overconfident, Josh. You recut the pilot last night and we haven't tested it beyond a small focus group. Flat could be where it's at."

"Everyone knows Josh does his best work in the crunch," Kat fawned, perhaps trying to get back in his good graces despite yesterday's insistence that she'd never go to Vancouver. Best thing in the world would be Kat's renewed fervor for *Void*.

Josh wormed between Kat and Bea. "Have you met the cast yet? Want an introduction before everything gets crazy?"

Kat beamed at Josh and slid a hand along his elbow. "Yes, of course. I have sneaked some peaks at the recent dailies, you know, despite Bea hoarding them like nuts for the winter."

Bea let the burn sting. She was still the official villain of *K-Town*'s demise.

Philip offered his arm and Bea took it. He half-smiled at her and then let Kat take an extra step ahead. "Should I apologize for that?"

A prince. A true prince. Kat should propose to this man and be wed in a fortnight. "For that? No. I've taken a lot worse. She'll forgive me eventually."

"She will. I've heard all the best-friends-forever London shenanigans at least three times over. You're like sisters and all sisters fight."

"Maybe. I've never had a sister. And she deserves to feel a little upset over *K-Town*. She wanted that show; it had become very personal."

"She's one of those creators who make everything personal. *K-Town* had gone too far to be truly fixed. You can't sell a network a shoe and then give them a handbag. There's too much money at risk."

This was more than Philip had ever admitted, and the admission had terrible timing. Kat and Josh had paused to talk to a TV critic, and Bea and Philip nearly tripped over the pair on Philip's last sentence. Kat seemed not to notice. Philip moved them beyond her.

Bea squeezed his arm once they were clear of risk. "I'm hoping tonight helps her find her creative winds again. We're locked into three years at *Void*, and I want her to love what's happening there."

Bea reached out to shake the hand of a critic who swam past them on a reef of reporters. She said all the canned things she'd be saying all night, including handing off as much credit as possible to Kat.

"Hey, Eddie, Siena," Josh shouted above the crowd, behind her and Philip again. "Come join us. Meet our phantom producer."

Siena hung back to finish a conversation, her rear end perfectly encased in red velvet. She was a priceless jewel in a museum display case, not meant to be touched or bidden by the common man.

Eddie turned toward them, though. His curly black hair was more closely cut now that filming was on hiatus for the summer. He greeted them with that big, break-your-heart grin.

Eddie was toxic to Bea's composure, even after a month of not seeing him anywhere but on a screen. The fluttering jump in her gut disrupted equilibrium as a kaleidoscope of butterflies took flight.

Bea took five deep breaths. Butterflies were confirmed liars and mischief-makers. Their presence in her gut meant nothing. She forced the little beasties into a cage despite their insistence that Eddie looked happy to see her.

Kat reached forward to shake Eddie's hand, and her eyes caught on the black, edgy military-style modern jacket he'd worn in lieu of a tux. "Gods, I love this jacket. It's totally Sergeant Pepper," Kat said to Eddie, fingering the fringe at an epaulet. "You can't tell me it isn't."

"I can't and I wouldn't. Not given Bea's love for the Beatles." The light in his eyes danced as they met hers. He remembered their text messages? A silly little detail she'd tossed out when he'd quoted a lyric. She met his warm, amber eyes and a half-dozen butterflies escaped their lockdown. The world collapsed around her, and a single spotlight shone down that covered them alone.

Somewhere, Kat laughed at Bea and made a joke about Bea's distaste for classic English boy bands. But Bea couldn't break this gaze, not now, maybe not ever. And Eddie seemed okay with that.

"How doth the lady, Beatrice? You've been gone too long." Eddie's warm voice wove through the tinkling glasses and increasing buzz of voices.

He could mute the surrounding noise anytime he wanted her attention, but the micro-focus brought other things to light, confirmed rumors Bea had wanted to ignore. Red snakes wound around his irises, and his skin was sallow. A half-drunk glass of brown liquid dangled at his side. Drinking too much, as the gossip had said. Drinking all the time, as the whispers had warned.

"Get Siena over here. She needs to say hi, too," Josh said and the spell broke.

Eddie's arm snaked around Siena's waist to pull her into the conversation. She wore the world's sexiest dress, skin-tight and slit everywhere to reveal perfect skin. She was sex personified, and Eddie was *hers*. Not Bea's. Those were the lies the butterflies told. There was no special light, no magic. Bea was attracted to a man that thousands of women found attractive. She crossed her arms and smiled at the couple as Eddie brushed Siena's long, black hair from her neck to bestow a lover's kiss.

Kat laughed with her arms hugged around Philip's arm. "Did Eddie just call you Beatrice? He guessed your real name? He's got your name and your game, Bea. Every bit of it."

"I pilfered her mother's phone number. Any little detail I want is at my command. Elle Douglas is a very charming woman and a great conversationalist."

Siena slithered around Eddie, her head on his shoulder and arms wrapped about his waist. Her laugh joined his in complete awareness of every game. "Bea is a good sport. She puts up with his need to have a laugh, never complains when he teases her."

"That's me, the kid sister every guy loves to tease. Kat, meet Siena, third most beautiful woman in the world, per *Men's Quarterly*. Congratulations again, Siena."

"Though who needs magazines to tell us you're beautiful. Thank you for bringing Eddie along on this production, he's delightful."

"So they all say," Siena said and waved at someone beyond them. She tugged Eddie toward a group gathering at the front of the viewing salon.

"So, that's Eddie and the perfect Siena," Bea said to Philip and Kat, with a voice way too bright.

"Is it just me, or does she live up to her nasty reputation?" Kat wrinkled her nose.

Josh waved off Kat's response. "She's not that bad. A little full of herself, not wrong to be. Great sense of humor, but don't make her mad."

Philip offered his arm to Bea again as the lights around them dimmed for viewing. "Now, dear Beatrice, I am prepared to be amazed at the premiere episode of *Void*."

"You don't get to do that. I can't stop Eddie or my mom, but you're nice enough to obey. It's Bea. Just Bea."

"Alright, *Just Bea*. Let's go see success in the making." Bea grinned at Philip, grateful for his steady humor.

They found their seats amidst the cast and crew. The lights dimmed and the opening credits rolled. Kat nodded and hummed along with the score. Bea relaxed, a little. A good start could mean a great end. She kept Kat in her periphery throughout the viewing. Lots of smiles—good. A few eyebrow crinkles—she'd ask about that later. She still worried about her solo work, her inadequacy heightened by Kat's presence beside her.

Most of Bea's script changes had been tweaks. Lines shuffled among characters. Scenes rearranged. Character choices clarified. Dom's evil undercurrent shaded each interaction. The heroes became more complicated, and the funny lines took on an interesting tinge of self-preservation. And the sex—clothes on or off, Dom and Claudette buzzed with sexual tension and danger. Bea marveled at the collective audience response, more ardent than she'd imagined. There were gasps at the unexpected twists of character and giggles at the fiery banter.

Kat sat forward as Siena appeared on screen, obviously nude. She inhaled audibly when Claudette's nails marked Dom's back.

Kat elbowed Bea, hard. "Oh my gods, Bea. You wrote this? Are you having sex finally?" Then she gasped. "Are you having sex with Edward Wolverton? Because he likes you. Really, really likes you. And you like him. Are you and he . . . Bea . . . I've never been more proud of you."

"No. Of course not. He's practically married to Siena. I used this thing called imagination."

"Your imagination is very, very vivid."

Bea hushed her. She wanted Kat's reaction to the next piece. Kat tapped her fingers against the chair in front of her and then flung them to her mouth and gasped as Eddie killed the officer. "Wow. That was . . . he's amazing. You *should* have sex with him."

"I think his schedule is booked out for at least a lifetime," Bea mumbled, hoping no one around them decided to publish Kat's assessment of Bea's interaction with *Void*'s leading man. They'd publicized Eddie and Siena as a couple as much as Dom and Claudette.

"This is a hit, no question." Kat squeezed Bea's hand, but there was a tremble in her fingers and her body had gone too still.

Bea squeezed back. She leaned in to try and inflate the ego that made Kat the irresistible *Kat Porter*. "You did this. That's your vision, on-screen. Be proud of it."

But Kat went pandering best friend instead of inflated artist. Her mouth settled into a benign, soft smile. "No, this is you and Josh. Despite your claims that you couldn't succeed at sci-fi." The statement was an accusation.

Not good. Kat had to connect. Bea could stay in LA and work that side. Kat should be in Vancouver, on creative, side-by-side with Josh. "Well, if this is what Josh and I can do, I can't wait for the second half of the season. With you at the helm, this will be the show everyone still talks about in a hundred years."

Philip leaned over, his eyes on Kat, too. He offered salvation in a soft whisper. "Kat, this is the one, the one that makes you a household name. It's fantastic."

Josh beckoned them forward to the stage to accept the raucous applause that continued even after the lights came up. Kat hung back, as much as she could without breaking the moment, but Bea felt it.

This wasn't Kat being shy. This was Kat running *K-Town* and *Void* around in her head to decide on a winner. Kat couldn't not compete. And second place was never good enough. If *Void* won, and Kat gave credit to Bea, then *Void* became the competition, not the project.

And then what? Bea chewed her scar and worried through all of Josh's speech.

Kat smiled brilliantly when Josh mentioned her and called her to the podium. "All I did was rant an idea at Josh one night and then a few months later find a totally conceptualized show on my desk. All credit to Josh and Bea and the amazing cast and crew of *Void,* who have poured their hearts into what is definitely the next appointment-viewing show."

Competition.

Void had been slated under competition. Kat had given the big sign-off. Bea tried not to huff on stage. Somehow, she'd need to find Kat a new project, one that Kat could use to beat *Void* in the ratings.

Josh guided Bea to the press gauntlet. He was full of praise for her. But around the third interview, Bea noticed that Kat was nowhere to be found.

CHAPTER 14

So wie dort in blauer Tiefe,
Hell und herrlich, jener Stern,
Also er an meinem Himmel,
Hell und herrlich, und fern.

Just as yonder in the blue depths,
bright and glorious, that star,
so he is in my heavens,
bright and glorious, and distant.

—*Robert Schumann, Frauenliebe und -leben*

Kat

I don't *want* to feel this way. Heartbreak and rage have been at equal boils under my skin all week. Now they have company—jealousy, fear of irrelevance. I wish I'd gone nuclear, had the guts to say fuck off to the suits and their holy numbers and tiny unimaginative souls.

Including Bea.

Fuck off, Bea.

But my disappointment and anger can't explode over the top of Monkey & Me's future. *Void* is as sure a hit as I've ever seen. Edward Wolverton will bring the fangirls, and then they'll stay for the diverse ensemble and time-travel intrigue. Whatever I tried to do with *K-Town,* Bea has done it better.

So, I do the only reasonable thing I can think of—I run away. From Bea, who would say I'm being petulant. From Philip, who compared my baby to a handbag.

Not home. The premiere will go late, but Bea will be at the apartment eventually. No, I need to find some other way to spend the rest of Saturday evening. Luckily, I have at least three other options outlined *tentative* on my calendar. I direct the driver to my favorite theater in Los Feliz—an art house treasure where I have a standing invitation, not easy to come by—featuring a short film perspective tonight. *Art* beckons me.

I've missed the pre-mingling, but I enter the theater before the lights dim for the first showcase. Familiar faces—a cross-section of local artists across multiple mediums—greet me and my jangled emotions settle a little. I belong here.

A deep laugh from the front of the auditorium disrupts my composure, conjures up a kaleidoscope of intimate memories. I shouldn't look, I should turn around and walk away, but I have to confirm it with my eyes—what the hell is Ian doing here?

And I'm wearing the dress. The cosmos dress I bought with sex and love and Ian on the brain.

Hope bubbles in my heart—impossible, silly. I have been *so over* Ian Graham. And this isn't the Globes, this is not the height of my success, it's the goddamn bottom. I slink down into a seat next to an art columnist and we make small talk, avoiding the subject of my failed show, until the lights fade and the first film begins.

The Love of Zero draws me in, pulls me out of painful reality, offers destruction of the status quo and the nobility of suffering for one's art. I wipe away tears as it ends. This is exactly what I need tonight—catharsis, connection to something greater. Heart-shaped silhouettes burn into my brain, though—ridiculous hope born out of being in the same room as Ian. *Leave,* half of me says, but *Stay* wins the argument.

I mingle my way out to the bar, make a joke about being red carpet–ready when someone asks about my dress. All the way, I'm aware of Ian holding court in a corner of the theater's anteroom. I get a glass of wine and before I can turn away from the bar, I feel the welcome rush of tingling awareness. *Stay* dances, giddy, on my shoulder.

When I turn, the reality of Ian's proximity startles me and I almost drop the glass.

"Hullo, Kat," he drawls out in that wicked brogue. "This is a surprise."

"Good or bad?" I arch an eyebrow.

His eyes study me for a long moment, up and down, over every bare length of skin. The dress is destiny. "Quite nice."

"What brings you here?"

"Enjoying a short film showcase." His mouth quirks, and he nods toward an unoccupied spot away from the bar, underneath a vintage poster for a Taylor and Burton film. The alcoholic literary one. "Can we talk?"

We stand in silence for too long. I shift my weight and sip my Chardonnay.

"Ah, Kat." He rubs the back of his neck. "I want to apologize."

"And you couldn't do that any time over the past four months?"

"It's been complicated."

"Standing me up and not answering my calls seemed pretty straightforward."

"I handled it badly, I know. But I haven't stopped thinking of you."

Leave and *Stay* make their angelic and devilish cases while I try to digest this news. "I don't know what to say to that yet. Can we—can we just make normal conversation?"

"Willing to try." He raises his eyebrows.

"So, what do you think of it, *The Love of Zero*." A nice, normal, ran into an old friend at a film night question.

"I get something new every time. One of the greats, really. You?"

"I've only seen it once before. Ages ago. The music was different, Debussy, so it had a more impressionistic quality. More hopeful. The classic silent film accompaniment is so tragic. I don't know. Are all true artists doomed to heartbreak and death, or a life without love, or is it a self-constructed mythology?"

"Are we always tragically torn apart by the forces of that so-called real world?" He lifts his drink and sips Scotch and I'm caught by his gaze.

The unbroken eye contact calls up that kaleidoscope again. Bliss wrapped up in Ian's loch-deep blue eyes. "Or is tragedy something we bring upon ourselves, by caring too much?" I'm seeing something new in Ian, the something more I've always sensed. Ian the artist, more than his public persona. "This is one of my favorite places in LA. It's a really lovely escape from the pedestrian."

"My escape, too. Helps me remember there's a world beyond action movies."

"It's a good thing to remember. You should remember it more often."

"Well, Ian Graham's muscles must satisfy Ian Graham's fans. Then I look for summat to satisfy the artist as well." He takes my wrist and a thrill shoots up my arm as he turns it over to examine my new tattoo, a bit of Latin text for my *K-Town* losses. "Life is short?"

"But art is eternal."

"Couldn't agree more." Ian smiles at me. Not one of those trademark grins—softer, more personal.

"You're more than a collection of muscles." My voice sounds thin and strange. Ian's fingers are still on my skin, and intimacy twines around us.

"But they're fine muscles," Ian grins, the laugh lines at the corners of his eyes crinkling with deadly charm.

"I won't disagree." The lights flicker, signaling the next film, while *Leave* and *Stay* gladiate their advice.

"Care to watch with me, Kat?"

Leave whimpers in defeat. "I would like that."

Ian offers his arm and I wind my fingers around his forearm, feel the muscle underneath fabric, unlocking another kaleidoscope of memories and sensation. We sit in the back of the theater, where we can watch and comment without interruption or being disruptive.

The next film is a new science fiction piece, taut and stark, with a contrasting bold score. I shush Ian twice as we watch, I'm so engrossed. And then I babble as soon as it ends. "How brilliant was that? That line between truth and psychosis, reality and escape—nobody explores it this way on film."

"Nah. Wouldn't sell a single ticket. But it was brilliant. Care to meet Karl, the filmmaker? He's right over there."

"You're kidding. Of course I would love to." I slap Ian's arm lightly. I don't know what our touches mean, I don't want to analyze this moment.

We mingle and float between groups of people—me and Ian, it's another bubble moment, a couple moment. Though I know half of everyone here, he keeps introducing me as *Kat Porter, a brilliant producer.*

"Oh, you're not *that* Kat Porter, are you?" A woman with spiked, purple hair bounces as her head bobs in recognition I don't share.

"There's more than one of me?" I reply, attempting to convey light humor, though I dread what I'm sure is coming next—a rehash of my spectacular fall from television grace. My face is already heating, and I can feel the question in Ian's raised eyebrow.

The purple-haired woman continues, though. "No. I can't, can't, can't believe it. Since it happened, I've said if there was one person I want to meet it's *that* Kat Porter. And here you are. I've been quite simply *destroyed* over what happened with your *amazing* show." She reaches across to grasp my hand, and tears well in her eyes. "If no one else ever says thank you, then let me say it now. Thank you, Katrine Porter, for daring to tell such brave, brave stories."

"Well, thank you." I nod uncomfortably, unsure what else to do. The social media fallout was nasty and unrelenting, but I had some hopes for anonymity when I came here tonight. Not to hear it all told again. But that's exactly what happens. The purple-haired woman's partner continues the story and it buzzes around the rest of the group. The power of my art, the destruction of my heart.

"They made it *palatable.* Fucked up the whole thing."

More bobbing heads take their turn in the dialogue. "No understanding of art. Art is pain. If it doesn't hurt, why do it?"

Purple hair gushes forward. "The network releases this statement—oh, it's such a laugh—that the storyline change removing the religious elements is about respect for all represented points of view and a desire to be a safe space for all viewers."

"God, that screams investor manipulation, doesn't it? Oh, the joy of being a social group with rich, white pockets, right? What I'd give for some honest, cutting commentary, like we might have had."

"Bigots and hypocrites in Christian clothing. Thirteen of them in every dozen."

The group laughs, but I struggle against an old memory. The same kind of talk at the GLAAD awards. Meaningless banter among like-minded friends, not intended for public consumption. Yet that happened, it happens. And I can't let it happen to me again. Then I really will be done, dead, irrelevant. But when Ian squeezes my hand, everything calms again. He'll fix this, his hand seems to say.

"I said it months ago. Let the suits bury the suits. Kat here is no suit."

I force a smile and follow his lead. "That's true. It's a mutual hate affair, I guess."

"Fuck them all, right? After you take their money." Another laugh ripples through the group.

"That's not really—" I try to protest, but it's a runaway train and there's no stopping this.

"And this other show, the sci-fi one? As artistic as a bar of soap, I hear."

Apparently, nothing is safe. Bash Bea, sure, but *Void* belongs to Monkey & Me, too. I turn to Ian. "I think I need some air. Lovely to meet you all."

"O'course. Let's walk outside a bit." Ian steers me away from the theater and people, to a semi-secluded corner against the railing outside the theater. "Is that really what happened?"

"Yes, no, maybe. I sold them a shoe and delivered a handbag. And now my show is dead." Oh, that hurts.

"Some people don't know art, not at all. Bea wouldn't know it if it came with a label. She has all the vision of a world atlas—put the money here and the people there and follow a course straight to TV Land." He taps out a smoke and holds the pack out to me. I accept gratefully—both the cigarette and the ritual of Ian holding the lighter for me.

But Dom and Claudette declare Ian a liar. Every tinged and twisted line of dialogue in *Void* protests his assumption. Bea sold a nice durable shoe, and then delivered the designer version.

Ian continues on without my reply. "You, on the other hand, are brilliant and passionate, everything an artist should be. Pains me to see some of the fire banked. But this could be good. You shouldn't be commercial. You're an artist. I can help get you some meetings."

"Thank you, you're sweet." I look up at him. "You're not usually sweet."

"I owe you. I made a mistake in January, birdy. I shouldna walked away. I've regretted it every day. Not been sure how to make it up to you. And now I know."

Hope clutches at my throat. The space around us is still too small, intimacy enhanced in the delicate night air. I inhale deeply. I know what I'm running from, but Ian's eyes are the same as mine with reasons much less clear.

"It's a miserable business, sometimes, trying to do the right thing," Ian says quietly, and it resonates. He faces me, crowds into my space—big, commanding and sexy and every Ian Graham thing I love him to be. "Let's go to dinner, spend some time together while I'm here."

"I—"

He runs a hand up my free arm, tugs me forward a little. "Come on, birdy. Seeing you tonight, being here with you—the best surprise."

My eyes water. I want all of Ian, not just sometimes or surprise times. "I won't survive another heartbreak, not from you."

"Don't cry, birdy—" Ian's voice is thick with the same painful desire that keeps me rooted to this spot, unable or unwilling to walk away. "I won't ask you to."

"Ian, what are you saying? You can't say things like that. You just can't. And you—you can't walk me around a room full of artists and let me hear everything I want to hear—"

"Even if it's true?" Ian grins and reaches for my hand. I lace my fingers through his, feel the rightness of touching him. He believes in me and my art, makes me feel, makes me *burn.* As no one ever has. "You scare me to death, birdy. And I canna let you walk away."

Every piece of me trembles, on the precipice of my most achingly insistent dream coming true. "I'm in love with you. I'm stupid in love with you."

"I know, lass. I know." Ian brushes away my tears, slow and tender, the scrape of his thumb against my cheek more intimate than a kiss.

Ian wraps a hand into my hair at the base of my neck, lifts me to him. "I want you, Kat. Not just in my bed. In all the ways." He kisses the side of my face, whispers it over and over—*all the ways*—until the threat of tears is long past. Happiness bursts out of me in cosmic, radiant rays. Our kisses deepen and find more significance. Ian is every beautiful dream. He's Scotch and smoke, oak and honeysuckle and wild serendipity.

And love.

CHAPTER 15

Es blicket die Verlass'ne vor sich hin,
Die Welt ist leer.

The abandoned one gazes straight ahead,
the world is void.

—*Robert Schumann, Frauenliebe und -leben*

Bea

The sounds of family banged overhead, bringing Bea her first moment of zen in way too long. Home. All the sounds of home. There were basketballs being tossed around, good food being scarfed off every surface, and, best of all, the whole host of nieces and nephews running around.

Bea had offered to be on baby duty while Alex's wife napped upstairs. The newest addition had sapped its mom of milk and energy during her two-week growth spurt. Bea sheltered the baby in her arms and made soft coos to echo the infant's early attempts at speech.

There was something perfect about a newborn's nose. Sweetly angled and slightly upturned, offering up little puffs of breath. Bea traced the nose and accepted baby-breath blessings that minimized the negative effects of the noxious parts of her day.

Kat's disappearance had ruined most of the last two days. Her reappearance threatened to ruin this one, too.

Kat wasn't dead.

Not in Germany, either.

Nope.

Kat was wrapped around Ian at his house in Scotland. In L-O-V-E, love.

Despite her very real, very devastated boyfriend whom Bea had had the awesomely awesome task of breaking up with. Because that's what Bea did for Kat.

The dirty work.

Thanks to Kat's love of ghosting as a relationship exit strategy, Bea knew men cried. They sobbed, too. And this sob session had sucked. Philip was perfect for Kat. Absolutely perfect. But after three days in a panic-ridden boyfriend hell, worrying and calling and worrying some more, Bea, not Kat, had called to inform him that Kat was naked in Scotland with someone else.

Oops. Sorry, Philip. Better luck next time.

Bea leaned down to inhale baby-scent and kiss soft skin rolls along the tiny neck. Happiness. Sheer bliss. Perfectly-timed baby joy that kept Bea from telling Kat where to stick her production company. Bea couldn't quit and move back home, not if she wanted one of these little creatures for herself. She needed stability and money. One more year on *Void* gave her both. Then, she could quit.

Her phone buzzed with the zombie logo. Josh. She picked it up.

Josh half-yelled into the phone, livid over today's other crisis. "Have you seen this, Bea? Roger. Roger! His baby is due any day now."

Bea flipped over to Matthias's email and the photo he'd obtained of Siena and Roger having a public liaison that would be illegal in even the most liberal countries. Her inner cynic wasn't surprised by anything anymore. The world seemed full of people who chased momentary pleasure at everyone else's expense.

Bea swiped the phone to disappear the photo forever. "His wife gave up ballet and acting for him. There's a lovely life lesson in that somewhere."

"Killed our publicity. Killed it. Do you think Eddie knows? Hell, he was already drunk most of the time. What happens now?"

"I don't know. He's out of the country, right? His manager said he couldn't be booked this month because of some retreat. I'm hoping retreat equals rehab."

"Could this get worse? I know, you told me not to cast a couple. But they were solid, good as engaged. They were buying a house, planning a family."

That part of her heart that kept Eddie tucked deep inside heaved for his loss. Nothing wrong with Eddie that a little moderation didn't fix.

"And I don't know how you had enough of an idea of the risk to have a contingency plan in place. I hate the plan and can't morally sanction it, but do it anyway. Make it look like a cell phone shot. We'll fake-fire a fake employee tomorrow."

Bea disconnected and then hit send on the email she'd composed to Matthias an hour ago. She was sliding the phone back under her thigh when three of her brothers descended and woke up her small charge.

"You better hide that phone. Mom's coming in. She gets the idea you're working, she'll run that phone through the dishwasher like she threatened yesterday." Gabe, the family's other redhead, draped himself along the back of the couch. He reached around Bea to stroke the baby's head, a proud father of five and uncle of eleven.

"What's the latest in Hollywood? Who did what to whom and requires you to fix it? I want a producer. Life would be so much better if I had a producer to solve all my problems." Alex extracted his daughter. He tucked the baby into his elbow and made silly faces the baby probably couldn't see yet.

"Nah, that's not it. Major set design catastrophe. The producers bought pens from 1884 instead of 1882." Micah took a bite of apple as he hovered over Bea. Spittle and apple juice sprayed her cheek. She wiped them away as she rolled her eyes dramatically at her baby brother.

"Bea. No. The world will crash on such a mistake." Gabe made choking noises. "I can barely breathe."

Micah extracted the phone from where it tucked under his sister's leg to hand it back to her. "It's okay, Bea. With so much in the balance, we'll protect you from Mom. Arm that cell phone. Save the planet."

Elle Douglas appeared at the base of the steps, wiping her hands on a dishcloth that she tossed on the laundry pile. "Shut up, you three, and take your kids to the park, as promised. Dinner will be ready in an hour if I can get everyone to stop pilfering the ingredients." The three boys heard and obeyed; Elle wasn't a woman who was ever disobeyed.

When the men rushed out as noisily as they'd come, Elle sat next to her daughter in similar posture. Their knees drawn up to their chins, Bea and Elle were mirrors except for hair color.

"So, how are you doing after this morning? A little less tearful, I see."

Bea sighed as her mom rubbed her back. "I'm hurt. And sad. A lot confused. I don't know how this even happens. How are you everything in the world to someone one day and a ghost the next?"

"Well, that's Kat's life, right? Everything got wrapped up and changed in a blink of an eye when her dad had to transfer. It's what she knows, honey. Not much you can do about it."

"How do I stay friends with someone who treats me—and everyone—like that?"

"It's this little thing called Christianity. Hard to master. Beautiful, once you do."

Bea accepted her mom's hug and then laid her head on her mom's shoulder.

"Can I ask one more intrusive question?" Elle spoke next to Bea's ear.

"I've never been able to stop you."

"Oh, you love me so much. You embarrass me. The way you heap praise on your old mother. I'm having visions of jewels and motherhood awards."

Bea laughed at her mother. Home. Nothing was ever so wrong that home couldn't fix it, even if her mom did act like insanity's stepdaughter.

Elle *tsked* at Bea and then kissed her head before speaking. "Is this your life, sweetie? Funding shows you don't like? Cleaning up after other people?"

"It works. Makes money. Makes people happy."

"Makes you happy? Or makes Kat happy?"

Bea lifted her head to let the sights of home speak to her. Beige walls with children's scribblings on the baseboards. A worn, orange sectional that had seen too many wrestling matches. The faces in all the photos staring back from mantels and shelves. These four walls held all her happy thoughts. If she could get enough money, she'd come home and be a nurse and raise her own child in the happiness she'd known, but it was always a dozen sacrifices away from being reality.

Elle looked up the stairs to where Bea's dad sat in deep council with Ryan, Bea's eldest brother whose farm was on the verge of failing. A soft grin always tugged at Elle's mouth when she looked at Richard.

"Until I met your dad, I'd never had a thought that didn't get contradicted a dozen times over. My mom was full of politics and movements and rallies and ideals that hurt as many people as they helped, but she could never see that. When we rolled into Salt Lake City for a rally, I did exactly what she wanted to be the good daughter I'd always been. Then I met your dad at a café: a white boy in an ROTC uniform who wished he could go to war. Everything I'd been taught to dislike since I was born."

Bea rallied to her favorite part. "But Dad was too handsome, so you missed the bus back to Oakland."

"I did. I stayed to talk to the cute farm boy who listened as though I had something to say, and then I never left. My mom didn't talk to me for ten years, but it was worth it to have the life I live now. So, where are you, sweet girl? Are you on the bus? Or are you in the life that's worth missing the bus to live?"

Bea hid her eyes in her mother's soft pink wool sweater and cried a little. She was on the bus. Stuck on the bus.

Her phone quivered and buzzed beneath the couch cushion. Elle raised a single eyebrow. She leaned forward to kiss Bea's hair and then handed her daughter the complaining technology. "Get off the bus, sweetie, before the bus is all there is."

Bea glanced at the phone to see Matthias's floppy bangs. She tapped the green button.

Matthias started speaking the moment they had connection. His voice jumped with excitement and greed. "*Gattina.* Are you serious? That's *all* of Siena Russo. Do you know what that's worth?"

"Put a few filters over it, make it grainy enough that they watch *Void* to put together the missing pieces of the puzzle. Distract the Internet for a few days. We'll match whatever the *Mail* bonus is. She deserves a little bad press, but we want to control the message."

Matthias hesitated and Bea exhaled. He was a good negotiator, and their friendship seemed to buy less and less with every scandal. If he didn't take the money, she'd have to offer up the only other thing she had. Kat would never forgive her, but maybe she needed to get off the bus. The bus had shown how little it cared.

"*Gattina,* it's a great offer, but—"

"I can give you an Ian Graham story."

She heard a swish and squeak as Matthias's chair spun to hide himself from his prying coworkers. Then his voice came back, hushed, his hunter side fully engaged. "There are rumors about this one. Make it good."

"He's holed up in Scotland—"

"With his ex-wife and kid. Everyone knows that. Publicity stunt, if you ask me, after his last go-around with the squealing virgin in Barbados. He's trying to look like a family man."

"No. Not ex-wife and no squealing virgin."

"Fucking-A. Rumor was that he was going to marry the ex again."

Bea bit her worry spot so hard it bled. That jerk. Loser. Oh, every time she thought of Ian she wanted to spit and make assassination plots. "Ian is a raging bastard. Nail him for me."

"*Che figatta, gattina.* You know I love your cutthroat side. Get back to England so we can celebrate. I'm sick of you being in Canada."

Bea spun her phone in a slow circle on her palm after she disconnected the video call. She'd loved her cutthroat side more a year ago. But with each passing day, she hated everything she had to do, everything she'd become.

She hit the number for Eddie's manager. She was certain Eddie didn't know about Siena. Heartbreak number two coming right up. Two good men in one day. The bus was fan-freakin-tastic.

♦ ♦ ♦

Kat

I don't know why I'm here. Coming back to London in the deadest of the night, to chase after Eden who has run off. Eden with the artist's temperament and promising future. Ian's pride and joy, baby girl, apple of his eye—every cliché a father could use, I've heard said about Eden. I've loved him for each one. I was Eden once, to my own father.

Ian rarely speaks. He checks his phone every other minute. They've looked in all the usual places. Eden is nowhere she usually runs.

Usually runs.

The idea warps my vision of the curious youngling from her *21 Things* set visit and the adorable blonde girl in pictures on Ian's phone. Ian's youngest is a sullen eleven-year-old who runs away with enough regularity that there's a finding plan and a PI on retainer.

We race across London in Ian's fancy sports car. It's imperative that I be with Ian, but the long, silent hours from our Scotland retreat to London open cracks where doubt creeps in.

We pull into Fulham in a dead-of-night quiet. The trees along the street loom, monsters casting fear and hiding villains near neat Victorian row houses with beautiful pickets that seem to summon a visit from Mary Poppins.

Ian glances over his shoulder. His paranoia has been amped up by at least four phone calls from publicists—his publicist and the publicists for each of his ex-wives. He's set up plan after plan that sounds like it belongs in a James Bond movie, with me as the silent Bond girl.

I'm not Eden's mother, not part of this family no matter what fantasies I've drawn up when snuggled naked next to Ian. In reality, I'm an intruder—another new woman in tow, the next girlfriend on a very long list. I met Eden the once, and I've been a happy receptacle for Ian's proud-papa tales of his bright, smart daughters—Laura and Daphne, who are Tess's daughters, and Eden, from Addy. But the family doesn't know me, will certainly know less about me than I do about them. This feels real, though, like Ian bringing me into the fold, making me real. All the things he's promised.

Ian walks up the stairs to the nondescript door framing three unfamiliar faces. The pained expressions that greet me amplify my discomfort, agree with it, and mock me for ever thinking I was anything other than Ian's latest fling. Tess casts Ian a quick look that encapsulates a thousand shouted lectures. Ian shoves his hands in his pockets and pushes past her into the house.

Addy's eyes spew hatred. I screw up my face at her and roll my eyes. I don't need her approval. She's lost her eleven-year-old daughter.

Rosie gives me a sympathetic smile. The last ex-wife, the childless one. She's terrifyingly beautiful—long waves of black hair around a perfect pale cream and rose complexion. She beams like Snow White in the magic mirror.

Ian locks into quiet conversation with Tess. He smokes his seventh cigarette of the night next to an open window. Tess links arms with him and then drops her head to his shoulder.

Coffee appears from somewhere and a sort of vigil commences. Addy sits on the chintz couch, her legs pulled up to her chest. Tears slip down her cheeks. Not silent tears. Goopy and too dramatic. She slaps at her face with the back of her hand and snuffles.

Drunk. She's drunk. Un-fucking-believable.

I sip coffee to contain disgusted huffs. I know a bit about maternal wastelands. You should have to get a license to use the term *mother*. Women like my mother and Addy shouldn't be allowed five minutes with a baby.

Addy gags on a sob. Ian's groan covers my own.

"What in seven hells, Addy? Can't watch the gel one bloody night? Tess is busy and you canna be bothered to actually stay with your own daughter?"

"Don't you pick bones. It was your bloody weekend. Just following the schedule you had delivered to me by messenger. Not even the decency to discuss our daughter. Your manager drew up a schedule." Addy's made of nasty edges, just like her too-clean, too-modern house with Victorian skin.

Addy points at Ian, her nails flashing bright red except for the jagged gaps of two missing fake nails. "You promised, Ian, that you'd do it right, but two weeks and you're off with your latest accessory." She tries to accentuate her words by standing but can't hold the floor. She tips and overcorrects. A gesture in my direction almost throws her over. "I'm trying to restart my life. Then I get a call—from your assistant—that you've taken that *thing* to the Scotland house. Well, too late. My weekend had already begun."

Tess intervenes. "Addy, you should've called again. Yes, we were out on Friday, but we would've come for her that night. We all know Ian's schedule changes frequently."

"You lie," Addy lifts a finger to wag in odd crazy-eights, too close to Tess's face. "Eden says you're tired of her, too. Poor baby girl with a drunk mother and a dad who wants a piece of ass more than his family. So, she runs away, tries to find summat to love her." She rotates toward Ian, and then a raging fight commences.

Tess motions to Rosie. The two women advance toward me, the piece of ass accessory. "Best let them at it," Tess whispers.

I nod and follow. Addy is wrong about me and Ian but I couldn't give a shit what she thinks of me.

Tess pulls bowls and ingredients out of cupboards. Her familiarity with Addy's kitchen shocks me. Not the first vigil.

Rosie pulls out a chair and sits at an angle from the table. "I leave the baking to Tess. She won't let me near it, even if I offer."

"Well, you have the gift of baking bricks, nothing more," Tess teases. I've stepped into a Twilight Zone episode. I'm in a sorority of Ian's women, led by Tess as alpha mother. The strength and dominance of these women force another crack in the image I've carried of Ian's family. Somehow, in my fangirling, these two women had become sad, pathetic, pulsar wannabes that quivered for a moment near the center of the galaxy. Life that close to a quasar made everything pale in comparison, perhaps, because these women command the planets that surround them, even as they orbit around Ian.

Fucks fly in the other room as the argument escalates. Grievances roll out and are countered without pause as if on script. My name is the only bump to a predictable, well-rehearsed cadence. Addy shouts it. Ian silences her. Then the script resumes.

Tess stares out the door with pursed lips at the second repeat of my name. She motions me to the counter. "Come. Helps to have summat to do with your hands."

Tess plops a pie tin and a lump of pastry dough in front of me. Really? The pie crust? The most difficult part of a pie, always, and something I haven't done since Thanksgivings with my dad. I start rolling out dough while Tess gathers more ingredients to the stove with more noise than a grand band. She turns on the oven fan. She bangs pots. She hums. It's impossible to hear the details of the argument.

"So, how was Scotland? What took you there?" Rosie asks with a too-bright smile.

I smile back, filled with the wary feeling of the nice girl at school asked to escort the new military move-in. "It was a lovely getaway. Ian's house there is all old stone and—" *surrounded by green hills,* I stumble and don't finish. Rosie would know exactly what the house is like.

My silence after the fumble is too long. I should apologize, but I can't think of an appropriate correction. This sorority thing is ridiculous. Instead, I patch a gap in the dough.

A door slams. Addy and Ian have gone outside. Honesty rushes in with the sound.

"I should have given her my new address, Tess. I didn't even think about it. I needed out of the house he bought me and I just moved when a flat came available. I feel terrible. I'm so sorry, but honestly it didn't occur to me," Rosie says.

"We're all a little to blame, Rosie. I had no clue she overheard me vent to Alan during her last unexpected visit. How can I raise my own when—" Tess whisks faster, bangs another pot.

"I know, Tess, I know. I've missed her since the divorce, but I have to move on. I thought she was doing better, but then—"

"But then me?" My voice echoes too loud and a half-step sharp.

Tess shakes her head. Rosie has compassion in her eyes again. "Then her parents made an interesting series of choices that further confused a confused girl." A political answer. Practiced.

"It's not any of our faults." My errant tongue won't be silent. "With a mother like that, who doesn't bail every chance she's got? A raging alcoholic with claws? Gods, I'd be so gone."

Maybe it's because I kind of suck with people that I know so well what uncomfortable glances look like. Rosie and Tess exchange one now. Discomfort makes my skin itch.

Rosie licks her lips and coughs once before responding. "Addy can be really fun and loving. She's worse right now than I've ever seen her. Been a difficult few weeks."

"How do you even—" I shake my head. How do they all even speak to each other?

Tess spins to face us, me and Rosie. She's fierce, eyes flashing, mouth hard. "Ian brings you into our children's lives with nary a thought or word of introduction. So, once you are in, you stay. We stay. That's our family rule. Honored from the day he brought in Addy. She may be trouble, but she's one of us and we're all Eden has."

Tess's voice cracks on a sob. Rosie leans across the counter to cover her hands with her own. "We'll find her, Tess. I'll make sure she knows where I am."

Ian bursts into the kitchen. "The PI has got her. Found her. Tess, she's—she'll need a mum."

Tess dries her hands. She points me toward the recipe. "Follow that. Hard part is done. This is Eden's favorite, so do your best, please." She and Ian walk away without another word. Rosie joins me and takes up Tess's whisk to finish off the chocolate.

"Well isn't this quaint?" Addy's voice strikes at us from the doorway. "Ian's women all cozy-like in the kitchen. We should be one of those groups—those Mormons, is that it?—who all live together. One man and all we women eager to please him, keep him so happy."

"Right, really fucking cozy," I strike back. "Even got ourselves a family drunk."

"And a whore who fucked my man after we'd promised our little girl we'd give her family a chance. So, stop judging me, you little slut. You're the reason Eden ran. Then you were so goddamn selfish that my little girl didn't even get her weekend with daddy."

Rosie abandons her whisk to calm Addy. "Whores are in good company here, Addy. Only Tess has a clean record. Stop baiting Kat and let me help you to bed."

"No. I want to stay and talk to our newest sister." Addy cackles at her joke.

Each word feels like a kidney punch. I turn back to the stove to try to read the recipe, but everything blurs. It can't be true. She's a lying drunk, a mean drunk.

Addy laughs. "Oh, I've hurt the tender little flower. Look at her, she's almost in tears."

"Enough!" Ian bellows from the doorway. "Rosie, take Addy up to bed. Kat, come with me. You shouldn't have to listen to her ravings."

The pie isn't in the oven yet. One thing to do, and I haven't done it. I open the oven, despite Ian's impatient puffs of air above me. Anger and hurt coil tight in my chest as I set the timer and put the pastry bowl and caramel pan in the sink. "Is it true? You were with her right before—have you been with her all these months?"

"She's drunk, birdy, spouting rubbish." Ian clasps my hand—the first touch in hours, and I hold on tight.

Tess waits in the living room. "They're close. She'll park down the street and bring her in under the dark. I've turned all but this light off. If anyone is out there, they'll get a grainy shot at best." Tess flips the switch on the lamp. We stand in near-complete darkness.

We hear footsteps outside—one set firm, the other a slurred drag. The door opens. Both Eden and the PI are dressed in all black with dark hoods over their faces. Tess rushes to Eden. As soon as her hood pushes back, Eden is revealed to be as drunk as her mother. Maybe something else, too. Her skin has that gray-white pallor of too much everything.

"Everyone's here, sweet one." Tess coos.

"Everyone? Even Rosie?" Eden mumbles.

"I'm here!" Rosie bounds down the stairs.

Eden's eyes focus in the relit lamplight. Her nostrils flare and lungs churn faster when her eyes fall on me. Addy's rage is genetic.

Ian releases my hand. He steps in front of Eden, kisses her forehead. "Love you, pretty thing. I'll see you on Monday. Mind Tess and Rosie."

Eden turns ashen and Tess hurries her down the hall to the bathroom to vomit. I could have said a dozen things to Eden. A dozen nice, reassuring things. But I was speechless.

The silent Bond girl. No different than a piece of technology. Or a car.

I play my part all the way back to the hotel and after, even as Ian uses me as a placeholder between cigarettes. I serve my purpose. A fitting accessory.

CHAPTER 16

"The time at length arrives when grief is rather an indulgence than a necessity; and the smile that plays upon the lips, although it may be deemed a sacrilege, is not banished."

—Mary Shelley, Frankenstein

Kat

Eden never hits the tabloids as was so feared that night, and Ian and I are free to resume our uninterrupted bliss. *21 Things* is filming again, and Ian is shooting a movie at Pinewood studios. We work all day and then play all night. Weekends pass in lazy domesticity in the house Ian bought for us that I'm crafting into a home.

Our home.

"A woman needs a house," Ian said to me the day after we returned from Scotland. "Birdy, I'm taking you house shopping."

I've heard horror stories about real estate hunting, and it was difficult enough to find a flat to rent, so I imagined we'd continue to live in a hotel suite for a few more months. But I didn't count on the power of Ian Graham's name and money opening the schedules of agents and the doors of beautiful homes that are empty but unlisted unless the price is right.

One of those unlisted treasures, in a quiet and stately corner of Hampstead, won my heart the moment I crossed the threshold. Rich wooden floors and wide airy rooms full of architectural detail beckoned me to explore every inch. The agent prattled on about the types of wood and what century the moldings are from, but I only half-listened. At the end of the ground floor hall were a set of steps and I gasped with delight at what they led down to—a conservatory.

I walked to a side wall of exposed brick. My fingers skimmed window ledges and panes of antique glass. The house whispered as certainty flooded me—*this is mine.* My living spaces have always been temporary, places I was carried to by my dad's job and then my own career, so falling in love with a house was new, a strange thrill.

"You like it, birdy?" Ian asked, low in my ear. The window reflected his large, comforting presence behind me, and whatever crazy seduction this house had worked over me was complete.

"Ian, I love it," I whispered back, afraid of the agent knowing how eager I was.

"Then yours it will be. Ours. Make us a home, birdy."

And, I did. Almost two months later, it is undeniably our home. I've filled it with books and layered, patterned rugs. We've scoured galleries and chosen stark abstract paintings and colored glass sculptures to surround comfortable sofas and the best high-tech entertainment gadgets. There's a bedroom with a fanciful window seat that will be perfect for Eden. And Ian filled the wine cellar with all my favorites.

Now, Ian calls for me from down the hall. I'm in my conservatory with the floor-to-ceiling windows. And my concert-size grand piano. No more silently tapping out piano pieces. I fill our house with sonatas when the urge takes me.

Some days, I'm silent. Like today. I've huddled in my giant, green chair. My knees pull up to my chin. A laptop perches on top and rocks back and forth as I jab at keys, lost in the world I'm creating on the white space of the screen.

"Are we going for lunch or what?" His approach breaks me out of my writing tunnel. I've lost track of time. I'm still in my pajama shorts. I promised I would put my workaholic tendencies away for the day, but when Ian dove into a football game, I retreated to my corner.

"Oh, sorry. I'm really almost done with this. I just—it's so close." I keep typing—driven, furious typing. I'm afraid the scene will slip away. I've struggled with this one. The nuance, the set design—I'm trying something completely new that I've wanted to do forever.

Ian sits down on the wide white sofa scattered with colored pillows. Oversized album posters and floor-to-ceiling movie posters complete the decor. Papers are scattered about, usually held down by a pile of CD cases. Ian bought me new sound mixing equipment, and the room is equipped with full surround sound. I can drop blackout screens over the windows and a projection screen from the ceiling to create a private viewing room. I live in here—the center of my creative whirlwind, Ian calls it.

"What's got you so intent?" He runs a hand along my arm and angles to see the screen.

"What? Oh. No." I snap the laptop closed and shake my head.

"I could make you show me." He traces a finger along the ticklish edge of my ribcage.

"That is not going to work, Ian!"

"I've barely begun." His hand moves under my shirt.

"You can't see it. Nobody can see it. I'm playing around, just skill practice stuff." My metaphorical heels dig in and cement in place.

"Fairly intense practice. Don't think I don't notice you losing sleep over this, getting up in the middle of the night to write."

"I get like this when I need to finish something." I shrug against my nerves. "Which is silly because it's a side project. I needed to be creative, to find my drive after *K-Town*. This is helping. Even if I'm the only person who ever reads it."

"Well, I'd hate to see all this passion wasted, tossed in a drawer to never be seen. What's stopping you?" Ian runs a finger under my chin. He tips my eyes up to his.

"Oh, fine. I'm adapting a science fiction novel. Something I've always wanted to try. But there's a huge copyright issue. Monkey & Me is cash-strapped at the moment, so I couldn't afford to get the rights if I wanted."

"The rights to this?" Ian picks up the novel at the top of the stack of references on the side table. He slips on his reading glasses and skims the back cover.

"Yep, the rights to *Birds of the Air*. The most amazing piece of literary science fiction in decades. Everyone wants it. A million rumors, but no one has it. The author is holding out. And I just wanted to play at it, pretend I could be in the running. Even though I can't."

"A true artist never says can't, birdy. So, how's it coming?"

"I think it might be good." All the nerves I have built up around this strike again.

"Let me read it? I'll tell you straight," Ian coaxes. He arches an eyebrow.

I bite my lip and tip my head to the side. "Maybe. Just to know if it's any good . . ." I don't tell Ian that I've done it again, written a part in his voice because I hear him in my head as I listen to the character.

"No doubt it's good. Now hand over the screenplay." He hugs me to his side and I feel it, that connection. More than our hearts. Like when he came home last week with this glee in his eyes over a project in Madagascar. We hear this song, Ian and I, this call to art. He's the only person I've ever known who hears it, gets it.

I hand him the laptop, cued to the first page. "It's not completely finished, missing scenes, needs a better setup for—" I stop myself. "I'm just going—I'll, yeah." Ian steps past me. He walks down the hall toward his office. I grab my headphones to work on music for *21 Things,* but I'm too nervous to concentrate. I tiptoe down the hall to watch Ian read. His office is beside the kitchen. He sits in his giant armchair with his feet on the media center—his soccer pose—while I pretend at doing dishes.

I know every word on every page, as Ian scans and arrows down. Then he arrows back up to the beginning after the first scene and reads the voice-over intro again. I watch him get lost in the words, utterly engrossed—the way I feel when I'm writing. He hasn't read the book, I am his introduction to this story. Every emotion plays out on his face, and he starts to mouth the dialogue.

Halfway through, I can't handle the suspense anymore, so I retreat. I shower, get dressed for what will be a late lunch, the movie playing in my mind the whole time. Then I pace outside the office until I see that Ian has hit the finale—the emotional peak and release in a series of reveals so shocking, it brings me to tears every time. The truth rips wide open, the confessor is as affected as the afflicted, and a broken man finally finds peace.

When Ian finally looks up from the screen, there is respect in his eyes.

"Is it good?" I ask.

"Is it good? It's bloody brilliant, birdy." Ian nods and reaches for me, putting the laptop aside. "This movie needs to get made and I know who to call to make sure it does. With your screenplay. Destiny is calling."

"Really, really? Because if this is for real, then—oh my god, Ian, I have something to do. I have a next step. I don't have to go to Vancouver and pretend to love someone else's baby."

"You shouldn't be on the sidelines of anything, birdy. Leave Bea to her television. You're headed to movies."

We both forget about lunch as Ian makes several phone calls. By evening, I'm talking to the largest studio production team in New Zealand about securing rights and that dovetails into production details and actor wish lists. And no one mentions budgets or ratings. Ian has done it. He's given me back my art.

♦ ♦ ♦

Bea

Bea slid in next to Matthias in the crowd of paparazzi huddled at a back entrance. His hand wrapped her waist for a whispered conversation.

"Thank you for keeping your eyes open. I figured he'd surface eventually."

"One breath isn't exactly a call for help. You're on a fool's errand, *gattina*. He's as in love with fame as he is with himself."

"Looks can be deceiving. Where is he?"

"Losing his guts on a curb around the corner. But any minute, he'll be stable enough to rejoin the party."

"Likelihood of a story beyond a quick byline?"

Matthias shook his head. "Everybody got a few shots of him draped in women and drugs. Normal single guy stuff, and normal doesn't sell papers."

Matthias tugged at her waist until she turned into him a bit. "Why worry about this? Let him alone. I'm almost done here. We could get a late dinner."

"Not tonight. I can't have this bleed into *Void.* The affair already dominates the discussion. I want them talking about the onscreen drama, not this disaster."

"Any publicity is good publicity."

"*K-Town* already proved you wrong."

The door opened and released a flood of light. Matthias pivoted, raising his camera to capture whomever had emerged. Bea slid away amidst the distraction. She hurried around a large trash container to where Matthias had said Eddie waited.

In the darkness once again, she blinked twice before her eyes could focus on the solitary man beside the bin. Her brain refused to accept that this half-beaten derelict who reeked of sweat and dirt and sick could be Eddie. A mixture of frothy bile and blue pills lay at his feet. He stared at it with his fingers threaded through sopping wet black curls, lost and disoriented and too alone.

Encounters with Ben had long ago taught her that pity got her nowhere. Bea walked up to him, placed one hand on her hip and shook her black getaway hoodie in front of his face, letting the zipper clink in rhythm.

Eddie's head came up, but his eyes didn't raise. The rhinestones on her shoes reflected spots of light on his face. He ran a finger along the top strap. "That foot is the reason designers make shoes."

"Thanks. Don't vomit on them, or you'll ruin the effect." Bea shook the hoodie again, and ignored the tingle in her foot where he'd touched her shoe.

Eddie's gaze followed her leg up to the hem, paused, and then continued upwards until it settled on her face. He raised his eyebrows as he blinked glassy, bloodshot eyes.

Bea tapped her toe, which called his attention back to her foot. "Oh, get up. You look more train wreck than man on that curb."

Eddie covered his mouth to hold back a giggle. Bea huffed, frustration shoving attraction aside. "Geez, Eddie. Get up, put this on, and stop making a ridiculous arse of yourself on a public street." Bea reached down to tug him up.

Eddie wobbled to his feet. Bea slid his arms into the jacket and zipped him in like a child. He leered at her, clueless as to who she was. Bea rolled her eyes before tucking herself under his arm to guide him back to the waiting sedan.

Matthias held open the door to Bea's cab. His head wagged left to right, a wry grimace in place. "You could be having *cannoli* at Gioli's," he said as he maneuvered Eddie into the cab.

"How about you bring some by the apartment when you're done for the night?" Bea placed a hand on his arm and reached up to kiss his cheek. "And thanks again."

Matthias sighed, a soft breath against her ear. "Anything for you, *gattina.* If I can luck into something truly tragic, I'll bring a whole meal."

Bea pressed another quick kiss as she laughed. "You can be quite the horrible piece of humanity, Perrini. See you soon."

Bea slid into the sedan beside Eddie. As she settled, Eddie's gaze travelled down to where Bea crossed her ankles. Bea almost couldn't contain her amusement as his intoxication bumped her attractiveness into the desirable range, but, in Eddie's defense, the shoes did look amazing on her.

Bea grabbed Eddie's forearms and turned them over. Small puncture wounds. Dull, not fresh. "How long ago were these?"

"Two . . . maybe three hours." His eyes rolled backward.

"In the meantime? What else is rumbling around your bloodstream?" His pulse was fast and thready; she could barely get a count. His skin felt like cool clay.

"Hey! Eddie, hey!" She shook his shoulder, hard. His head lolled, but then his eyes fluttered open.

"Heroin, not my usual, does me in . . ." Every other word slurred as he rolled in and out of awareness. Bea chewed her lip and contemplated action as the list of drugs covered the lexicon. ". . . a lot of ex . . . something white . . . a line or two, maybe . . . and some purple thing, didn't like it much . . . peyote? No, that was another party, and I definitely liked it . . . a joint? Probably . . . loads of alcohol . . ." His voice faded away on a goofy grin.

Bea rubbed her temples. Did they need a hospital? Or could Joelle handle this? Maybe she could find a concierge doctor. Discreet, but somewhat risky. First, she needed a blood alcohol level.

Bea banged on the glass until the driver turned around. "I need to borrow your breath analyzer."

The cabbie made a token protest. Bea banged the window again. "Don't pretend with me. I know you've got one. I saw you hide the beer bottle."

The man produced the small, yellow device. Bea shuddered a little at the number called up by the recall function. Then she shook Eddie back awake to check his breath in a frustrating game of parrot. Open mouth. Close mouth. Breathe. No, not sleep. Breathe. Finally, Eddie completed the test and laid back down. The results read 0.35. Bad, but not dangerous.

"Well, buddy. You just won yourself a detox on my couch. But any trouble and we're in an ambulance, PR problems be damned."

Her apartment wasn't far from the party. The car pulled up. Bea pushed the door open and then helped Eddie out. He leaned on her for the entire walk up three flights of stairs to her dingy place. The gray couch seemed way too common for Edward Wolverton, but it was all she had. She slid Eddie off her shoulder and onto the upholstery.

Bea pressed the back of her hand to his forehead, and then let her fingers fall down his face in a caress. "I'm so sorry about Siena, Eddie. So, so sorry. I don't know what else to say. You deserved better than this."

Eddie's eyes found hers, but the pupils slipped about erratically, unable to focus through the haze. Bea guided Eddie's head onto a pillow in her lap, and then ran her fingers through his hair until he fell asleep.

♦ ♦ ♦

The next morning, Bea awoke to the sounds of someone rattling around her kitchen. She'd slept in Kat's room, an uncomfortable intrusion into a place that used to feel like home. She grabbed her blankets and walked back to the connecting door.

Eddie was cooking.

He toweled off his black hair in between sips of the coffee Bea had pilfered from Kat and left on the cupboard last night.

Bea tapped the doorframe to alert him to her presence. He spun, spatula in hand. A real Eddie smile lit his whole face. "Given the male paraphernalia in the shower, who deserves an apology for anything I said or did last night?"

"No one. You were fine." The shampoo and soap were two years old, left by Gabe after a quick visit. Bea kept them for the occasions when Ben stayed to sober up and wanted a shower. "I'm glad you won't have to spend the day smelling of lilacs."

"There's nothing wrong with the way you smell," Eddie said. He grabbed two plates. "I made omelettes. As a thank you."

"Consider me thanked. And you're welcome."

They ate in silence, Bea greedily, Eddie with more restraint. Or maybe disgust. His plate was more vegetable than egg. No reason to rush that flavorless mess into the gullet.

After she'd finished, Bea put down her fork and rested her chin on her hand. "How much should I worry about last night?"

Eddie shrugged and swallowed another small bite. "Needn't. Simply a party."

"A party. In a series of parties? And you can quit anytime, right?"

Eddie smiled at her, another attempt at charm. "I've had a rotten summer."

"Yeah. I know. But killing yourself over Siena isn't exactly the best solution."

"Better than returning to *Void*, which I'm not doing. I'd thought you'd have heard already."

"I did. I've read your lawyer's letter. Josh is a little resistant to your release."

"I've already heard from his lawyers. Gave me an excellent reason to drink."

Bea reached across to cover his hand with hers. "I'm sorry for that, too."

"But Dom makes Josh a lot of money."

"That's true, too."

Bea studied him, watched the tightened jaw that pushed back pain, as though he could wrestle addiction into submission. "You're planning to go cold turkey?"

"I've made a few attempts since the breakup. Almost to twenty-four hours the last time."

"So, you've mastered *not* getting sober."

Eddie quirked an eyebrow. "You neglected to mention detox came with a side of sarcasm."

"At least you've still got your vocabulary. Many say it's the last to go."

Eddie laughed, then rubbed a hand over his face as pain seized his whole body. He limped to the couch. His head fell into his hands, and he trembled head to foot. Then he laid down in fetal position. Detox had effectively disabled his swagger.

Bea crossed to him and pulled a blanket over him. "Oh, you poor thing," she cooed to cover a laugh. "Let's get you something to take the edge off."

From under the couch, she pulled out a box of detox supplies. She'd stashed away anything that helped Ben feel better on the worst of days. Perhaps some of these items would help Eddie as well. Bea handed over two Ibuprofen and what remained of the Diet Coke she'd had with her eggs.

Eddie wrinkled his nose.

Bea tipped her head to the side. "You filled your body full of dangerous chemicals over the past few days, but you're going to flip out over artificial sugar? I'm out of bottled water and the city water tastes like thousand-year-old sewage." Eddie accepted the pills and soda.

"So . . . marijuana or nicotine for short-term relief? Gotta stop the shakes. I can probably get you methadone later today."

"Is this a licensed apothecary?" Eddie joked through chattering teeth as he perused her collection of legal and illegal drugs. Bea hushed him.

"Nicotine. Marijuana best after sex," he said.

"I'll take your word on it." Bea helped him light a cigarette. Normally, she'd force him outside but he couldn't move three inches. He managed to hold the cigarette while Bea moved to the patio to open the door.

"How did this happen to me?" Eddie said. Compassion overwhelmed her again. Detoxing on a friendly couch isn't written on anyone's life plan.

Before she could respond, though, Eddie chuckled, and then moaned in pain.

Bea followed his gaze. Ah, crap. Ladies' sex toys on the television. Why couldn't Great Britain have just a few broadcasting decency laws?

"You got a problem with facilitated sex play?" she joked, hoping her own blush didn't make her the brunt of a dozen virgin jokes.

"Not at all, but I am wondering if this entire moment could possibly be stranger."

"Never say never. That's my philosophy. So, cold turkey is not really the best way to go. Can I make a few suggestions?" Bea opened the browser on her phone and handed it to Eddie. Eddie pursed his lips as he scanned the list of rehab sites. Then he sat back and smoked.

Bea softened her tone as much as possible. "You don't have to play Dom ever again. That's not what this is about. You deserve to have a life after this and I want to help you find it."

Eddie nodded, then shook his head and looked out the window. "I'll take the closest one. I need to go now if I'm to go at all."

"You want me to call someone to take you?"

"No. I prefer you. My mother's temper is hell on a hangover."

Bea walked Eddie the three blocks to the brownstone treatment facility. The check-in process tugged at her—leaving someone alone to face the monster. She stayed the whole time, at least an hour, until the nurse beckoned Eddie to the back. She hugged him, held him until he let go, and then waved at him when he glanced back before the door swung shut.

Yeah, she hated this part.

Then she pulled her collar up against a late spring squall to hurry back home alone.

She hated that part, too.

CHAPTER 17

"Nothing is more painful to the human mind than, after the feelings have been worked up by a quick succession of events, the dead calmness of inaction and certainty which follows and deprives the soul both of hope and fear."

—Mary Shelley, Frankenstein

Bea

Nicola placed a plain brown envelope on Bea's desk the moment she walked in from lunch. "This came by messenger an hour ago."

Bea handed her back the proofs from the morning photo shoot. "I need you to set me up a meeting with publicity. Kat hated all the official cast photos. Every last one. It's our final season and she demands perfection."

Nicola's perfectly arched eyebrows raised into an even more perfectly arched arch. "Would be easier to approve things if she ever worked on-site."

"She'll be on set, never misses an on-set day. Schedule a new shoot and try not to drunk dial Philip again."

"No guarantees," Nicola sang over her shoulder.

Bea slit open the envelope. She was doing this thing, forgiving Kat and accepting her choices, dealing with Kat's abandonment with a cheerful attitude and plenty of love. Not unusual for friends to feel abandoned when a new lover came along. One day, if Bea were patient and kind, everything would go back to normal.

The contents tumbled out of the envelope onto her desk. Bea rifled through the images that made no sense. Kat and . . . no. No.

Not right, not real. She placed everything in a neat pile on her desktop, closed her eyes, and took centering breaths. Then she repeated the process while a thousand alarms sounded and resounded in her head.

After the third cycle, with internal sirens so loud her head ached, she glared at the pile and waited for paper to apologize. It wasn't possible. What she'd read, what the photos contained, it wasn't—no, she was overworked and confused and upset over Kat and so she was misinterpreting things. There had to be something she didn't understand. If she could think through this noise, then she'd find what she couldn't see. But her eyes blurred on tears as she tried to re-read the contract in her hand.

A movie.

Kat had signed onto a movie. A big one. With the New Zealand crew.

Kat alone. Only Kat.

Bea's name nowhere on the contract. Monkey & Me, nowhere on the contract.

Her temples started to pound as an unseen scalpel ripped open her gut. Nausea struck, hard and unforgiving, with something that burned her throat.

Kat's promises. *I'll never push you out, silly. We're friends. More than friends. Sisters.* That's what she'd said when Bea discovered the original contract for *21 Things* that listed Kat as the sole proprietor.

But Kat had done it again. Drawn up a contract without Bea, created a property to which Bea had no claim.

Her heart seized, that little half-beat that accompanied adrenaline.

Fight or flight. Which is it, Bea?

Bea brushed the photos and papers into a desk drawer, then dug under her desk for the bag with her scrubs and hit the intercom for Nicola. She needed Bea, the nurse. Bea, the nurse, the reliable—the only reliable part of her other than family. The proof of that lay hidden in a drawer.

"I'm gone. Out. Until at least Monday." She disconnected before Nicola could sputter.

Joelle greeted her with a hug at the refugee center. Bea was in an exam room not an hour after she'd opened the envelope.

Bea pondered the envelope for hours with her hands buried in hard, heartbreaking work. Kat's sad songs played in her head. She'd listened to thousands of depressing tunes as friendship dues because Kat loved sad songs. The songs had been harbingers gone unheeded.

Bea's hand stumbled as she sniffled. The elderly man jumped and the vein slipped away, but not before Bea nicked the outer wall. A red bubble followed her needle out. She grabbed purple dressing tape from the metal drawer and wrapped the elderly man's arm, but the bruise had already begun to form. She turned over his other arm to find a new vein. Her first repeated IV poke since school. She was out of practice, so thinking caused mistakes. Bea quieted her brain and delved back into work. Work would drive away the pain.

The panacea blissfully carried her well into the night.

"You leaving soon, honey?" Joelle asked.

Bea shook her head. "You know I'm good for another shift. Nights are quiet."

Joelle's full lips formed a thin, thin line. Her eyebrows met above her nose. "You're not seeing patients for an hour, though. Go rest on the couch in my office."

In the office, Bea stared at the ceiling, her hands in fists, knees raised. The contents of the envelope haunted the area behind her eyelids. She went back to work as soon as she heard Joelle's loud farewells to staff.

But in the morning, Joelle physically blocked her as she exited the bathroom. "Baby, you gotta go home. You've been here twenty hours. I can't even read your writing anymore. You want me to call someone, honey?"

Bea shook her head. Her lip quivered. "There's no one to call."

Joelle's eyes softened. "Oh, honey, I'm so sorry. You want I could take you home?"

The tears fell at the idea of the apartment. Bea shook her head harder, forced breath through her constricted throat. "I'm fine. I can walk home."

"Okay, baby, but you be careful, okay?"

Bea stumbled over the step at the bathroom door despite the warning. She forced a bright smile and a laugh—all so false. Joelle's face tightened. More worry. Too much worry.

Bea turned and walked away as fast as she could. It was early, not even six in the morning. Her stomach churned angrily. She'd fed it only danishes, crackers, and gallons of Diet Coke since breakfast on Friday.

Her shuffling feet carried her to Big Ben. He was a relic, like her, a part of an earlier world made mock-worthy by modern mores. She curled up in a ball on the nearest bench, like the forgotten woman she was.

Bea stared at the bright-lit face of the bell tower and counted each tick that carried time along an endless path. Old Ben shouted the hour. Bea smiled back. "Hullo, Ben. Got any advice for me?"

Almost on cue, a reminder sounded on her phone, the very tech that made this clock irrelevant. *Check on Eddie.* And stupid as it was, six a.m. seemed as good a time as any to send a simple text.

How are you?

Bea jumped when the response came before she stowed her phone. *Been better. Sober cells feel like shite.*

Poorly kept secret of the sober. Sorry.

Where are you? Fancy some company?

I'm at Big Ben. Fancied myself a tourist.

To eat or shag? I'm game for either.

Haha. Then I'll see you soon.

Eddie appeared ten minutes later, dripping sweat and running in long strides. He was thinner than ever; his skin sagged over wasting muscle.

Bea guffawed. Harsh. Loud. Full of hilarity. "Oh! You look horrendous! Did you lose a fight—several fights?"

"I never lose a fight, but these fucking sober cells hate me. Can't breathe. Can't run. Can't train. I'll never be handsome again." Eddie gasped as he regulated his breathing. "What's your excuse for looking like death?"

"I've been on my own kind of bender. Different type of drug. Same result."

Eddie raised an eyebrow. He sat next to her to down an entire glass canister of water. He still smelled sexy, even if robust no longer applied.

"So, what have you been up to since rehab?"

"Not a lot. Avoiding friends. Running. Pretending I don't know every place to get a drink or score a high. But it's better than sitting in a silent flat while my mother knits her disappointment. Skein after skein of pursed lips and punctuated failure grate the nerves. And you? What have you been doing these past six weeks?"

"Working too much and pretending life doesn't suck."

"Fine plan. But if we're bound to be miserable today, we should do so together."

"Misery does love company."

"And breakfast. Come along. I know a great place."

Bea slipped her hand in his sweaty elbow. The reality of having to go home and to work pressed on her. She couldn't face this, not even with a good meal in her stomach and some decent conversation.

Eddie was lucky. His time with Siena had carried him all around the world. Bea's adult world had never grown much; it was exactly three cities wide. London. Vancouver. Los Angeles. The only place in Europe she'd seen was Germany once, years ago, at Kat's command.

"What if I proposed something more adventurous than breakfast?" she said on impulse.

Eddie leaned in close enough that she could smell the hint of anise beneath his sweat. An inquisitive twinkle of humor played in those amber eyes. "I'd say buy the bloke a meal, first. Stamina matters for ego. It's only respectful to give us our best shot."

Bea laughed, her first real bit of humor in a day. "Something much more platonic but less responsible."

"I'm intrigued. Go on."

"I want to run away and see the world, or at least Europe. A good interpreter could be handy. You speak, what? Five languages? And I'm a really good sober friend. I can teach you fun without adult beverages."

"I'll come along simply to discover how long a workaholic can go without making a to-do list."

"Moment's already passed. I'm making one in my head already."

"Then I accept the challenge of teaching Bea Douglas life unfettered."

The conversation shifted to countries and adventures and experiences Bea had never had. Curiosity bloomed and shoved aside everything else. By the time she said good-bye to Eddie, she was full of hope.

"In forty-eight hours, I'll be standing on a train platform. Don't make me a cliché, Beatrice." Eddie said with a waggle of eyebrows and broad grin before he took off on the day's second run.

She wouldn't. She could never turn Eddie into a cliché.

♦ ♦ ♦

Kat

"What the fuck?" I almost spill my coffee at the text of Bea's brief email.

"Something wrong?" Ian motions for my phone but I hold it back.

"Bea. Another four-day weekend." I shake my head. "I swear I don't even know her anymore, she's so checked out of work. She has a meeting on Monday with network brass, that now I'll have to take. Ugh."

"Good to have your own face in those meetings, Kat. It's your show, they should remember it."

"I hate those meetings. Have I told you how much I detest Royce Rudkins?"

"More than once," Ian laughs.

"Yeah, you can laugh. I'm the one who has to look at his stupid face and smile and nod at his stupid words coming out of his stupid mouth."

"Here." Ian slides a plate in front of me. "Eat. You'll be less irritable."

"Only slightly." I've got my own meetings to worry about. I'm skipping out of *21 Things* early today for the first logistics meeting on *Birds*—schedules, budgets, the nitty-gritty of starting a production. "Seriously, though. How can Bea just take off like this?"

"Maybe it's not a bad thing."

"But I was going to tell her about *Birds*. And now—I need her help on the business side, Ian. *21 Things* and *Birds*, both." I chew, thinking. "I should have told her weeks ago."

"Nothing was certain, you can't be faulted for not talking about it until it was signed."

"It should have been a big moment for the company. Making that leap, you know."

"It's your moment, birdy. You did it all. It's happening because of you, your brilliance."

"And a whole lot of help from you."

"I only made introductions. Everything else is you."

"I'm so bad at the business stuff, though. Bea understands it all."

"You will, too. This is your time, Kat. *Birds* is yours."

"I don't know." Bea's email legitimizes this growing feeling of separation. The looming end of *21 Things* shades everything between us. Maybe more than that. *K-Town*, too. Art versus business. All our little disagreements.

And Ian. Bea doesn't like Ian.

"It's something you can be certain of, birdy. It's yours. Bea didn't sweat over the best screenplay I've read in years, didn't meet with one of the biggest directors in the world and sell the idea of this movie. Partnerships end, Kat. Not the worst thing in the world. I've said it before, she doesn't understand art, and you're headed to bigger and better things. Let her have *Void*, let her keep her commercial telly stuff."

"You're talking about dissolving Monkey & Me?"

"If it makes sense."

"It doesn't, though. I built this brand, it's mine."

"So, expand it—add a movie division, yours alone. You can do what you want, Kat."

A movie division. Movies have always been part of the dream, the plan. *Birds* will be the beginning, and there will be more movies. More stories from my fingers and creative vision to the silver screen. My heart races at the idea all morning, and every sound—on the *21 Things* set and then on the Tube out to Chiswick—tattoos out a rhythm of movies, movies, movies.

Iona meets me in the small London offices of Jack's production company inside the parent studio's larger building. Everyone video conferences in—Jack and Nan are in New York, the cinematographer is in LA, and the production designer and location guy are in New Zealand, early morning hours everywhere except London, but Jack's schedule dictates when this meeting can happen.

Our laptops open to the shared production bible document, a mere skeleton at this point, and everyone's heads are too big on the video projection screen in the conference room.

Jack sits in a chair two sizes too small for his considerable size. He's a grizzly bear in human form, all hair and mass. He spins as he speaks, reaching for things in books and random items on his cartoonishly messy desk. "Alright. Who's going first? We've got location nailed down. You want to talk money or schedule first?"

Oh, cringe—I never want to talk money first. "On locations, there's still scouting to be done, right? What are we looking at building on a set and what are we going to shoot on location?" New Zealand isn't a nailed down location, it's an entire country, and I'm hoping this is a clever ruse to distract everyone from the money talk.

Jack unfolds noisy, ancient paper maps, shares others from his computer. He and Iona argue over past productions and the feasibility of various geography.

"Can we find a place to build out the alien village, in the landscape, crops and everything?" I ask.

"Don't see why not. We've built universes before," Jack says.

"Creates a lovely tourist industry, if done well," Iona adds in her soft burr.

"More money from the film commission maybe?" Dan, the location manager, pipes in. "It's tropical, right? We'll need to go further north than usual for that."

Jack and Ward, the production designer, devolve into an argument of CGI versus real landscape, the risks and benefits. "Kat, how important is it to have real versus CGI here? I mean, really." Jack throws the question to me.

"CGI goes a long way, but how grounded is this new world going to feel if it's all done in post prod? The landing site and the village are going to be incredibly important to establishing the new reality." No CGI trees. Blech. Artificial universes look artificial.

"Then clear-cut me a forest, Dan."

"I can't clear-cut a forest, Jack. The environmental offset fee alone would bankrupt us."

"Could we maybe look outside New Zealand, then? There were some lovely spots in Costa Rica and the taxes aren't as awful as they once were." Iona chimes in. She's slid glasses on her nose and makes marks in her notebook as everyone talks.

Can we do that? Fly to an entirely different country just for a tropical location? My location shooting expertise is limited to Hyde Park. How expensive will Costa Rica be? I've got that out-of-my-depth feeling again, and I try to school my face to hide it.

"Options would be lovely," Nan speaks finally. "Let Dan explore Costa Rica a bit or see if we can find a nice already cleared tract on the North Island to lease and build out."

"Can we get back to schedule, please?" Iona adds. "Jack, I can barely find time for lunch on yours. Where are you planning to put this? How far back are we willing to push?"

"Not pushing back. Three years. I want this cut and covered in three years."

"Then show us the slot," Nan says.

Jack grumbles. He pulls over a giant desk calendar and then fumbles with an electronic tablet. There are more lines and colors and names than I've ever seen as his schedule jumps onto the screen. Iona groans and both Ward and Dan laugh.

"I'm not sure what I'm looking at." I really don't know what I'm looking at. I pull up my calendar on my laptop and try to match existing dates and events to the mess Jack presents.

"Here, let me." Nan's soft voice comes through again. An invitation to a shared calendar pops up, and there it is. The *Birds* schedule.

It's insane. Absolutely insane.

A three-year timeline with barely a day free. Seven days a week. For three years.

"Welcome to my world." Iona winks at me. "This is a mess, Jack. We'll have to clean it up. And I was right. Not a slot for at least several years. You're overbooked, big time."

"Yeah, yeah. Here—I'm bumping that next trilogy out three months. No harm there. Those fans will wait forever. So, I'm available for three months starting next September. You've got to get this ready by then."

"Okay, thanks Jack. That gives me a timeline." Nan starts barking orders. To me. To everyone. I've heard about Nan, so quiet in public, so in-control in the background.

The timeline draws out on our shared screens with dizzying complexity—a huge commitment from each of us. A year of preproduction, filming in New Zealand's summer, another year for post-production, and a summer release date already penciled into the grand scheme. Alongside mine and Ian's combined calendars, it's boggling. Wrapping *21 Things* post-production while Ian is in Belgium for a short project, then Madagascar, then another movie in London, and a dozen pond hops to LA for smaller things—events, appearances. My involvement in preproduction will be accomplished via email and video until next spring. And I have until the end of November to finalize script changes necessitated by things like location scouting results and the author's notes.

It's lunacy, and I love it. That same sex and rock 'n' roll feeling I had running the *K-Town* writers' room. Everyone here thinks big, sees the themes, then narrows down to the details that will bring the vision to life.

This is the dream. I'm living the dream.

Except—I can't deliver on my first action item. I clear my throat and interject. "I don't have the author notes yet. I know it's part of her condition for selling the rights, but is it bound to a deadline or not? I'll need time with whatever she sends."

Nan purses her lips, then stares at the schedule. "We need a finished script soon, Kat. Best work some magic."

"Of course."

There are other irksome pieces, too, as I listen and try to swim upstream. There are suggested changes and overrides based on cost or feasibility. Then chunks are marked in red on my script. Storyline elements on the chopping block based on things I could make happen, but I'm only asked story-based questions, not the bigger picture things I usually manage.

I'm the writer, here as the writer. Consult only.

Frustration prickles across my skin. Money talks in this business. I've brought nothing but a script. I need buy-in to be a producer, to be a creator—an action-maker. Or I'll lose my baby. Again. Maybe I lose it to a crackerjack team of undeniable genius, but still—it's my baby.

I'll never get what I want without cash on the table. My mind begins to spin out plans and ideas while I ratchet up my confidence. I'm Katrine-fucking-Porter. I get what I want. Anything I want. And this is what I want.

The monthly income reports from Monkey & Me help me find my ballsiest set of balls. When the meeting ends, I grab Iona as she passes me.

"What would you think of a Monkey & Me production credit in the title cards?"

Iona raises an eyebrow. "I'd think I needed to talk it over with Jack, but he's been open to secondary companies in the past. But, to put this delicately, does Monkey & Me have the capital? Production is a buy-in, it always is at this level." Iona has that look—that you need to prove yourself look. I know that look.

"I—we—can pull it together." Barely. Maybe. If. But I need full involvement on *Birds*. I bet Bea can get us a loan somewhere. She's done it before. Or maybe—I shake my head, no that's probably too much to ask—but Ian does have a lot of money.

I'll make it happen. Whatever it needs to be. I, Katrine Porter, will make it happen.

I look more brazen than I feel, an act I mastered at thirteen. "Get me the figures. I have ideas for this movie that are worth using. It's a waste of my talents if I'm sitting here as the writer and nothing more."

Iona peers at me over those glasses like my last grade school teacher trying to reign in the wild artist ruining her happy group of conformists. "We all started as writers, Kat. You're still young in this business. I'll put together some numbers for buy-in, but don't expect EP. We've all earned our chops. You'll get yours soon enough."

I swallow a retort about golden statues and did she have any at my age. I'm a fucking creative genius. I should have that stamped on my Golden Globe.

By evening, I'm exhausted and on edge, but jazzed with a plan, as Ian pours wine and I replay every moment of my masterpiece taking shape. "The calendar is color-coded, a dozen colors, half a dozen weekly check-ins. Everything laid out. It's insane but so amazing. And Jack, oh my god—he's brilliant."

"He is at that," Ian chuckles. "Should I be jealous? You gonna throw me over for a director?"

I laugh and throw my arms around his neck. "No, you're my guy."

"Bloody right, birdy." He nips at my earlobe.

"But it's not my calendar. Everyone has action plans, to-do lists. Mine? Write. That's it. That's what I am. Maybe a sort of producer, but not really. I'm only in this because Jack and Iona get it, respect the writing. But I need more."

"More?" Ian pulls me down into a chair, a different more clearly on his brain.

"Mm-hm, Executive Producer Katrine Porter." It's now or never, Kat, my mercenary side announces as I stare at him. I grin and lick my lips so he's nice and pliable. "Front me half the money to make it happen?"

Ian laughs, the dimple in his chin grows pronounced as he grins at me. "Anything you need. I'm all yours."

A squeal erupts from deep within me. Monkey & Me cash plus Ian's investment means I'm in. Producer Katrine Porter is on her way to an Oscar.

CHAPTER 18

Grüß' ich mit Wehmuth,
Freudig scheidend aus eurer Schaar.

I greet with melancholy,
joyfully departing from your midst.

—Robert Schumann, Frauenliebe und -leben

Bea

Leaves floated and swirled along the lazy current of the Seine in the Sunday evening sun as Bea sipped expensive water and drank peacefulness during one last light supper. Their grand runaway adventures ended right here. The list of stops seemed endless. Burlesque in Prague—that had been an education—museums in Berlin, art in Holland, and fairytale castles at Neuschwanstein. Eddie knew a party in every city. Bea had taught him the art of the mocktini and demonstrated you didn't need alcohol to dance on a table.

They'd saved France for last. Kat called the country dirty, but Eddie called it lived-in. Perhaps the people here simply had better things to do than scrub buildings. Conversation, art, lovers, and food filled the collective French priority list. She and Eddie had enjoyed all but one. On this last day, they paused to read along the Seine and soak up what remained of the rose-colored light in the world's most romantic city.

Eddie read *L'Élégance du hérisson* across from her. His expression modified in time with the novel text, engrossed in whatever elegance a hedgehog might have. His long fingers embraced the book spine. A breeze rustled his dark curls. He'd found handsome again, more than ever. His muscles had taken form beneath the skin, and happiness re-etched itself in each line of his face.

His raspberry-infused sparkling water cast triangles of color on his now-taut chest as the liquid sloshed in the wine glass. Bea leaned forward to tease him. "No matter how often you swirl that, the water won't turn to wine."

Eddie looked up from his book. "Doesn't hurt to hope. Wine in France is one of life's great pleasures."

Eddie covered her hand with his free one. He pressed the pads of his fingers into hers to create a steeple. "You haven't told me where you disappeared to this morning?"

"I went to see a church."

Eddie's face soured at even the generic mention of organized religion. He was an agnostic, a hobby Buddhist if pressed, and as closed to the topic of Christianity as Kat had always been. He was too like Kat, sometimes. "I know. You hate churches."

"Not my fault. I've an allergy to oppression."

Bea pulled her fingers into a fist but forced a half-laugh, as she did when Kat made similar jokes. If he knew she'd actually attended the church, the whole trip could take a nasty turn. "So, my morning was no great mystery. But how to speak this language remains a puzzle."

"Not really, though your choice in French literature may need to mature a few decades for mastery." Eddie nodded at the preschool primer beside Bea's plate.

"Very funny. I'm shocked these children learn to read. Why use that many vowels per syllable? It's wasteful, pure and simple."

"A matter in frank discussion amongst the country's leadership, I'm sure." His sarcastic chuckle echoed in the glass before he took a sip.

"I'll write those forward-thinking parliamentarians a letter of support."

Eddie grinned over the rim of the glass. "In words of no more than one syllable—"

"And no more than three words per sentence." Bea tried not to grin.

Eddie was *it*—exactly her type, intellectually. When he'd noted that Bea'd incorrectly attributed a theory of time to Vasiliev that belonged to

Popescu while they stared at Umberto Boccioni's *Dynamism of a Cyclist* in the Louvre, Bea had wanted to have his babies. She warded off a sigh. Enough, Bea. Enough pining for Eddie. She was no Siena Russo, or any of the other women Eddie had chosen for long-term love affairs. And she was Mormon, more so every time she took another step toward getting off the Kat train for good.

Eddie leaned across the table to caress an errant strand of hair escaped from her braid. "Your hair is remarkable in this light. It's the color of your heart, full of fire and light."

Bea felt her skin heat and pushed that back down, too. "Someone woke up on the poetic side of the bed today."

Eddie raised her freckled hand to his lips as he winked at her and said something lovely and French. An incorrigible flirt. He'd done something similar to a waitress because he wanted his scallops prepared in a particular way. Bea pulled her hand back, grinned, and then quoted Humpty Dumpty in bad French. Eddie laughed as only he could, bright and full of joy, but loud enough to attract harsh looks from passerby.

"Come on. Let's go before you lose your French street cred. Mind if we walk back to the apartment rather than grab the Metro?"

"Not at all, my lovely one. I'm at your command."

Eddie offered his hand and then pulled her in tight to his side once she stood. She'd become his platonic cuddle-buddy, as she had been for so many other past guy friends. But she didn't mind. Crazy-good shivers rushed through her whenever he touched her.

And this night, he couldn't stop touching her.

They stopped along the river. Eddie's thumb ran across her collarbone while they watched children play with geese. When they resumed their walk, his hand settled on her hip with his thumb hooked around her jeans waistband. Her stomach rode a roller-coaster whenever his knuckle made contact with her stomach. Then, when Eddie settled his hand in the space between her jeans-covered thighs while they leaned against a wall to listen to two street performers play guitar duets, a battle between her amygdala and frontal cortex almost undid her entire life plan. She'd never been so turned on in her life.

Something had changed in Eddie. His touches spread warm chocolate over her skin with a silent promise to remove it in a dozen sensual ways, part of a sweet and molten seduction that left her quivering on a public street. Eddie wanted *her* as a souvenir from France, and it was sexy—the sexiest, most amazing thing she'd ever felt.

But, think, Bea. Think how to get out of this without ruining everything else.

Except she *couldn't* think because of earworms tunneling holes in her brain. Eddie wouldn't stop humming stupid Beatles songs just to annoy her.

Bea elbowed him at the second chorus of "All You Need Is Love." "You're an arse. You know that, right? A complete arse. That will be in my head all night."

Eddie stepped behind her. He splayed a hand across her stomach and nipped at her ear. Happy tingles chased down her neck and then disappeared behind her shoulder blade.

They began an aimless walk along the river. Small steps full of sway—not enough movement to make progress, but plenty to enhance friction and sensation. Another step down the path that promised even more friction and sensation and happy, sated giggles.

Eddie pushed her braid off her neck and ran two fingers along the tendon. "Let's go find a private moment to tell each other all the things we've never said."

His lips on her neck sent an electric jolt that re-enervated her brain. Bea removed the hand that curved around her rear. He'd gone far enough. Every relationship these days, no matter the type, seemed hell-bent on sex, but that wasn't what Bea wanted. Not at all. She wasn't available to be Eddie's rebound.

"Enough flirting, Eddie. You know all you need to know about me."

Bea needed to get off the rose-colored streets filled with lovers, escape the twinkling lights and soft clink of glasses and the lusty, romantic music that filled the air. She jogged across the street and entered the Metro for a screeching, jolting train ride back to the apartment.

Eddie grabbed her hand as the train squealed into the station. "Bea, talk to me."

"I'm fine. Tired from so much travel, I guess. Stressed about the move." She squeezed Eddie's hand to accentuate each lie.

Eddie dropped the subject and her hand.

The train lurched to a stop. Street performers played more love songs, and everyone seemed to be kissing. Paris. Stupid, sexy Paris. From here on out, Bea would only travel to frozen areas with icy libidos.

Eddie held the door as Bea entered his uncle's Paris apartment where they'd spent the weekend. She stormed down the hall and collapsed on the wide, white bed that invited her to sink down and endure misery with class.

After who-knew-how-long, Eddie entered to sit at the end of the bed. His hand wrapped her ankle, but Bea felt almost nothing. Back to friendship. Back to platonic. Back to bearable.

"Bea, I've made a decision about *Void*."

His thumb made a small circle around her ankle bone, and all the blissful emotions from earlier returned. Why couldn't she manage this feeling?

Eddie didn't wait on her response. "Tell Josh I'll be at work a week from Tuesday. I'll fulfill my contract."

Bea's eyes flew open. She pushed up on her elbow. "Good. Because it would have been tragic if you'd let those idiots ruin this for you."

Eddie smiled at her, mostly in his eyes. "Not going to let anyone ruin this for me. Not even me. Don't you worry." Then he stood and walked back out the door.

Bea collapsed back on the bed, the whole of her misery returned to greet her. The pending end to her travels. The *21 Things* wrap party. All the dismissals of her life.

Eddie made sense, of course. No one went from Siena Russo to Bea Douglas; even a blind man would know he'd scooped from the bottom of the female barrel. Unless, of course, that man were in France after a long, dry spell. Then Bea Douglas became an acceptable body in a bed. No more, no less.

But Kat . . . there was no rationalizing the mess with Kat. Bea let one tear slip down her cheek before she batted it away. She wouldn't cry. Not for Kat or anyone.

♦ ♦ ♦

Kat

"That's a wrap. Thanks, everyone, this has been one for the memory books," Ralph says with a slight catch in his voice. He slides off his chair by the main camera and places his headphones on the seat. This is the end, the last day filming *21 Things*. Unknown workers will strike the bookstore set tomorrow, and our studio will go to the next small, new show with big dreams.

Ben pops open champagne, spilling it recklessly. Anna laughs, then cries. Then Quinn cries. Jamie hugs Bea and tucks her into his side for a whispered conversation, the only kind you can have with Jamie. The crew gathers around. I queue up my *21 Things* wrap party soundtrack and the party begins. We sit on the café stools and barter for set souvenirs. There will be an official *21 Things* media event when we post the last episode, but this is the farewell party we'll remember.

The finite storyline plan was brilliant when Bea and I conceived it, but four seasons have passed without reckoning. There's a lump in my throat. It's over. My first successful production is over.

Ben drapes himself over me. He wiggles the bottle in front of my face and dangles two champagne flutes in his other hand. "A bit of the bubbly, Creative Genius Kat Porter?"

I grab a glass and hold it steady as the golden liquid pours. "Ah, Ben. I do love you, dear idiot brother I never needed."

"A brother doesn't do this, does he?" Ben plants a sloppy kiss on my cheek, and then takes time to make it weird and laughable.

I push him off with my free hand. I'm full of giggles, even without champagne. "Oh, shut your face. I'm not available, dumbass."

"Story of my life, Kat."

"I could find you someone. She should be sweet in the sack but mean in the streets. Slap you when you deserve it, possibly every day. Almost definitely every day."

"You'll never find Ben a woman that perfect, Kat, but I'll show up and slap him. Fuck knows, I've enough practice." Quinn wiggles under Ben's arm. Seems a loss they never had that ménage à trois that Ben wanted. I think Ben wanted more than his gross jokes suggested, but Quinn never gave him a look. I've thought it wise on her part, but now it's sad.

Anna joins us. "Are we slapping Ben? One more time for good luck? I want two, thanks." The game is on. The jokes fly around. Jamie and Adhira join us, then the crew and Ralph. One camera operator is circling with a handheld, recording this last joke, a final saved memory.

We've all moved on to tearful remembrances and favorite funny stories when Bea jostles my arm. "Hey, do you have a minute?"

"Yeah. I was going to find you and ask you the same thing."

"Great minds, right?" Bea pushes her long hair off her face. Her mouth smiles but her eyes barely make contact. She's been odd lately. I've meant to ask her, but some item on my to-do list always pushes the moment aside. It's not a sad kind of odd—more distanced, her head in other places. Maybe Bea is seeing someone. Actually dating. A reasonable explanation for most of her recent odd behavior. The only guy she spends time with here is Ralph, though. Maybe Bea is having a fling with Ralph. But that's ludicrous—I almost laugh—Ralph is married. Even if Bea were madly in love with a bespectacled, waist-shirted man three decades her senior, she would never, ever entertain an affair. Back to zero in the viable theory count.

I reach out to squeeze her hand, but it feels strange so I pull back. "Um, how about we sneak off to my office? "

Bea nods, oddly amenable lately. Anything I ask, she agrees. Ben drops an arm over her and whispers something. She nods again. Wow. Two *yes* responses in twenty seconds. Love . . . or whatever it is, has worked miracles with Bea.

We walk down the silent hallway. Very silent Bea is shorter than usual. She's not wearing heels. Her whole style is weird. Wide-legged black pants and a long, oversized white blouse with ridiculous costume jewelry. As usual, I only know fashion when my stylist puts it on me, and my stylist keeps putting me in these barely-there, androgynous jumpsuits with no bra or else slacks and sexy-slutty silk dress shirts left unbuttoned to my waist—which is what I wore in *Vanity Fair*. Ian loves them, but I feel naked.

Bea glances back at the studio. She rubs her hands on her pants and then chatters at me in nervous small talk. "This whole thing is funny, right? Add a yearbook signing and it'd be Ririe High School Class of 2006 all over again. Love you. Friends forever. But we won't be. Obviously. I don't like endings. Never have."

"I don't like thinking of it as ending. It's a chance for new beginnings. Maybe I'll be one of those producers that has favorite actors who show up in everything I do."

Bea looks at me. Pointedly. Then her eyes change. Sadness and disappointment parade across her face until she erases both with a giant sigh and smiles at me, but it's her polite and careful smile, nothing real. I can't find my Bea anywhere in her careful up-do and perfect makeup. "I'll get to the point. We shouldn't be gone long. It's our last day with everyone."

Bea hands me a cream-wrapped package with long, golden ribbons. "I've got you something. An apology for *K-Town* and a thank you for *21 Things*."

I pick up the box. I should tell her about the movie, but all I can think are lies. Half-truths. Hedges. I untie the ribbon and tear at the paper to find a simple flat box with elegant lettering across the top—*Teatro alla Scalla*. Season tickets to the premiere opera house in the world. "You didn't!"

Bea smiles her first real smile.

"It's perfect! I've only been once, and it was so transcendent. Bea, thank you so much!" There's a lump then, not in my throat. Closer to my heart. This is Bea, who always knows what I need. And I'm—no, I won't feel guilty.

I'm doing what I need. There's nothing wrong with putting yourself first. Only misogynistic bullshit says otherwise.

I don't have a gift in return. Bea is always more thoughtful that way, but I've been driving on a plan, not thinking about wrap-party presents. The package tucks into my chest and excitement naturally flows. "I think it's time for another move with the company."

Bea smiles and crosses her arms, like she does in negotiations. Her apple cheeks go high and her eyes sparkle. She's a cheerleader and student body president with the mental chops of a bank president, completely unreadable and impassable but thoroughly likable.

My confidence falters, but I push on. It's a great plan and Ian has offered even more cash to make it happen. "It's time for a movie division because I have a movie. I wrote a movie. And people love it. So, I'm making that leap, we're making the leap to movies."

There, out on the table.

But Bea doesn't pick it up. Her cheeks fall and her mouth forms a hard, hard line. Her voice echoes slow drips of water forming icicles on a frozen roof. "I heard. Congratulations."

"You knew?" I swallow but my throat has gone dry and it turns into a cough. Was this what the weirdness was about? Not some mysterious lover in Paris? I wanted the mysterious lover in Paris.

Bea's arms come undone. She reaches for a package behind her encased in her favorite brand of Manila envelope. "Yes. I've known for a while. And I know my name's not on it anywhere. So, I think your division is really more of a split, isn't it?"

"Well, maybe. If you want to see it that way. I'll run movies, you'll run TV. It stays Monkey & Me." I didn't plan on this. Not immovable Bea with eyes flashing as brightly as her hair. But this idea is golden. She needs to listen. I need amenable Bea from the party. "We've got a movie with the New Zealand gang, and a production credit if we can gather the capital for producing buy-in."

"The money we have—given our less-than-ideal financial situation after *K-Town*'s poor showing—is sitting in escrow. We're 15k short per Iona's request." Bea hands me the documents. "But I'm not sailing down this river again, Kat. I'm not listening to pretty stories and pretending everything will get better with time. You've got a great new life. I get it. I know your ghost routine. I've been cleaning up after it for years."

The veil falls from Bea's face. No more friendly high school seniors in residence. Her fingernails dig into her arms where they're crossed—she's all rage. Bea's been avoiding me because she's angry at me.

Really, really angry.

Maybe I deserve a little of that. I can't remember the last time we talked. Probably Los Angeles, before the *Void* premiere. Yeah. The night before the *Void* premiere, we had ice cream and girls' movie night.

And then I ran off with Ian. But Bea knows what I'm like when I'm with someone new. I always drop off the face of the planet until the sex calms down, and sex with Ian could take a long, long time to calm down. She knows this. Why is she glaring at me like she's wishing for a wild animal to escape the zoo and hunt me down?

"No. Bea, please. I know I've been missing lately. But you have to understand. This isn't how any of this was going to go. I wrote it on a whim, it wasn't real, and then it got so big and I couldn't tell you and then you were never here."

One hand comes loose for a giant, harsh stop sign. "Shut up, Kat. I promised I would do this calmly. You've had so much time to make this right and you chose not to do so. Did you lose your cell phone? Or just my number? Forgot how to send emails? You obviously forgot our address after you had a delivery company gather your stuff. How is Ian's house? I wouldn't know. I've never had an invite. Nor have you stopped by the offices for a chat, though I've been not three hundred feet from where you filmed three out of seven days of the week for the past six weeks."

The hand six inches from my face starts to quiver. Bea fists it slowly and then tucks the hand back in her armpit.

"I've been part of everything, whether I liked it or not, for seven years. I've done everything you asked, including hiding who I really am because my religion brought up bad memories. I spent a year in Vancouver at your request—on a show I barely understood—feeling like an overpaid intern every stinking day. You ruined the *Void* premiere for me by disappearing. You made me break up with your boyfriend for you. So, you take your movie and ride to success on Ian's tail end. But you don't get *21 Things*."

Bea takes the documents from me and flips to the back page. It's a division of assets page. "Nothing I can do about proprietorship, but marketing was all me. This document splits that out. Any marketing of *21 Things* must bear my name and logo as long as Monkey & Me exists, and you can't sell *21 Things* without my approval. Split the company any way you like. Fire me, for all I care. But you can't remove me from the record."

My hackles rise and then this slow burn awakens ashes I forget lie dormant. This beastly piece of me that I always regret but can't control. The risen beast roars from my mouth and hurls every weapon I have at the person I thought I loved most.

"I haven't done anything wrong here, and I'm not taking any puritanical moralizing bullshit from some dumb girl who's never had a dream of her own except to live the life her uterus handed her at birth. I've worked for what I wanted, taken what I needed. I have everything I ever wanted and you're no one, no one at all. You never were. You'd be nothing but a nurse in a random rural hospital crying over your lonely state if it weren't for me."

For one moment, every barb cuts open grand gashes on Bea's face. But she sews them up quick, as neatly as any stitch she's ever placed. "Thanks, Kat. That made this easier." She hands me a card. "That's my new lawyer. We're prepared to fight for anything. And Josh wants me to remind you that Monkey & Me is on contract for three years at *Void*, and he wants me to lead that project, since you're not taking his calls either. We both wish you well with your new people."

I wrestle the beast, I do. Inside, part of me screams to make things right, but the card in my hand summons the beast again. A lawyer. How dare she. "I. Don't. Need. You," I snarl.

"Good. Because you don't have me. Not after this." Bea shrugs and then walks past me to slide into the hall without a bit of noise, magically silent, as though she was never there at all.

Bea won. I didn't even know it was a competition, but she won. I'm left with a broke company and her blasted name—and new logo—on everything Monkey & Me creates from now until the day I die.

"Fuck!" I grab the first thing off my desk, throw a House Stark mug at the wall, but I feel zero satisfaction when it cracks into pieces. Then I head back to the studio to enjoy what's left of the party because she can't take *21 Things* from me, either.

Bea and Ben lean against a wall near the entrance. My heart thumps at the thought of even making eye contact, but as I near, Ben hands Bea a red poker chip. She throws her arms around Ben's neck and cries into his shoulder. In all the years I've known Bea, she's never cried, not even on the day I made her watch every tear-jerker movie in the world. Nothing. Stoic, impassable, always-right Bea.

There are tears for poker and Ben.

But none over the end of our partnership.

CHAPTER 19

Nur eine Mutter weiß allein,
Was lieben heißt und glücklich sein.

Only a mother knows alone
what it is to love and be happy.

—Robert Schumann, Frauenliebe und -leben

Kat

Several weeks slide by before I'm really okay with the end of Monkey & Me. Ian came through with his promise to front more than a division; he helped me set up a whole new business that Bea can't touch. Ian and I are partners now, in everything: life, love, business.

And family. This week, we're going to make a family: me, Ian, and Eden.

Addy's had one chance too many and Ian has decided—maybe with a few pushes from me and Tess—to be a regular kind of dad. Custody negotiations with Addy failed despite every attempt, but yielded a temporary ceasefire pending the next court hearing. Ian gets Eden for a week every month instead of two days whenever the whim strikes. Since my run-in with the disaster that is Addy, I've been lobbying for a better life for Eden and real parenthood for myself. Ian stepped up, albeit with plenty of coaxing and promises that our sex life won't suffer.

A middling fee, and one I'd pay twice to reimburse what Marian did for me.

Marian. I miss Marian so much. Losing people is normal for me, but Marian and my dad have left a hollow spot in my heart. My dad died of heart disease my senior year of college, the year I met Bea. Marian died of ovarian cancer two years after we moved to London. My two hard losses, that's what I call them.

The anniversary of Marian's death came and went with the usual video conference and toast with John, but with Eden about to arrive, Marian seems to be hovering outside my vision field, as though I could see her if I only turned my head fast enough.

Marian. Closest thing I'll ever know to a mother.

When I was twelve, my dad got promoted to Master Sergeant and afforded his pick of squadron engineer assignments, which took us to Croughton Air Force Base in Brackley—*this* close to London. I had recently discovered the Beatles, and I might have begged for us to be stationed in England.

I attended the private school in Northampton, but after school, I'd drift around the base and wait for my dad. I'd been a girl without a mother for my whole life, as evidenced by my wardrobe of Star Trek t-shirts, jean overalls, and thick-rimmed purple glasses bought at the base exchange on the cheap. I was a fumbling, hopeless fawn with none of the grace.

Which is where Marian came in.

She was a civilian secretary on base. Every day, she'd pass by and see me with my nose buried in novels far away from the cursing, clanging ambiance of Dad's shop. Then one day, she sat down with an almond croissant from the bakery in town. She asked me all the questions no one but Dad ever asked. Then she told me her husband, John, worked as a publicist for television shows. Marian made a friend for life with that statement. I lived at her cubicle every day after school, talked her ear off for hours, and then begged her to take me to the BBC. She did. Along the way, we bought new clothes, and she introduced me to contact lenses and tampons.

Marian was my useless mother's official stand-in, and that's what I hope to become for Eden. We've had a rocky start, but I know I can be Eden's person—her safe space—to guide a little girl into womanhood. Now is my chance, here in Madagascar as Ian films and I rework my *Birds* draft based on the author's notes.

I make a final circuit of the sprawling beach house to check my preparations. The breeze off the ocean blows through the screens that open to our private patio and beach. The house has three bedrooms and a great room. The ocean expanse incorporates island paradise into our private and exclusive rental cottage. I've stocked Eden's room with everything the *Teen Vogue* back-to-school issue lists as a *must have* for preteens. An iTunes gift card, a new iPad Air loaded with every possible game, a stylish bag that isn't a backpack, and black silk bedding highlighted with bright blue pillows. Dozens of pillows.

I've placed a few gifts from me around the room. Nothing wrapped or fancy or trying too hard—some old favorites from when I was her age, and a couple of albums the Internet assures me are all the rage with teenage girls everywhere, a demo from an indie band that submitted it to *21 Things*, and a highly recommended young adult novel based on Greek mythology that I've forced myself not to read a dozen times since I bought it at the airport.

Back in the kitchen, I check on the food side of my campaign by topping a banoffee pie, Eden's favorite, with copious amounts of whipped cream. And there are other recipes and ingredients. Baking is mothering time, per Marian. Nothing to do but talk about boys and dreams and issues while you wait on a pudding.

I hope I've done it all right. I long for Marian's gift of seeing a need and filling it.

Bea has the same gift, a tiny traitorous voice interjects. Mustn't think of Bea. Something bad happens in my gut when I think of her. But last night, I dreamed of her in her pajama bottoms and X-Files shirt with messy bun. She talked to me, but I couldn't hear her. Then I made myself wake up. I have other things to focus on. Endings happen. Best not to puzzle over them.

A flash of red catches my eyes. Dammit. I pull a lacy red bra from between the cushions of the large sofa. I thought I found all the sex evidence and put it away. I don't think there's a single surface, indoor or out, that Ian and I haven't had sex on. We've left mementos everywhere. It's been quite the job, finding them all.

Mother figures don't advertise their sex lives. They give small, insightful details at the perfect moment.

Two cigarettes lay together on the side table. Gah. How did I miss this? Mothers don't smoke just because their sex partner hands off a cigarette or because everyone seems to do it here. How many lectures have I heard about the horrors of smoking? We're risking Eden's lungs having those beastly things in the house.

Cigarettes. Sex. Slightly hung over from last night's party. I'm failing at adulthood. I can't be a *mother*.

Tears sting my eyes that have nothing to do with the acrid scent left by this morning's smoke-and-dine with Ian. Ian had demanded me on his lap after the smokes. Ian demands me all the time and I'm a willing plaything. But how do I be the lover Ian demands and the mother Eden needs? Dad never had girlfriends, not that I knew, so all my vision of parenthood is a sexual wasteland. Bea's parents still chase each other around the house and the whole family banters in sexual innuendo, but none of them sit pantyless on the veranda and finish off the second batch of smokes while doing things too risqué for a gentleman's magazine.

Of that, I'm sure.

So, pull it together, Kat. I reach over and toss the cigarettes on the beach. Teach responsibility.

I know that one.

Marian gave me all the right info—smoking, drinking, sex. I've ignored them too much, but that doesn't mean she was wrong.

The door opens and I scramble to my feet but stop nervously in front of a mirror. If it wasn't myself I was looking at, I suppose I'd be impressed. From my cat-eye purple glasses to barely-there jean shorts to bare feet and toe rings—artistic, young, and hip. That's what's written on the style sheets Ian's publicity team emails me.

"Hey, you two." I walk out to the reception area of the house. Ian engulfs me in a hug and kisses me. I push him off. Best start the less-sex life now.

Eden stares at me in sullen neutrality. I remember sullen, disrupted-family preteen too well to expect a hug. "Eden, I haven't seen you in ages. How was your flight?"

Bulky headphones hang around her neck. Her blond hair is mixed with chunky streaks of black that match the heavy black eyeliner smudged around her blue eyes. She's wearing thick makeup, false eyelashes, and black lipstick. She looks eleven going on zombie.

Eden flashes a fake grin. "Fantastic. I love flying alone. Super great to be here!" Eden starts to slip on the headphones. Ian shakes his head and she drops them back to her shoulders.

"Are you hungry? Airline food is always so awful." Ian mouths *good luck* as he disappears around the corner with Eden's luggage. "I made your favorite pie."

"Dad got me something healthy. I'm over pie." Eden tromps after her father down the hall. Her heavy boots are all wrong for the beachy beauty of the island.

My inner traitor conjures Bea again. No, I don't need Bea's input even if she is great with kids. I'll figure out Eden, and I'll do it on my own. We'll start with space. Then pie. I was prickly at her age, and she has even more reason than I did—so, patience.

Small bass and treble sounds float down the hallway as Ian and Eden talk. Eden cues up the indie band. I like the sound. Like home. Like my dad and me.

Ian emerges and takes up the space behind me. His hands find my breasts, his breath warm on my neck. "Pie, hm? Wine, too? What else you got for me?"

I wiggle away from his hands. "Later, Ian. We're not alone."

"Ah, she'll keep to her room tonight and we've got ours." Ian nips at my ear.

"Did you see her makeup, Ian?"

"Yeah, and it's what teenage girls do to try to get a rise of their ol' Da', trust me. Leave Eden to her sulking. I got new lines today and need your help to perfect them."

The night disappears in routine, my hope for motherhood negated. Ian and I do the usual things in the usual places until almost midnight.

Then I tiptoe out for tea and deep thoughts. The tea pot hisses as I tap out a Rachmaninoff prelude on the counter.

Eden wanders into the kitchen bleary-eyed, her makeup now a mess on her face. Eden grunts and grabs a mug from a cabinet to make instant coffee. Before I can wonder too hard or even offer sugar or cream, Eden sips it straight, black.

"You want something to eat? Midnight is the best time for pie." I open the refrigerator.

Eden scrunches her nose. She stares at the whipped cream and her mouth works. Then her eyes slide down to her stomach. "No. No pie. Just coffee."

"Look, you're hungry—I can tell—and you need fuel. Coffee isn't enough. So, I'm going to cook and you're going to eat."

"Egg whites and spinach. No oil. Maybe some fruit. And I'll eat in my room." She lifts her arms to sip coffee. The shirt rises all the way up to the unnecessary wire in a way-too-sexy, padded black lace bra. Too much skin. The only sign of her real age is a zit forming in an unwashed swath of makeup.

I close my eyes for a moment. What would Marian do? What would Bea do? *Care for the problem at hand*, they speak in chorus.

"Hey, I found this incredible makeup remover. If you want to try it, you can. I'll leave some in your bathroom." No response except the sound of one of the bar stools being pulled out. Not bad. "I'll go to market tomorrow, if you want to come, and we can get you some of your own. Maybe a whole facial."

"Are there peppers?"

I smile as I separate the last egg for Eden's omelet. "Red or green or both?"

"Both." I don't have to see the shrug, I can hear it in her voice. Trying for coolness. "Do they have sandals at the market?"

"Oh, there's everything on the market street. A couple fun jewelry places, swimsuits, beachwear, you name it." Egg whites flip onto a plate, surrounded by tropical fruits.

We eat in silence. Eden tosses her hair or fiddles with her oversized concert t-shirt. "I just have my Docs. I'll need some sandals." Eden tugs on a dark chunk of her hair, avoiding my eyes.

"Sure. We can get some tomorrow." I panic at the end of conversation. I can't think of a thing to say. I've covered all the topics Tess told me would work.

Then I see the book I bought her. It's dog-eared a few chapters in. I point to it. "Is it good? I opened to the first page and I was hooked. Been killing me not to read."

"It's not bad." Eden forgets to shrug. She looks away and then back at me. "I like the main girl. She's tough. And the monsters are cool."

I slide my stool around the bar to sit by her. "Oh, show me. I love mythology."

We read together on the counter as we eat omelets and banoffee pie. Ian finds us hours later, the book cradled between us.

The next morning, Eden has transformed. She wears my butterfly tank over a horrifyingly inappropriate bikini with peek-a-boo cutouts in the form of dollar signs and obvious padding to make her breast buds into an A-cup. She's got on my jean shorts. On me, they're short and sexy, but they cover her to her knees. She has yet to choose among the ten pairs of sandals scattered on the floor. Instead, she stands at the mirror, trying on every piece of jewelry I own.

"I want to get my nose pierced." She slips dangling chandelier earrings into her ears.

"It would be adorable. You have the perfect nose. Want a cuff for now?" I dig through another jewelry box until I find the nose ring cuff I wore in a staged happy couple shopping trip with Ian a few weeks ago. More publicity than fun, and it worked. We are the buzziest coupled bees to ever make the cover of *US Weekly*. "Here. This one's got turquoise, it will match your eyes."

"My mom said I can get my belly pierced next year on my birthday. Then I have to convince Da about a tattoo."

"Oh, really?" I choke on the idea of a 12-year-old getting a belly piercing and a tattoo. The inappropriate bikini, the false eyelashes—all Addy, all the way.

Eden removes the chandeliers and replaces them with black skeleton heads with ruby eyes. "I wanted a dragon but daddy said no because Tess said no, but if you said yes . . ."

My brain sputters and finds a hint of inspiration. "My friend, Bea, always says that anything permanent risks being permanently out of fashion. That's why she plays with henna tattoos and nonpermanent stuff. Maybe we should try that, find what you think is perfect before we talk to your dad."

I veer away from the topic before I stick my foot in it and ignite a family feud. I made a mom-list of necessary safety items this morning. Item 1: No smoking. Item 2: Sunscreen. "Hey, did you try that new sunscreen? Doesn't it feel like silk on your skin?"

Eden pokes through all the bottles on the vanity while I find the sunscreen. "I love your perfume." Eden spritzes perfume into the air.

"I bet we can find an amazing floral scent for you. Something jasmine or plumeria." I will make the little girl emerge from beneath layers of too-soon sexuality. I hand her a pair of turquoise spiral earrings to replace the skeletons. Without the fake eyelashes and cake makeup, she already looks closer to her age. She just needs clothes that wouldn't double as wardrobe in ads for Pedophilia Quarterly.

"Okay, girly, slip on a pair of sandals. Your dad's money won't spend itself."

We walk the short ways to the market. The black wardrobe finds some color. Eden's first choices are always too mature, but if I look first at something younger and mention I wish I could wear it if only I were blonder or shorter or had Eden's true-blue eyes, the item acquires immediate value. Even the awful bikini ends up hidden in a bag, replaced by a darling tankini.

My memory slips back to shopping trips with Marian. My problem had been the opposite—my dad refused to see me out of my baby years—but I'd assumed Marian loved shopping. The pretense was always that Marian needed a little something or other. Never once did I stop to consider that Marian may have been more motivated by my needs than her own.

"Can we make Thai for dinner?" Eden shocks me out of reverie.

We decide to try handmade potstickers just for the fun of it, which is where Ian finds us much later—attempting to summon a feast of Asian food.

I chop onions while Eden laughs at my cartoon tears. "Isn't there a way to avoid that? Tess does something."

I laugh and wave fumes away from my face. "I don't usually cry. I swear Madagascar onions are nuclear."

"What's gone on in here? Laughing. Crying. Piles of bags everywhere. What's kept my women so busy today?" Ian kisses Eden and then wraps his arms around me.

I turn into him to languish in a good day, a family day. "Well, girly, get the fashion show started. He'll want to see everything."

Ian sucks at the soft spot behind my ear once Eden disappears. I float away on happiness and the promise of sex. Then I hear Eden's feet in the hall and push away, like a good mom should. "We had loads of fun today. We may have spent a whole lot of money on what she's about to show you."

Ian shrugs—money is something of a meaningless word to him—and goes back to work on my erogenous zones hidden behind the counter.

Eden walks in wearing an adorable mid-length A-line gray skirt and retro 80s pink tee with a rainbow. She looks stylishly almost-twelve.

Ian is dumbstruck enough that he forgets his less-fatherly behavior beneath the counter. He walks to Eden, turns her around in a slow spin. "This really my gel?"

Eden giggles, and then wiggles close for a hug. "Oh, but you have to see my new shoes. Hold on. I'll change into the next outfit." Eden sprints back down the hall.

Ian rubs the back of his neck and laughs. "Unbelievable. Kat, you're a worker of miracles." He drapes his arms around me as I chop vegetables. "Ask me about my day, birdy."

"Mm, how was your day, love?" I turn to kiss him.

"One take. Pin drop silence when I finished. Best work in decades they said."

Ian tells me play-by-play about his good day while Eden runs in and out to show off clothes and shoes. I feel like a mom, like everything a mom should be. Sexy. Connected. In the center of everything. The reason it all works. The happy still tingles in my toes as I put away dinner. Ian retreats to the back room to rehearse. Eden video chats with Tess and the girls. I sway and sing along to Florence + The Machine, triumphantly feminine.

I was born to be here, to be Ian's woman and Eden's mother. I've found home.

CHAPTER 20

"The different accidents of life are not so changeable as the feelings of human nature."

—Mary Shelley, Frankenstein

Kat

Three months later, we're in LA. I don't remember this from last year—endless pre-parties and luncheons for the Golden Globes. But here I am, attending every possible event and smiling throughout. Confirming continued success after last year's trophy grab and charming any potential investors in *Birds*. Word is out in Hollywood, and everyone is interested. But we still need that last investment-level interest from a someone or studio with deep pockets.

With the investment from InK, mine and Ian's production company, my place as an executive producer is secured, but preproduction and pre-viz have revealed a worrisome money gap.

Another luncheon, another wedge salad barely eaten. "I swear to gods, Ian, if one more person suggests the Weinsteins I will strangle someone. I don't need their meddling fingers in my movie."

Ian runs a comforting hand down my back as we get back to the hotel suite.

"This is the stuff I'm not good at. I wish Bea were here." I kick off my heels and fall into the couch. I wish I hadn't pushed Bea away.

"You don't need her, birdy. You're doing spectacular on your own."

I feel myself flailing in the ocean, a little fish among the sharks. We were always little fish, but Bea could project the image and confidence of a shark.

Nic knocks on the door before entering with her key card. I've kept her on as my personal assistant, at Ian's insistence that I need one. It feels a little ridiculous to me at the moment, having her manage my social calendar, but she keeps me on schedule.

"Your final dress fitting is tomorrow morning, moved to make room for the BAFTA Tea Party," Nic reads from her Galaxy phone. "And I need to know what you're wearing tonight for *W Magazine*."

"The Stella McCartney paisley."

"Nope. This is a fashion party, you have to wear something new. And edgy. I ordered up three dresses yesterday, did you even look at them?"

"No. Help me pick?" What is the point of owning a fabulous designer dress if I can only wear it once?

Nic follows me to my dressing room, through the sitting room where Ian is on the phone with Jace and watching rugby at the same time. The options lined up on a separate rack are—edgy, at the very least. Another moment I miss Bea. She knows fashion, while I blindly navigate, mostly doing what I'm told or what's comfortable. Golden Globes week is not for comfort, though.

I hold up each dress in front of me in the mirror and sigh. I don't really like any of them that much. At least not compared to the silver paisley dress.

"The graffiti print—the Moschino," Nic says. "That's the one. I'll let Jace know so he can order up the right jewelry."

"Is anyone else coming?"

"Anna is confirmed, a nice little co-presenting moment. Bea sent regrets."

"What? Why? Why wouldn't she come?" I guess I know the answer. I thought that maybe we could all be together again, here—instead of scattered to the wind—a triumphant return a year later, but there's too much damage. I'm not even sure I want to see her again.

Nic pulls a large envelope out of her bag. "Also, Sundance catalog and credentials arrived this morning." The catalog—Sundance's directory of who, what, when, where for all movies being screened at the festival—is more than an inch thick with an artsy cover obviously printed on recycled paper. "I'll keep your credentials until we're there, but you should look at the catalog. And you need to call John."

Nic takes the rejected dresses back out to the main area of the suite. "I'll return these. Don't forget the diamonds are coming for tonight."

"Thanks, Nic."

"Just doing what you pay me quite handsomely for."

"Do I pay you?" I joke, but it falls flat. Everything with Nic falls flat these days. I don't know why she agreed to the position when I offered it, except that Bea already has an assistant in Vancouver. There are times, in the office, when Nic seems like the good old Nic. I'll bring her coffee and perch on the edge of her desk while we swap stories. But then something always happens, something that pulls Nic back into this barely contained space of anger and frustration.

"Why else do you think I do this every day?" No smile to soften the sarcasm. "Don't forget to call John. Pick up your phone and do it now."

"Yes, ma'am." I salute and obediently pick up my phone as Nic exits.

"Kat," John's familiar and perpetually worried voice greets me after a single ring.

"What's up? Nic said you needed to talk to me."

"Ian's custody battle is getting more and more play in the rags here, and it's bound to bleed over to the more independent press types at Sundance."

"The bloggers? John, you worry too much."

"It's my job to worry. Did Nic give you the catalog?"

"Yeah."

"Page 73, please?"

Lithophilia, the page title reads. "Oh, it's Ian's movie. What's the problem?" But I find the problem as I ask the question. In the cast list, next to Ian Graham—Adelaide Andres. What? The art movie *for an old friend* involved Addy? Ian never mentioned her in September except once to say they'd had drinks and worked out a visitation schedule for Eden.

"I'm concerned that this could be construed as something worthy of more than a passing glance, given Ian's past reputation with costars. Do you know if they share screen time?"

"It's nothing. Seriously. He'd made a commitment to this movie months earlier, so he did it. But that's it." I choke on my cover up. Not entirely sure why I'm lying to John, except I don't want him to know I don't have the whole story.

"Alright, Kat. Just wanting to prepare you. Don't read the stories. It'll be better if you can stay focused on your life and not feel defensive when reporters come to call. Do we need to prep you for questions?"

"Questions? Prep? John, you're scaring me."

"That's my job. If you're going to Sundance, you're going to face the press."

"Really, it's nothing. I'll be fine. The movie is fine. You're getting worried over nothing."

"The press is unpredictable, especially when it comes to Ian Graham. I'm coming to Sundance. I've already arranged it with Nic, alright?"

"Okay, okay. It'll be nice to have you there. You'll have some fun and nothing is going to happen."

"Better prepared now than sorry later, Kat. But I hope you're right."

"I'm sure it's fine, John. Nothing to worry about."

"I'll see you in a few days."

I hang up the phone and stare hard at Ian, who's been listening since I mentioned his movie. He rubs the back of his neck and breaks eye contact, his nervous tell.

"Tell me again about Belgium? Little part in a little movie, just a couple weeks, right? No big deal? But we'll get to go to some festivals, hopefully?"

Ian huffs an annoyed sigh. "Yeah, we're going to Sundance, right."

"Addy will be there, too, because Addy is in the little movie that's no big deal, right?"

Ian crosses the room and puts his hands on my arms. "I meant it, birdy. It's no big deal. It's a good little film. Perfect for festivals. That's what's important."

"But Addy—"

"Addy doesna matter, birdy."

"She better not." I poke at his chest, hard. Addy makes me crazy and he knows it.

"I promise."

He soothes me away from the cliff of my Addy-driven temper. If I see her at Sundance, though, I think I will cheerfully strangle her.

♦ ♦ ♦

Bea

Josh sauntered up beside Bea to pass her a cup of coffee that warmed her hands, though it would do nothing for her frozen innards. "I don't know how you did it. All my money was on Eddie leaving. You told me not to flinch, that you thought he'd come around, but I doubted. Yet here he is, proving we wasted our money on Matt."

Eddie stood a football field away, rechoreographing their expensive battle scene while Matt, the actual choreographer, graciously stepped aside. Eddie redid every step of footwork. The result was brilliant, fast and full of mayhem and violence, perfect for *Void.*

"Kudos to Matt for being humble enough to admit that's better."

"Kudos to you for everything else." Josh deflected Bea's dodge.

Bea blew into the cup to send up a burst of steam to warm her nose in the early dawn chill. "Eddie likes to be happy. I figured if he could find happy, he'd find ambition. Then I made sure he found happy."

"Helps that we scrunch up all his filming, too. You seem to have a gift for getting him off set just when it looks like he'll throw that punch Roger so completely deserves. And in your spare time, you've made us a top show. I wanted top ten. Never considered top five."

Bea didn't respond. Neither humble nor boastful responses seemed adequate. She rotated and jiggled the cup in search of a hot spot.

Josh dropped his cup in a cardboard, makeshift trash bin. He rubbed the back of his neck and then pushed his hands into his armpits. "You're the real deal, Bea Douglas. The real fucking deal. I could turn this thing over to you tomorrow and *Void* would be the better for it."

Bea watched the full scene play out. Their winter premiere would be fantastic, full of drama and blood and sex—though that part took a huge chunk from Eddie every time. She was trying to sell Josh on an affair storyline for Claudette to let Eddie have a break from kissing his cheating ex, but Josh felt the storyline hit a little too close to reality.

And Bea didn't have a right to an opinion anymore. Monkey & Me was belly-up. This was likely her last day. She'd gotten here early to break the news to Eddie, but he'd been too caught up in choreography to take a break.

"Despite your praise, Josh, I'm broke. I didn't expect Kat to abandon Monkey & Me. Big misstep. She took all the money and ran. So, stop the pretty words and tell me if you're willing to buy my shares in *Void* or not."

"Maybe. Maybe not. Come to the office. Let's see what we can work out."

The welcome blast of heat sapped her energy. She unwrapped her scarf and placed her gray coat on the hook while the exhaustion of the last four hard months hit her. If only she'd been able to stretch the money two more months. But expenses for *21 Things* had piled up and everyone had heard Kat left Monkey & Me to start a company with Ian Graham. If Bea even got anyone to take a phone call, she was politely told that *21 Things* was now dead and they were holding onto revenue to invest in the next big thing.

Kat. She was the next big thing. Always.

Despite all Bea's clever machinations, Kat had not only ghosted Bea, but she'd convinced an entire industry to do the same.

Josh gestured for her to sit in the plastic chairs around his makeshift office in a company trailer. "You're sure you need a whole buyout to stay afloat?"

"All of it. I can't let Monkey & Me sink or I lose my name on *21 Things*. We're paid up on all our commitments to *Void* and production costs for *21 Things*, but I have nothing left for marketing and launch. I could let *21 Things* float this year in a bad time slot with no PR, but it's too good for that. You can keep going here without me, but, if I fold, *21 Things* ends with me."

"What happens to you once I buy you out?"

"You could use another nurse. I had to stitch up Ezra again the other day. Eddie threatened to make him film with a dummy blade if he can't control a real one."

"You spending your life patching up actors would be a damnable loss to the industry. You're the real fucking deal. I'm so disappointed in Kat. Not saying I wouldn't lick her ass if she asked me to, but I'm still disappointed."

Josh grabbed a paper from his desk drawer and then walked around to the front of his desk. He perched on the edge. "Okay. Then I buy you out, but first—you got any change on you? A dollar? Anything?"

"What do you need money for? I need to save my pennies. I haven't paid myself since October. I'm broke on all sides."

"Don't argue. I'm the Grand EP. Plop some change on my damn desk."

Bea dug thirty-five cents out of her purse. Josh counted the coins and then scribbled on the paper before handing it to Bea.

"Alright, so Faux Monster buys *Void* at original investment plus twenty percent, as agreed. But Monkey & Me repurchases a thirty-five cent interest in the production at original royalty payout. That sound fair?"

"That sounds impossible. And really stupid."

Josh pointed his pen at Bea's face. "Don't bicker with the dude saving your bacon, little lassie."

"I also hate to dither," Bea drawled. "But the check is short by a dollar."

"Oh, that's the poetic part." Josh pulled out a framed photo of a silver dollar. "Here's your last dollar. Framed. Encased in museum glass. Will take effort to get this out. And you don't. Because as long as you have this dollar, Monkey & Me is never bankrupt."

"Is that legal?"

"Probably not, but it's hopeful. And sometimes hope makes for good business. I stayed afloat on my last dollar for a good while before the tides turned. You can, too."

Bea ran her hand over the glass. The symbol did ignite a small light. It burned low, almost smothered in despair, but the coals were warm.

"Never let the fuckers win, Bea. Never let them win. I'll see you at two for editing. Paycheck or not, I expect good work."

"You'll get it. Always."

Bea pushed out the door, puzzled and pleased and a little dazed. Eddie snagged her elbow after she'd passed him. He handed her a large white cup. The sweet smell of chocolate woke her salivary glands when she blew into the small hole.

"Bless your beautiful hide," she sighed as she sipped warm, rich chocolate with touches of vanilla, nutmeg, and cinnamon. And something else that made it creamier and richer than ever. "It's perfect today. What did you add?"

"My secret. I'll never tell." He fell into step beside her, his hands wrapped around a soy chai latte per the scribbles on the cup. "I've noticed my favorite producer has a few empty calendar dates. Is it finally time you proved to me that you can snowboard?"

"I don't know. Do you own any of those weird high-waisted pants that make every European skier look like a villain from a Sean Connery Bond film?"

"I bring sexy back in those pants. You'll be distracted and fall flat on your back. No, wait, that's simply snowboarding's grand feat—the fine art of falling forward or backward."

"Oh, you are so toasted. Mock my skills and eat my powder, ski bum."

"I thought perhaps we could avail ourselves of a quiet fireplace and—"

Bea's phone buzzed with a ringtone she'd not heard in many, many months. She held up a finger as Eddie said something about deserving a reward.

"Hi, John. What's happening?"

"Bea. I'm so glad you answered. There's a crisis brewing and, well, I need to neutralize a bit of gossip. No one does that better than you."

"Not for Kat. If that's what this is about—"

"It is. But Nic and I are hoping you'd do the favor for us, regardless of Kat."

Bea tapped the phone to her head. Eddie shook his head no. She'd much rather spend the weekend laughing at Eddie in his stupid-looking snow gear, but she did owe John a favor or two.

"Okay. Where am I heading?"

"Park City, Utah. On me. Maybe you can see family. I'll give you details when you arrive."

Sundance? In time for her birthday. Bea could probably convince Gabe or Micah to make the drive. That might take the edge off whatever John needed her to do.

Eddie's eyebrows were raised when she looked back. "You owe them nothing, Beatrice."

"I know. But she's still attached to my company. It must be big for John to call, and I can't let Kat tank me right now. Can I have a raincheck on that ski trip and six-month celebration? Do you mind waiting?" Bea leaned up to kiss his cheek.

Eddie hugged her with one arm and then dropped his own kiss on her cheek. "Yes, I'll wait. As long as I need to wait, I'll wait."

Bea rushed off, dialing Nic as she ran. "Tell me you've got me booked. Flight and hotel and a big tab because I can't pay for a vending machine sandwich right now."

"Would I let you down? It's all done. Don't make me do a minute of this alone." Bea flagged down a cab and began to plan a film festival wardrobe.

CHAPTER 21

Ich hab' im Traum geweinet,
mir träumt' du verließest mich.
Ich wachte auf, und ich weinte
noch lange bitterlich.

I have in my dreams wept,
I dreamed you forsook me.
I woke up and I wept
for a long time and bitterly.

—*Robert Schumann, Dichterliebe*

Kat

The dance floor called my name, but after three songs, I've lost Ian in the melee of one of Sundance's never-ending series of parties. This is a regular people's party, so it's packed with gawkers and hobby artists, but it's sponsored by one of Ian's long-time friends so we're here, too, to let people see Ian and to whip up positive press in preparation for tomorrow's premiere.

Swanky pop-up club atmosphere is set to a deliberate fever to contrast the freezing temperatures outside. I wind my way through the crowd to get to the bar for a glass of sponsored wine and then find Ian. More than every other face is famous or familiar by industry reputation.

My stomach clenches with nerves as a too-familiar dark head bobs into sight. Philip.

My eyes find Ian. He's halfway across the room in conversation with Cusack, surrounded by their respective entourages—a half-nameless gaggle of business types, helper monkeys, and the stars they orbit. And Philip blocks me from it all.

Philip. I don't want to see Philip or even think about Philip or remember he ever existed. The whole point of ghosting is to never ever see them again, so your insides don't seize up with remorse or, worse, fond memories.

There are enough people that I snake in between taller bodies to wind my way past my past. But, as I think I'm free, someone knocks me from behind and I almost spill wine onto Philip's back. I save his shirt by putting my hand out to stop me from tumbling forward. My hand falls on a favorite soft spot just below his shoulder blade and I recoil as if burned.

"Sorry, sorry." People press in all around the bar, collapsing me into the spot the universe insists I stay to face my sins. Philip turns, two glasses and a bottle of beer balanced in his hands.

"Not to worry. It's packed in . . ." his voice trails off as he sees who hit him. "Kat." A statement of fact, but I'm caught.

Yeah, so this isn't awkward at all.

"Philip. Hi. What brings you to Sun—" I stop as I remember the answer to my banal small-talk question. Philip loves Sundance, comes every year.

"The usual. Love films. Love Sundance. No change here." He grins, but looks past me.

"Oh, good. Good to see you."

"Yeah. Good to see you, too, Kat."

Retreat, retreat alarm bells ring in my head so loud I can't hear the eighties remixes from the dance floor anymore, but my damn twisty, remorseful insides replay the last time I saw Philip and how I ran, ran, ran without a word good-bye.

"I'm sorry," I blurt out.

Philip looks at me, briefly, and then back the direction he was headed. So much plays across his face, the good guy wants both to hear me and to escape.

My tongue trips over every possible extension of my apology. I did it all wrong? I behaved badly, but I'm not very sorry for what my life is now? I don't know what to say, so I give up. I'm crap at apologies.

"I won't keep you from—whoever you're with."

"Thanks. Um, it's okay, Kat. Do you need that? I'm okay. We can leave this be with that, right?" He glances back the same direction again. His mouth screws up and he shrugs at someone unseen.

"It was most definitely me, not you, so, um, yeah. I'm glad you're okay."

"I am. Now. Finally. Anyway, good to be seen, Kat."

Philip moves in the direction of his many glances. The crowd parts, and I don't quite comprehend what I see. Bea and Nicola, at a table, clearly looking at Philip, expecting him but not me. Bea's eyes grow wide, and then she and Nicola look away, as if on cue. But Bea looks back, breaks. She gives me a wry wave with no happy smile.

Philip looks at me as natural kindness overwhelms his need for escape. "Yeah—we met up for drinks." He lies. He's a terrible liar, but he lies to me anyway. Because Bea who couldn't come to the Globes did not suddenly decide to gallivant to a freaking film festival for drinks.

"I'll join you," I invite myself.

"Hey. I can tell them you said hi. I'm sure he doesn't want you gone long." There's a lot of emphasis on the *he.*

"I want to say hi." I shrug him off.

I can't see Philip but I know he, Nic, and Bea have a facial expression conversation over my head. The women's faces contort like the terminator at the end of T2. That makes me Linda Hamilton, and that's okay.

"Hey!" I smile brightly when I reach the table. "What's up? Great party. This DJ is amazing."

"Definitely, boss. You need a seat?" Nic is too formal. Of course, Nic and Bea are still friends. Of course, Nic has been in communication with Bea all these months. Bea must hate me; that's why Nic hates me.

"No, I'm fine."

Bea forces a smile at me, but her eyes look past my shoulder. "Hey, Kat. Great look. Who is that?"

My eyes look down at the paisley tank and black velvet dress I'm wearing. I loved the burnt orange crocheted fringe. But who designed it? My stylist came in with a bright young thing and a huge collection of Euromodern looks. I like the brocades and the strong, dark colors. Of course, I lost all the sweaters and slacks I liked most in lieu of the half-exposed items completely at odds with a Utah winter. A name pops in my head, though. Maybe designer. Maybe brand. I never know the difference. "Um. Etro. I think."

"Good choice. The fringe is incredible."

"I can't take any credit. I'm still hopeless, someone else picked it out."

"The joys of an endless bank account, right?" Little barbs shoot out of everyone's eyes.

"So, Ian's film is tomorrow, right?" Philip steps in to hand off the drinks. Nic smiles and winks at him, then takes a huge gulp of wine. Philip tips up his bottle, and I swear Bea looks jealous. They all prefer alcohol to me.

The monster wants to roar but hides under my regrets instead. I've spent months studying Eden's every facial expression, learning nuance I didn't realize existed. Those skills have transferred here. There's real hurt on every face hiding behind the disinterest and rejection. They're not being mean or selfish or sucking on sour grapes. They're being honest. Whatever balloon has kept me above all this for months springs a leak. The longer I stand here, the more I sink.

"Yeah. Premiere is tomorrow at the Egyptian on Main. You should all come." No, please don't come. Don't come watch me bask in the life I won by hurting you.

"What luck. We'll all be there." That's funny to them all somehow. An inside joke.

"You do look great, Kat," Philip says. That seems to be all they can think to say.

The awkward grows exponentially, but I can't leave. If I'm crap at apologies, I'm worse at fixing. Bea fixes. And if I could maybe get her to look at me and see . . . I don't know what. Everything got me where I wanted to be. Maybe only ego insists I also need to be at this table, too. But now that Bea is here, I can't ignore the empty space in my life. "I missed you at the Globes, Bea. I'm surprised to see you away from Vancouver."

A polite smile replaces Bea's wry one. Maybe that's progress. "It's my birthday. Thought I deserved a break."

Oh, hell. Oh, fuck. I deleted the reminder after our fight. I've stood here like a dumbass and ruined her party for my own selfish reasons. "Of course. Happy birthday! Here's to still being in our twenties." I've reached pinnacle awkward. Misery grips at me and tears my dignity away.

"Just barely. Hanging on with my teeth."

An Adele sort of wistfulness punches me in the gut. We were supposed to reach thirty and beyond together, but I ruined it.

My only recourse is to leave before I cry. "Well, congratulations. Maybe I'll see you around. The joy of a film festival—so many places, events."

"Sure. Because we run in the same circles." Bea shoots, she scores. And I find the apology. The on-my-knees, please-God apology I've never uttered.

But a rustle among the group blocks my moment. Everyone gets nervous and shifts about. Then Ian's hand wraps my waist.

"Kat." He kisses my cheek. "I wondered what was keeping you."

Then he lifts an eyebrow at the entire group.

Bea's polite smile amplifies. More polite. More fake.

"I was on my way to finally drag you to the dance floor." I try to soften Ian's mood—that eyebrow is not good—but he ignores my teasing.

"Introduce me, birdy."

"Well, you know Bea and Nicola, obviously. This is Philip. He was the casting director on *K-Town*." Ian's fingers dig into my side and I'm sure he remembers Philip's name very well.

Philip reaches out a hand. "Hey, Ian. Your work is legendary. I've been a fan."

Philip is taller than Ian by at least an inch and a few inches broader in the shoulder. I've never put them side by side in my head, not like this. Ian is my guy, but Philip may be more objectively handsome.

Ian doesn't seem to appreciate the comparison. His hand tightens on my waist. "Unless you're casting something, can't imagine this needs much more of your time, eh? We've people waiting."

Bea's attempts at politeness disappear. That quirk of disgust lifts the right side of her upper lip. Bea's disgust encompasses me now, too. I earned it. I ghosted her. I'm done lying to myself about this. All her painful words that last day were true.

The two ghosts I created stare into blank space.

The people I turned to nothing.

It's ghastly to be haunted by the living.

I did everything wrong, or the wrong way, and I want to say that, but Ian tugs me away.

And for the first time, I notice the look of distaste he casts at Bea, which makes my self-righteous balloon whine out air until it's a wasted, flat piece of plastic on the ground.

Bea doesn't dislike or disapprove easily. I can't pinpoint another person in all our years who provoked a negative reaction from her.

An idea rocks my world, a thought I've never explored. What if Ian started this?

Yes, Bea disliked the money and the fame-pandering, but she's dealt with Siena without an all-out feud. Only here has she unleashed claws and bared her teeth.

Only against a man who looks at her with contempt and who guides me up to the dais and proposes a game of *top and bottom of the resumé,* a guessing game about the fake career highlights of people around us. It's cruel more than anything, meant to elevate the group and belittle the rest. It's not the first time Bea or Philip's name has made the rounds, but it's the first time I've hated myself for being part of the in crowd.

♦ ♦ ♦

Bea

Nicola leaned across the table, her chest attracting attention. She was drunk enough to have forgotten about any semblance of grace or modesty. Philip didn't seem to mind, and Nicola didn't mind him not minding.

"So. Seriously, I have a theory. Because *that* woman is not Kat. No way. Can't be. She doesn't even look like Kat. So, I think Kat actually *did* go missing after the *Void* premiere. And that is one of those Japanese sex robots I saw on cable."

Philip groaned. He clinked his beer bottle with Nicola's wine glass. "Awful. But I grant you the win. Your theory is definitely worse than our reality."

Nic took a sip, then waved a finger in front of Bea. "Okay, okay. We survived and processed the Kat run-in for more than an hour. Now back to the topic she so rudely interrupted. 1,523 texts! Bea Douglas, why have you received 1,523 texts from sex bomb Edward Wolverton in a month."

Bea ran a finger around the top of her Diet Coke glass. "Not the topic. The topic was, why is my ex-assistant snooping on my phone when I go to the bathroom."

"No!" Philip jumped into the game. "The question is . . . why do you have *that* photo on your phone? That's the Fairmont Empress Hotel in Victoria. I've also spent a romantic weekend there, so don't try to lie to me, Bea."

"*Dishabille* photos. 1,523 texts and counting, since your phone beeps nonstop. I turned my head for a minute and you became a wanton woman."

"First—*dishabille* is Eddie's natural state. Harder to get a photo of him fully clothed than not. Second—we're friends who enjoy travelling together. Whole story."

"You're lying, and I need more wine. Be right back."

Bea bumped Philips knee as soon as Nic's perfect body disappeared in the crowd. "While she's gone, tell me about this romantic weekend in Victoria."

"I'll tell you mine if you tell me yours."

"Deal."

"I'm getting played, aren't I? I'm going to tell and you're going to ditch."

"I'm totally going to ditch and then claim I didn't. That's your third beer, and you get tipsy on wine. You're almost full-on drunk."

Philip laughed and launched his story. He'd just gotten to the sexy part when Nic pushed back in. "Oh, you won't believe this, Bea. Ian was at the bar. I almost vomited on him. Wish I had, actually."

"Wanting to vomit on Ian is no surprise."

"No. Not that he was there, what he was doing while there. Look for yourself."

Bea's head whipped toward the bar. Her lip curled up. Ian wasn't more than a few feet from them. "What in the . . ." Bea whispered.

Ian sat at the bar talking to a woman. Ian's hand brushed the girl's waist, then wound around her rump.

Unbelievable. That man was unbelievable. Ian whispered to this woman and she bit her lip in excitement. Gah, the girl couldn't be more than twenty.

Kat still sat on the dais, her head on Theo's shoulder. Unaware. Or maybe not. Maybe Kat knew. Ian wasn't hiding his flirtation, and Kat wasn't objecting to it. Bea sighed, loud and harsh. Philip's eyes had closed against old pain and Nic rubbed his arm. Once upon a time, Kat believed in romance and true love and fidelity. Now she was in an open relationship. The sex robot theory garnered evidence enough to become a hypothesis.

Ian looked up from the girl's neck. His eyes locked with Bea's in mutual distaste. Her fingers twitched and tightened around the glass in her hand. Gah, she hated him. Her bicep seized as his cocky grin led to a raised eyebrow. A challenge. And Bea had never backed down from a challenge.

She took aim and launched the glass across the short divide. The glass connected with force, sure as any baseball or football she'd thrown in her life.

A satisfying red line opened along a premature wrinkle in his forehead. Streaks dripped down into his storm-colored eyes.

Then reality crashed in on Bea. "Ah, crap. Now I have to fix him," she sighed.

Drunk Philip gaped at Ian with a wide-open mouth. Then he started to laugh. "You didn't just do that. You did. You assaulted Ian Graham."

Nic pawed at him. "This isn't funny. If anyone saw, if there's a picture—" But Nic couldn't stop laughing.

"If there's a picture, I've ruined everything. Nic's right. This actually isn't funny."

Bea dumped ice into a napkin and crossed to Ian. She pressed the napkin to his head without mercy. "You're a lousy excuse of a human being, if you wanted an explanation. A stupid, drunken, serial cheater," Bea muttered to Ian as she applied pressure to the wound.

"You threw a mug at my head. I should have you arrested. You assaulted me."

Nic arrived. "No one saw a thing, but I'd be happy to take a photo, get the word out, in case someone knows your assailant." She waved her cell phone.

"We came right over to help the moment we saw the damage." Philip brought a fresh napkin and more ice. "Odd crowd here in Sundance. Sometimes, it gets nuts."

"And the nuts get thrown out," Ian growled as he snapped at a nearby security guard.

"Is there a problem, Mr. Graham?"

"Yes. Get them out."

The group walked solemnly for about three feet before Philip couldn't resist a chuckle. Nic joined in. Bea sniffled but also found a laugh. They laughed through the entire obligatory speech by the security guard about how unwelcome they'd all be forevermore.

"I've been thrown out," Philip said in awe between chuckles. "I've never been thrown out of anywhere."

Nic wrapped her arms around him, drunk and laughing. "Bea, you remain undeniably, uncontrollably, indescribably—"

Philip tightened his arms around Nicola. "Bea is Bea. No other word describes her."

Nic pulled Bea into their embrace "Defender of truth and right, wielding the Diet Coke of Doom."

They walked down the street, arm in arm, interrupted by giggles, the occasional stumble, and Nic's unfortunate reaction to too much booze and bar food.

But as Nic emptied her stomach, Bea remained the sober one. She wasn't to blame. Ian was. Destruction personified. He barreled through life with some modern theory about consenting adults, never held accountable for the cheating and discarding and demeaning. The women couldn't ask for more. They had to be whatever he demanded.

She wanted him held accountable. She wanted every misdeed to come to light. She wanted Matthias to nail Ian's cheating ass to the wall.

CHAPTER 22

Die alten, bösen Lieder,
die Träume bös' und arg,
die laßt uns jetzt begraben,
holt einen großen Sarg.

The old, angry songs,
the dreams angry and nasty,
let us now bury them,
fetch a great coffin.

—Robert Schumann, Dichterliebe

Kat

I'm not looking forward to today. I want to hide in my cave and avoid my demons, so Ian's excitement for the premiere of *Lithophilia* chafes.

For one thing, I'm still hung over. I sobered up enough to cry over my actions at the party and then I drank more to forget that I'd let Ian make fools of Philip and Bea and that Addy was en route to ruin my life.

The sick feeling in my stomach may be more than alcohol withdrawal and regret. The whole movie makes me sick. He made a movie with Addy, Eden's wretched mother against whom we filed for full custody two weeks ago. My head spins with soap-opera-worthy scenarios of custody battle revenge and the bleached-blond villainess winning the day.

I reach for the wine bottle. Ten in the morning in Utah is five o'clock London, right?

All my Addy fears, rational or not, loom larger with every passing hour. John shares my worries—he asks me every day when Addy is meant to arrive, then retreats at my lack of knowledge with creases in his face set deep.

Addy has yet to show her face in exactly the setting she would normally be showing her face too much—promoting her role in a movie with Ian Graham at a prestigious film festival. And Ian dodges every question about the movie.

Ian shouts at me to get ready. The bottle joins me in the shower.

My stylist is there when I get out, and soon I'm glammed up good and proper for the main event. I hate my outfit. It's a full-length pantsuit with that no-bra plunge that's my *signature style*. I hate my signature style. I'm tired of being managed, dressed up, and paraded about.

But here I am on a red carpet, freezing my tits off and sure the sheer top shows more than how cold I am. Yet I smile and kiss and talk about how delighted I am.

Gods. It's such a show. I curse Utah's liquor laws that have cut me off from my panacea.

We settle into our seats at the front of the small theater on Main Street housing the premiere of Ian's film. Maybe Addy is too drunk to show up. She's hammered in Monaco and forgot all about the thing. That'd be a nice surprise.

A small commotion occurs near the VIP side entrance—Addy. She enters with her usual ridiculous preening, kissing cheeks and laughing too loud. She pauses to air-kiss the director a dozen times and waves at imaginary fans. Her eyes find me as she slithers along, and she smiles. My stomach churns at the glimpse of smug triumph. Her happiness feels like my undoing.

The lights dim and the director gives a boring spiel. Ian stands to raucous applause. So, I applaud, raucously, and smile proudly. I'm the best Hollywood girlfriend ever.

I'm not sure what to expect, or what I might have expected if I'd read anything but a film festival catalog description, but as the impressionistic plot and stark visuals progress I realize *why* Ian hasn't offered any expectations. The mild-mannered accountant's obsessions are a running parallel fantasy world, featuring none other than Ian and Addy in multiple, inappropriate sexual encounters. I can taste acid in my mouth as the depravity escalates. Ian next-to-me bleeds into Ian on-screen, looking at on-screen Addy with a hunger that is supposed to be mine alone. Ian's harem crowds into my mind to insist that look belongs to each one alone. We all believe that we're the only one he truly loves.

The audience reacts to every twist and turn, every surprising sexual moment and the correlating real-world problem-solving the accountant finds in his fantasies. It's not bad art, actually. If it were any other actor, I might be impressed by the existential commentary on the American obsession with sex. But I cannot believe he didn't warn me, didn't think I needed to know what he'd been doing in September, or what I would be faced with here.

The credits roll to more raucous applause, and a round of congratulatory handshakes move down the row of actors and filmmakers. The director takes the stage for the Q&A and I want to be anywhere but here.

Especially when weird things start happening. Buzzing surrounds me, and heads drop to stare at phones. Then eyes seek me out, wide and disbelieving. There's a murmur in the crowd, loud enough that the director takes notice. Reporters stand up, hands raised, to vie for attention. Every publicist in the room, including John, has gone to work tapping out messages and engaging whispered conversations.

Now no one looks at me. If they see me looking, they look away. I don't know what's going on. I'm panicked that I don't know what's going on.

Someone hisses my name from the side aisle. A bright, redheaded someone in killer heeled boots and a jeans-and-sweater ensemble emphasizing curves worthy of being painted on the side of a bomber.

Bea hisses again. "Kat, you need to come. Right now. Please. Before the questions start."

Bea reaches out her hand to offer escape, and I grab onto her. That's all that matters. I grab onto Bea.

The weirdness from the last day on *21 Things* is gone. She's my Bea again, and I hold her hand like it's the only thing that matters in the world.

Bea leads me away, out another side entrance into an empty hallway.

She turns toward me and rubs my arms, a familiar soothing motion. "Whatever you're about to unleash. Have your reaction right here where no one sees."

The door to the theater transforms into a movie screen where Ian and Addy—Addy, fucking Addy. Addy fucking Ian. My eyes go blind with tears.

My body can't decide between screaming and vomiting. And my head—over and over, Ian with Addy, every explicit lust-filled moment forever larger than life in my head. "I can't—I can't do this."

The bathroom beckons me to give in to weak knees and a weaker stomach. I can't remember the last time I vomited over pure emotion.

Bea kneels beside me. She holds my hair back as she always does when I stumble in, sick with drink or nerves or stupidity. She purrs and hums and does every comforting thing while I rock on my heels and cry between gags.

Then she helps me to my feet, lets me lay my head against hers as I used to do. She opens the door and walks to the sink to turn on the water. I slowly rinse my mouth out, and wipe at my face with harsh recycled paper towels until Bea hands me a makeup cloth.

"Shit. I forgot my purse. I had mints."

Bea digs in the large, white and green purse that's her go-to carryall. "I've got toothpaste, anything you need. I've even got some shampoo for that spot in your hair."

"In your Mary Poppins purse," I add with a smile. Everything is so right despite being so wrong. I do my best to fix the raccoon-effect mascara while Bea washes out my hair.

"Did you know what this was? The movie?" Bea asks.

I shake my head, afraid additional speech will bring me back to tears.

"Oh, honey. I'm so sorry. But actors really do—disconnect—from the roles, you know. He probably didn't think it would hurt you at all. You know Ian and art. You were always telling me how he chased art at any expense, how amazing that was to you. Critics will rave and this nightmare will pass. They always do, you know."

Bea wants to help, but every word tears me apart worse. Bea defending Ian. For me. Just to make me feel better. It's more kindness than I deserve from the person I least deserve it from.

Tears slip out the sides, carrying fresh mascara in lines toward my ears. Bea dabs them with a paper towel. "You're gonna need waterproof mascara today, hon. I have that, too. Sit up. We'll get your face back on, as my gran used to say."

I know that. I know the things gran used to say. I heard some of them from gran before she died. Bea's whole family seems present. Elle and Richard wrap arms around me as they did the week my dad died. Bea's brothers descend, all stupid and flirty, full of fun and humor.

And Bea.

Quiet, stoic, funny, always-there Bea.

The family I never asked for and never appreciated. More tears slide down my cheeks.

"You've got to stop this. The bag may have belonged to Mary Poppins, but this canister of mascara doesn't. It will run out."

Bea's phone beeps while she applies another coat. My eyes look amazing. She's done a cat-eye blend with purple shadow that makes my blue eyes even bluer.

The phone cradles between shoulder and ear as she finishes my makeup. "Okay. Yeah. I'll send her out the back way."

When I stand, Bea fusses with my barely-there outfit. Then from the Mary Poppins bag, she withdraws the same flimsy white shirt she wore the last day of *21 Things*.

"Here. Let's cover you up a little. It's cold outside."

The sleeves roll up halfway, the shirt buttons up to my clavicle, and a belt appears to pull it all together. Bea reaches up to restyle my hair into something simple, something timeless.

I look like me again.

For the first time in so long, I look like me.

"Okay, gorgeous. Walk out with your head high, just in case anyone sees. And no matter what happens over the next twenty-four hours, you remember that you are Katrine frikkin' Porter. No one can take that from you. You don't owe the world a thing because you're going to own the world one day. Okay? You ready? Don't forget what I said."

"Okay." I shiver against an imagined chill.

Bea loads me into the car, but doesn't follow. I need her to follow. I want to do that movie thing where I put my hand against the back glass and Bea runs after me while I scream for the car to stop.

But I don't. I only look back. Just once.

I can't imagine what the last ten minutes cost Bea. This was why she was here, to shelter me against Ian with no expectation of anything. I owe her the respect of staying on script. John and Nic and the spin brigade will tell me what to do next and I'm glad for that. Because I have no idea. All I want is T2 and ice cream and Bea to make everything better by mocking my movie and dancing hip-hop to the soundtrack.

CHAPTER 23

"There is love in me the likes of which you've never seen.
There is rage in me the likes of which should never escape.
If I am not satisfied in the one, I will indulge the other."

—Mary Shelley, Frankenstein

Kat

The car rolls to a stop at the kitchen entrance to my hotel. Even here, reporters gather to take advantage of America's lack of privacy restrictions on paparazzi. I'm to expect to be photographed and spied on every minute I'm in America.

"And for heaven's sake, Kat, smile," John reminds me again before the car door opens.

He holds my purse next to him, my phone buzzing inside. He won't let me have it, instead he issues polite orders. Smile, Kat. Hold your head up high. Keep up appearances, Kat. He looks too grim, even nauseated.

"I got it." I flash my biggest smile as I traverse the few feet of sidewalk from the car to the hotel—there are cameras to catch it all. The elevator doors close and I slouch into the wall. John remains silent and straight and it's beginning to unnerve me, even more than a buzzing theater and a hundred averted glances. There's more than the movie, something worse. But what could be worse than Ian fucking Addy while he was with me?

I fumble with the key card so long John takes it from me and unlocks the door to the empty suite. He places my purse on the red velvet settee while I pour myself another glass of wine at the mahogany bar.

"Please, John. What is it?" I ask, my voice strangely even, not as hysterical as I feel.

"Sit down," John gestures at the sofa and I robotically obey as he opens his portfolio, and then activates his tablet. He doesn't sit down, just hands me the tablet, open to the *Daily Mail* app.

Full Frontal! Ian and New Girlfriend Caught Having A Go with His Underage Daughter Only A Few Feet Away! the headline screams.

The picture below seems innocuous enough. Madagascar, Eden poolside. But half the photo has been blurred out. *Not Safe For Work* is hyperlinked over top. I click the link and then—I almost drop the tablet as if it had bitten me.

I didn't realize what a fine line separated mine and Ian's space from Eden's private patio. In the photo, Eden stands not three feet away from me riding Ian like the bull in a cheap cowboy bar. She has her noise-cancelling headphones on and can't see us over the fence, but I can't guarantee she didn't hear any of our full-daylight, voyeuristic, mind-blowing outdoor sex.

The proof of my terrible failure as a mother sits in front of me in full color. But there's more than Madagascar. The full slideshow has photos and Ian and I flirting on *21 Things* and one of Eden visiting the set—it looks like I befriended Eden to get to Ian. Photos of me shopping with Eden—in one, I hold up the skimpiest bikini you could imagine. I was talking her out of it, but without audio, it looks like I want a little girl to wear that thing.

Every muscle in my body quivers and longs for retreat, but I have to see it all. There are more pictures. Too many pictures. Most from the same encounter, but a few from other moments Ian and I thought we were alone and weren't. All behind NSFW links, each picture with its own nasty caption. *Ian Graham's Daughter Learns the Facts of Life . . . The Next Mrs. Graham Proves She's Not Your Average Housewife.*

A complete and depraved relationship history. Including LA, outside the theater of the short film showcase. And then in Scotland.

A midline title announces *Next . . . Ian's other holiday in Scotland NOT TWO WEEKS EARLIER*

Matching shots of Ian and Addy in Scotland with Eden. No crazy sex pictures of Addy. She's the happy mum, sober and smiling while Ian clutches one hand and Eden clings to the other.

I'm the whore in this story.

The text of the story follows. A chilling expose on me and what I've done to Eden, to my daughter. And it's why Addy beamed a winner's smile at the premiere. Not because she fucked my man, but because she fucked us over. Both of us.

Addy is the named source for the story. She's Eden's mother, so she approved the photos. Each and every one: Eden, her eyes bloodshot and wild as she argues with the PI, and Eden in her black hoodie outside her mom's house.

The words pass in front of me. My breath becomes more rapid and shallow at every sentence. My eyes scan the text again and again in search of the obvious lie that negates all the half-truths. The can't-be-trues. But I find nothing.

I'm sobbing by the second read-through. The highlights become my epitaph.

Graham and Andres reconciled in February and hid in Scotland for some alone time . . .

My heart hurts, squeezed from somewhere deep. Ian dismissed Addy's hateful words, and I never pressed for more explanation despite Tess's cryptic statements.

Porter's appearance was a disaster for young Eden, whose life came crashing down when her father left her mother AGAIN . . . she was found a drunk in a pub, cozying up to a powdered high and a twenty-six-year-old man named Jackson.

My stomach lurches. I'm almost as sick as I was at the premiere. She's only twelve. I've never asked these sorts of questions. Not about drugs. Or guys named Jackson. She's not ready, no one is ready for what might have happened to her.

And it's my fault. All my fault. Because I couldn't be happy for Bea and break up with Philip like an adult. No, I ran off and let the collateral damage pile up.

. . . But who could resist yet another saucy round with the amiable and ever-willing producer of 21 Things, *Katrine Porter. A Queen homewrecker beside her King (at least for now).*

Amiable and ever-willing. Yep, that's me. Truth, when it comes to Ian. An amiable, willing accomplice in the destruction of Eden's family and my own friendships.

"Who did this?" I demand. "How did they get these?"

John shakes his head, slow and sad. I scroll back up and see the byline: Matthias Perrini. Bea's pap friend. Betrayal threatens to bat away the hopeful loveliness of seeing Bea as a friend again. I thought she was here for me, but maybe guilt drove her back. Not about us at all.

Bea's friend has cost me everything.

No, I won't do this. Not again. This article is all me. I did this. Not Bea. Not Matthias. I, Kat Porter, carpet-bombed my own life.

Desolation, that's all I have left. A mirage in the desert where I thought I'd found paradise.

"The custody case is dead. We've lost Eden."

John sits beside me and puts his arm along the back of the couch. "I'm afraid so."

The sobs overtake me then. Eden. I've lost her, ruined her. John rubs my back and promises it'll be better one day, the father figure he's been since I moved to London. "It will take time to recover your reputation, I won't sugarcoat it, but we will get there, Kat. No doubts."

The door opens and bangs off the wall to announce Ian's entrance to the suite.

"Kat," Ian yells and I flinch. John's arm tightens protectively around my shoulder.

"Where the bloody hell did you disappear to?" His phone waves in his hand—can't be anything but the article—and he raises his arms to emphasize the question. Every line in his body reaches up in anger, not relief. He's not relieved to find me.

"My friends had the decency to get me out of that theater, unlike you, who dragged me there to witness that damn movie." I confront him. "You selfish ass. You're not going to say a word of apology about it, are you?"

"Naught to apologize for. It's a movie. A good one, at that. Got lots of nice praise. And we've got bigger problems than your battles with Addy." Ian waves his phone again.

"You think? We've lost Eden because you can't wait three hours for sex. Don't think I don't remember that day. I asked you to wait, but no. Ian Graham doesn't wait for anything. I'm supposed to put up with anything, give you everything without even getting a warning about something like that disgusting movie. No wonder you never told me what you were really doing in September."

His eyebrows snap together. "You could've come. I asked you to come, remember."

"I had a TV show to wrap up. I have a career, too, Ian. Not that anyone will remember that about me now, not after this story. Not after the fool you made of me today. I've become nothing but Ian Graham's accessory of the moment."

"Don't start this, birdy. The movie wasn't personal."

"How is making a movie—that movie—with your ex-wife not personal? While you were in the middle of a custody battle?"

Ian turns purple with anger, all hot, dangerous temper like I've never seen except on a screen. "We worked out a lot over drinks on that set. I don't owe you an explanation. My art, Kat. My life."

"So, you did fuck her."

Ian turns on me. He's got that smooth look, the one I saw most often when he tried to get under Bea's skin on set. "Nah, didn't fuck Addy. But I had a go with a lassie in wardrobe. I find my sex scenes go better when I've had a bit of it and you weren't on hand. All for the art, right? As a reminder, I did ask you to come along with me." Ian sits down in the large desk chair, his hands behind his neck, issuing a challenge. There's not a bit of apology in his attitude.

Something clarion reaches through the fog of my anger. "I'm not doing this. Sex scandals in the *Daily Mail,* mocking my friends, sitting at home in London while you get your rocks off with some poor girl in wardrobe." I shake my head as I stand my ground.

Ian laughs at me. He laughs. "What's this now? Self-righteous Kat? You weren't in those photos? You didn't laugh, too? You fucked me in a hotel room how many hours after running away from your boyfriend? I'm no more devil than you. Best accept it."

"For love. I went with you for love, but do I get any loyalty in return?"

"Loyalty?" Ian laughs again. "From the woman who dropped her best friend at my first suggestion? We don't do loyalty. We do what we want."

My arms wrap my middle as I turn away from Ian, from John. "I'm so glad my dad is dead, so he doesn't have to see what I've become."

"Enough, Kat. You can take the tragic heroine routine out of here. I've got a girl to save. You want a family? Or you want a fairy tale?"

"A fairy tale? Is that what you've given me? You've turned me into the wicked stepmother, you lousy, lying, cheating, bed-hopping, serial-divorcing bastard." My eyes land on one of the big blue vases decorating the suite. The color of Ian's eyes, I'd thought, when we checked in. Gods, I'm so stupid. But I'm strong, too. Linda fucking Hamilton. I pick it up and throw it at the wall with all the ferocity necessary to break my own heart.

The crash is loud, satisfying, but my anger deflates in the suspended stillness. My shattered hopes lie scattered on the carpet along with a hundred pieces of porcelain.

"Kat," John says from behind me and I jump. I forgot he was here. I can't believe I let him witness that. Any of this. He must be so disappointed. I picture Marian and my dad having tea together, their heads hung in shame.

"I'm sorry," I whisper. I want to slide to the floor, defeated, but I have to get out of here first. I whip to the bedroom and pull my bag out of the closet.

John comes to the bedroom. He folds my clothes as I pack and hiccough and cry some more. After the suitcase zips, he crosses to me and hugs me. I bury my face in his neck. He and Marian never had children, which is a ridiculous loss. I'm all they had. He's in father mode, now, not publicist, his eyes kind and soft. He knows me too well, knows I've given everything to Ian. And how fiercely my love encompasses Eden. We were all together a week ago. Eden sat in my arms, telling silly stories and singing to the radio.

"Let me offer some advice, as a man married a very long time. Don't make this decision in the heat of the moment. Let it all play out, on pause, until the crisis has passed. There will be plenty of time for decisions later." *Humor me,* his eyes say.

"And before you storm out of here, tell Ian what you need, m'girl. He might listen." An academic exercise, like all the PR lessons he tried to drill into me and Bea, and only Bea really took to.

"I'll listen, birdy," Ian says from the doorway. He leans against the frame, but his eyes won't meet mine.

"I'll leave you to it," John says after a long pause. "You have my number, Kat, and Theo plans to take you back to LA. He's waiting on your call."

Ian and I stare at each other as John exits. I try to impose my heart-image of Ian—my artist lover, in our quiet Hampstead home—over the angry, selfish cur I see in front of me. He's too different. I can't stay. Whatever demands I make will never be met.

"What will it take, birdy?" A verbal attempt to soften the conversation even as his color remains too high and his shoulders and jaw tense and flex.

I want it all. My goddamn fairy tale. I lay it out, everything I've never dared to ask for in my life. Not once with a man have I asked for what I really need. I need the life my dad gave my mom, the one she never appreciated.

"I want fidelity, real loyalty, full honesty. Probably counseling so you can learn to keep it in your pants. Our girl, home, where she belongs, with a father who loves her and pays attention to her, keeps her out of trouble, helps her with her homework." My voice cracks. I'm not only laying out our life together, I'm bargaining for a better life for Eden—the life I had with my dad. Maybe it will be enough, maybe Ian will get something right.

But not tonight. And not with me. Every nasty published word about Katrine Porter flashes across my brain. Eden can't be won with me here, and I don't want to be here.

"That's—" Ian rubs a hand over the back of his neck.

"Too tall an order. I thought it might be." I pick up my bag. "Good-bye."

Ian follows me. "Kat," he demands, his tone only marginally softer. "You canna let us be tumbled by a fucking tabloid article."

"Interesting word choice—tumbled. You don't get any more tumbles from me. Not until you can offer me more than being the next ex–Mrs. Graham." My heart twists and tears, my entire insides feel crushed and broken. It's a million times worse than anything I've ever felt before.

"I won't let you leave me, Kat. I can offer you a lot, even if it's not—"

He's not my guy. Not at all.

And I rail against the unfairness of having given up everything for the wrong person. "Oh, fuck you, Ian Graham. Because I am so done."

"Then go!" Ian shouts. "Get gone. I don't need this. I can fill that bed in an hour." His nostrils flare and his eyes flash bright with rage.

This is it. This is the end. I throw open the hotel room door and walk out.

My heart pounds and I feel shaky, though my hands are steady as I pull out my cell phone and dial Nic. "Hey, Nic. Can you book me my own room for tonight?"

There's a long pause. "You can have mine, actually. I'm flying out. I left you a note with John. I quit, Kat. The agency will have a replacement here tomorrow at 10:30."

So, this is the end of everything. They've all left me.

I slide down a wall to cry and try to make decisions. Everything I have is part Ian. I've got nothing. No one.

Over the past year, I've abandoned everything that wasn't Ian.

I'm truly alone.

I miss Bea. Terribly. But she doesn't answer my call.

I ring Nic again.

"What else could you possibly need, Kat?"

"I need Bea."

"How dare you even ask? She came and did what she could to help. She left hours ago, in tears. I've never seen Bea cry, no one had, but she did. Now you want more?—no. No. I've put up with so much shite the past few months. You've hurt almost everyone I love. So, no. No. Oh, it feels good to say no." The line goes dead.

Tears herald a collapse into a full-on pity party. Ian doesn't barge through the door in mad search for me. He doesn't care. No one cares.

Nic is wrong. Bea cares, I know she does. She washed vomit out of my hair. I don't know why she didn't answer her phone, but I will find a way back to us. To all my people, to all my *us*'s.

I send one text message before following John's instructions. To Eden, *Love you always. Never forget that.*

♦ ♦ ♦

Bea

Bea had wanted to walk away, go back to Vancouver, hit the slopes with Eddie, and let Kat stew in her own rotted porridge for a bit. But Kat's distressed face in the sedan glass haunted her like a personal Bloody Mary. She'd stood on the curb as Kat disappeared and read the article over and over until she spotted the lie. Then she'd walked back in and rained hell on Matthias until he confessed and agreed to help her.

To make things right.

They'd spent weeks cashing in every favor Bea or Matthias had amassed over their years of chasing gossip. More sacrifices for Kat. And tears for Kat and for herself—and for the distance that had inevitably inserted itself between her and Eddie.

But she'd done it. She and Matthias had found the path to set everything right again.

The countryside passed by in hills of green and yellow dotted with stone walls and bare trees. Matthias rode next to her, equally quiet in the sedan John had requested to carry them on this mission.

Matthias broke their silence as Cardiff appeared. "*Gattina*, please, it's my job. I didn't expect you, of all people, not to understand."

Bea dropped her head against the cool glass. Spring had pushed its way past winter, but winter still hovered at the periphery. The days held a touch of chill even as the sun shone brighter each morning and the rain changed from biting to refreshing.

"She's a child, Matthias. A little girl. Her life isn't even hers yet. But now the whole world has formed an opinion about her that she'll never shake."

"As you've said. A dozen times. But my job—"

"Shut up about your job. We're never going to agree on this. There have to be lines in the sand, things you won't do. Or this business will gobble you up whole."

Matthias's hand covered hers, as it had so many times over the past few days. This time, she didn't pull away. Anger had begun to eat holes too deep in her heart to be filled. The time had come to forgive, hard as it was. Or she'd end up gobbled whole, too.

She turned her hand up and let Matthias wrap his fingers around hers. Then she turned to look at him. "I've already lost Katrine. I don't want to lose you, too. Not to this business."

His eyes were slightly watery. "You won't, *gattina*. A few more years and I can leave it all. My photos can be my own. We'll travel the world taking pictures of adorable babies and rainbows and civil upheaval, as we planned."

Bea looked back out the window, but left her hand in his. Those dreams felt like they belonged to other people; their late-night chatter was a script to another show. They'd been such idealists back then, certain life would come together with one more promotion . . . one more series . . . a little more money . . . a lot more success.

"Nothing has changed, *gattina*. Stay in London this summer and you'll see."

Bea shrugged one shoulder, but the offer had merit. She missed London. *Eddie would be in London*, an eager inner voice reminded.

The sedan rolled to a stop outside a small café on Cardiff's outskirts. Ian had given them only fifteen minutes during tea time for this tête-à-tête. They'd meet him on the back patio.

Matthias pushed open the door to the café and whispered to her as she passed. "Not to ruin our peace treaty, but I'm not sure handing Eden over to Ian Graham does her any favors."

"We're choosing between devils. Ian has decent taste in women, at least, seventy-five percent of the time. Whether he and Kat survive or not, I think this is best."

"Then after you, *gattina*. Could we have a bit of fun with it? Or is the pall part of your process?"

Bea licked her lips and braided her hair back to avoid a mess in the seaside wind. "Fun. We can have some fun. After all, I'm about to nail Ian's ass to the wall."

Matthias placed a hand in the small of her back, increased touch after they'd circled each other hesitatingly for weeks. "This may not help my case, but I do love your cutthroat side."

Ian raised one eyebrow above his sunglasses. "Pistols or swords? I didn't bring a second, though. I've forgotten all about your little slap."

"Funny. Your head hasn't." Bea sat back, reclined to look lazy and at ease, but stared purposefully at the small scar above his left eyebrow. "He's not my second. He's my insurance policy."

Matthias summoned a waiter as Bea started the play. "As I said to Jace on the phone. I come with apologies and gifts. Everything you need to win a custody battle."

Bea slid a brown envelope toward Ian.

Ian pulled out a stack of photos and statements. The first was a photo of Eden. She was young, too young, maybe six years old. Crying and alone in a barely-furnished airport.

He raised an eyebrow and looked at Bea.

Bea leaned forward to offer explanation. "Addy left Eden in Manila. She boarded the plane without her. Eden was alone in that airport for almost six hours before she was recognized by the paparazzo that snapped that photo.

I've got signed letters from him and the airport staffer who watched over her. They report the same thing. Addy and her friends showed up drunk enough that no one could forget the entire group. No one remembers seeing Eden until the group dissipated. And there she was. Alone. Addy never came looking for her. The paparazzo called Addy's agent, who came back, with plenty of money to keep this story quiet. You owe the snapper quite a bit of money, by the way, for going back on that agreement."

Scarlet heat flashed around the collar of Ian's shirt. Bea had felt the same the day she and Matthias hunted down the story. The look on Eden's face—alone, afraid. The things that might have happened to her.

The next set of damning evidence included a photo of Addy passed out on a bar while Eden tried to move her mother. Might be sweet, but Eden had on three layers of makeup and a plunging neckline over a stuffed push-up bra. A cigarette hung out of her youthful mouth. Ian's lips pressed tightly and he swallowed a half-dozen times.

But there was more, so much more. Bea and Matthias had spent weeks investigating every minute of Eden's life, weighing the sins of her parents. Somehow, in the balance, Ian had emerged the more saintly, though far from untarnished.

Ian raised both eyebrows as he slid the photo of too-grown Eden behind the next. Then he jolted forward.

Bea grinned.

Ian's rear end had met the wall.

"But despite Addy's failings, you're also a bit of a louse. Not exactly father of the year, are you, Ian? Her name was Greta, right? The very friendly tailor? She couldn't wait to tell me all about your threesome in wardrobe. She posed with her playmate. Brittany, was that it? So cute. Did you tell Kat how busy it was in wardrobe that day? Somehow, I doubt it."

Ian's cheek muscle jumped as he clenched his teeth. "You blackmailing bitch."

Matthias leaned forward, a glass of Chardonnay reflecting the midday light over Ian's face like a classy interrogation lamp. "Not at all. To blackmail, you have to want something in return. Bea asks nothing. She gives you Eden, your baby girl. The rest is only a reminder that anything done, can be found out. She's the *gattina,* after all, the little cat who slips in all the windows and learns the secrets while she purrs and steals hearts. And she really wants you to be a more careful father figure."

Matthias flipped his business card on the table. Ian's breath stopped as he stared at the name. *Matthias Perrini, Editor.*

"You were the best big game I ever hunted, Ian. I'd love to go another round. I'm sure it won't be long until you give me the chance, though the *gattina* has high hopes you've changed your ways."

"Her *insurance policy*?" Ian gritted his teeth until his breathing returned to normal. He fumbled for a cigarette beneath the table.

Bea rolled her eyes and shook her head. This had been fun, maybe too much fun. "You know, smoking really does kill people."

Ian took a puff and released the smoke in Bea's face. He stood up, the photos of Eden tucked under his arm with a cigarette dangling from his mouth, a genetic match to his young and wayward daughter. He walked away from the table without a farewell.

"I don't think he likes us," Matthias said.

"Guess that means I'll never get my invite to Hampstead House."

Matthias stood and offered her a hand. "Being a professional gossip can be a fucking good time."

Bea lay her head on his shoulder. He smelled like leather and seedy back alleys, as he always had. "How about you take me to Gioli's and we pretend the last year never happened?"

Matthias opened the car door and let her slide in. "I'd say that's the best idea you ever had."

CHAPTER 24

Will mich freuen dann und weinen,
Selig, selig bin ich dann,
Sollte mir das Herz auch brechen,
Brich, o Herz, was liegt daran.

I will rejoice then and weep,
blissful, blissful I'll be then;
if my heart should also break,
break, O heart, what of it?

—*Robert Schumann, Frauenliebe und -leben*

Kat

It's fanciful—I know the geography of the city extends much further—but I feel as if I've traversed the whole of London over the past year. A flat in Dalston, a house in Hampstead, now a hotel in South Bank.

For its final season, *21 Things* gets the red carpet treatment. BBC has sprung for a premiere in Leicester Square, where all my past will greet me, because we now rank as one of their most successful shows.

I pick my own outfit, do my own makeup. A black knit top and a dark blue satin skirt with cascading black and silver stripes.

John is happy with my press, all the little photo ops he arranged, and LA wasn't so bad once I got down to a routine—work, eat, sleep, work.

But London is a minefield. Leicester Square is only five miles from Hampstead, from the house that was mine. That could be mine again, as daily bouquets of flowers and phone calls have declared for weeks, including a surprising one a few days ago where Ian offered to go to counseling and swore he'll never cheat again.

There's more, too—Ian's silent gifts are the most compelling—our production company, that he hasn't tried to dissolve it or buy me out or stall progress on *Birds*. All the waiting and worrying as someone else held my future in their hands—I get what I did to Bea, how it feels to have your name easily blotted out.

Oh, Bea. She responds to texts now, as this event has come closer. But I haven't seen her since Sundance, I don't know where she is except that she'll see me in Leicester Square and black is a good classic color to build a red carpet outfit around.

This will take more than texts or calls. Or thank you notes. Not that Bea has been ungracious about any of them. But this needs a bigger gesture. I've talked to three lawyers about how to undo my selfish choices for *21 Things*, *Birds*, and Monkey & Me, though, and no one knows. So, I've done something else, something grand even if I can't give her back what I took.

My final offering, the *pièce de résistance*, waits neatly wrapped—unassuming, sort of small. But half of everything Bea has always wanted.

I smooth over my outfit again and smile into the mirror. Red carpet, here I come.

It's a daylight premiere, in the early spring chill of London I've missed. I see Ben first, and I'm immediately wrapped up into the comfort and silliness of my *21 Things* family.

"What are you up to, you big lug?"

"Oh, not much."

"Liar. Big movie stuff, I hear. You gonna invite me to that premiere?"

"I don't know. You got that stinky pits problem under control yet?"

"What problem?" I wave my arms to show off my long sleeves and sweat-hiding black. "I don't know what you're talking about."

"Geez, Katrine. They'll report a dead animal died in here. Keep those arms down." Ben pushes my arms down and tucks me under his arm.

"You're the worst," I tease. I'm already this close to crying over the end of all my best things. He guides me to the rest of the crew. There's some awkwardness with Anna—she and Bea have always been close—but Quinn is the same as always.

"Well, Kat," she says. "It's your last chance for that shag. I'm single. You're single. Ben can watch, learn something." She kisses my cheeks, and winks at Ben. It's the kind of joke we will still make at the 10-year anniversary dinner I plan to have.

"Careful what you offer, Quinn. Might give Ben a heart attack."

"Please. Let this happen. Bea promised me rewards if I got sober. If this is what she meant, then it'll be worth every painful day." Sober? Oh my god, that's what the poker chip was. A sobriety coin. How oblivious to everything and everyone have I been? "Where is our busy Bea anyway? Did someone set off a bomb and she had to go save the day?"

Jamie wanders over, Adhira on his arm. "Nothing so sinister. Caterer brought the wrong something-or-other. She's reading them the riot act."

"Jamie," I motion him into our circle. I have them now, the four leads of *21 Things,* the people who breathed life into a dream. "I'm not going to cry." I sniff against the temptation. "But here I have you all, and I just have to say—you are brilliant, and I love you all, and *21 Things* will always be the best thing ever."

"Eloquent as ever, Kat," Ben kisses my temple. "And worth a toast."

"Hold up. I won't toast without Bea." Adhira's hands are on her hips. "I'm a little tired of her being treated like the redheaded stepchild."

Jamie elbows his wife. "It's fine, really. The rest of us understand, Kat."

Even Anna smiles. "Things change. It's fine. We can toast with Bea later." She glares at Adhira, who shrugs.

"Yeah. Bea'll have some suit in tow when she comes in. Let's get a moment before it's all business."

"And she doesn't drink, so it'll be less awkward," Quinn adds. The drinks get passed around.

I'm uncomfortably aware that they echo all the dismissive things I've said about Bea in the past. We toast and drink, and the official photographer captures us all smiling together.

All except one.

When Bea does enter, it's true to form. She's on Royce Rudkins's arm. Her smile is huge, charming him and shaking hands with the press, and her fashion is spectacular as ever—a white bandage skirt with black panels and a frothy, loose blouse.

"Uh oh. Suits. Time for us to make an exit. See you later, Kat." Ben licks my cheek.

"Oh, stop." I push him off and head toward Bea and the suitiest suit of them all.

Royce's large hand reaches toward me, as red as his nose. "Kat, so good to see you. How's your new company? The BBC would love to collaborate, you should come by and talk, soon as there's a spot in that busy schedule." He laughs and pumps my hand.

"I'll see what we can do," I say, noncommittally.

Bea nods at someone unseen, then smiles at us. "I'll leave you two to talk. I see Meg's on her way, too." She bows out of the conversation as Meg comes and wraps her arms around me.

"I told you, didn't I, Royce? Up and coming. I know my talent. Don't I know my talent?"

"You do, Meg. And I've kept that post-it note you stuck on my computer all those years ago about her. *Finest talent in a generation.* We gave her a start here. Never forget that. It was BBC that gave you your first studio."

"I will never forget, I promise," I say more to Meg than Royce.

But Bea is gone. Will I have to chase her all day across this event?

"Oh, we're just so proud of you. Can't wait for *Birds,* honey. I knew you'd be big. I just knew it."

"Still only a screenplay at this point, but moving closer every day." The calendar looms in my head. I'm to be in New Zealand in two months. So far from everything, from everyone. I need to find Bea.

We're working at opposite ends during the entire early mixer. If I'm with corporate people, she's with the cast. If I go to the cast, she's suddenly on the business side. Around and round with no luck, until I'm sitting through the whole first episode with a package in my lap and no idea where Bea has gone.

I take a chance and slip out under the closing credits to a side room where someone could watch everything but not be seen, but Bea isn't there. She isn't anywhere in the theater. Anxious urgency propels me to frantic searching.

I finally try my phone. "Where are you?"

"Getting some air. Is there a problem?"

"Can we talk?"

"Um. Sure. After the party?"

"No. Now. Where are you? Before everyone comes spilling out of the theater."

"Throwing coins into a fountain."

"I'll be there in a minute."

I semi-run in my heels and arrive at the fountain in the center of Leicester Square out of breath, my package clutched in front of me. "You hate Shakespeare. What are you doing here?"

"Making wishes." Bea's face screws up and she does this series of head shakes. "I don't much like good-byes. Anyway. What's up?"

I lean against a stone urn and try to remember the perfect apology I found months ago. "I brought you something." I hold up the package.

"Oh. Okay. Thank you."

"It's not an apology. I have to make that myself. I'm so sorry, for every way I wronged you and belittled you and your contributions. This is just—a token."

Bea's expression closes like the great gate to a medieval city. She does this, and I know this, the way she pulls back when people step too far inside. I took for granted that she let me in years ago.

"You could open it," I suggest.

Bea unwraps the gift with a hesitant expression, like it's possible I've gotten her a baby dragon. But I know the moment she realizes what's in her hand. Her lips quiver and then her mouth opens on a huge exhale.

"A . . . Monet . . . ," she whispers as she uncovers the last of the sketch. It's tiny, so small, but even with my large bank account, it's the most Monet I can afford. Three ships in pencil with the same delicate stroke of the master that created *Water-Lilies*.

That's where Bea goes, when life needs to slow down. She sits in the Tate and stares at *Water-Lilies*. Everything pseudo-modern about her slips away in front of Monet. He speaks to her soul, not to the layers of life she carries to try and make her way through a cruel world. When she's with Monet, she's full of light, living in a world of brilliant hues and peaceful moments.

The same thing happens to her now with the boats. Whatever brought her to the feet of her least favorite poet slips away and she smiles, a little, at the lines.

"Some dreams deserve to come true," I say with tears in my eyes.

"Thank you," she says, to me and Monet.

"Do we still have a chance?" A selfish question. But I can't say *you're welcome* for what Monet has wrought.

Bea's fingers caress the edge of the museum glass encasing the sketch. I spared no expense with the frame; the thing could survive a nuclear war. "I don't know. I thought no. I told John I wouldn't help you, but then . . ." Bea exhales again. "Sit down, Kat. I need to tell you something."

Stone digs painfully into my rear end, but I sit. "Tell me what?"

"Ian got custody of Eden today. He's on his way to Scotland to make the exchange. It'll hit the papers tomorrow. And I know John will disagree with what I'm going to say, but I think you should be there when Eden gets back."

My breath comes too fast and my chest starts to cave in. Eden. "To Hampstead?"

"I think that's the plan. It's not like Ian and I are on speaking terms. But that's the rumor."

"How do you—how do you know this? I haven't heard any of this."

Bea shrugs. She looks back at Shakespeare, her brows knit together. "I've been working this out since Sundance. I told Matthias about you and Ian in Scotland. I didn't know where it would lead or that it would ever touch Eden. I'm so sorry she got hurt."

She looks at me and her eyes grow sad. "So, you may want to keep this Monet for yourself." Bea stands then, the Monet abandoned on the stone.

"Custody? Really?" Sobs escape me. "Oh, my baby girl is coming home."

"You should go to them. I can make your excuses here." Bea leaves the Monet behind.

"No, no. Bea!" I pick up the frame and follow her. "It's yours. You can't—it's yours."

When I catch Bea, she's crying, blotting at tears before they fall to preserve her makeup. She's embarrassed I see them. "Sorry. It's been a tough few weeks."

"I'm sorry. I'm so sorry. And I know I shouldn't, can't, pretend like I know anymore where you are or what's hurting you. But I'm sorry for it, for every piece that's mine, because I'm sure a lot of them are. So, take it. What am I going to do with a Monet sketch anyway?"

"Oh, geez, Katrine," Bea half-laughs at me. "You really are the worst form of snob."

But the last comes with a bit of humor and affection. She takes the Monet and wraps it to her, next to her heart. "My future baby and I thank you."

"Baby? You're doing it?"

"Yeah. It's time. I've got a Monet. Can't leave the plan half undone." Bea and her no-man plans have always baffled me a little. Now I can only admire. "I'll make sure to tag you when I post the first picture online."

"Or call me?"

"I think you need to have a conversation with Ian before we make that leap." She leans up on her toes and kisses my cheek.

"This is about me and you, us. What does Ian matter?"

"Because he's your guy. Your future and all your dreams. And he mostly hates me, Kat. Sometimes, life makes you choose between paths."

She smiles at me, and my heart knows there won't be many more of these moments. We memorize each other, cement the past in place, and confirm that who we were and what we had held a value beyond what art or business could ever provide.

"Beatrice Elizabeth Douglas, you will always be my best friend."

Bea glances back at Shakespeare then leans close to me for a moment. "I kissed Edward Wolverton once. It was everything it was supposed to be—and then some. If wishes come true, then maybe I'll kiss him again."

It's the confession that echoes my sentiment. No matter where life takes us, I will always be Bea's best friend, too, the person who heard her dreams.

She walks ahead and then turns back for a final wave, tears in her eyes that she lets slip this time, carrying uncharacteristic smudges along her cheeks. Then business Bea rotates on her heels, back to work to make it possible for me to chase my dreams, as she's always done.

The key to Hampstead weighs heavier and heavier in my purse. Bea has disappeared from view. We each have a different place to be, a different place of belonging.

This is the terrible secret of adulthood, what no one tells you in your youth—that everyone moves on, finds their place. And sometimes, life makes you choose between new and old loves.

Even if you're best friends forever.

BONUS CONTENT

Nicola

Nicola dropped the flowing Bohemian mixed-print dress onto the counter. The sweet, young cashier at Tory Burch barely glanced at her. All part of the job. The androgynous salesperson at RAW had done the same. The stylist called to request items. Nicola picked them up. Kat wore them. Nicola returned them. An endless flow of duties that carried Nicola in and out of stores on Rodeo Drive. She was glad for the employment, but honestly, this didn't feel like a step up in the world. Kat didn't feel like a step up. She wasn't a cruel boss, not overly demanding. Just—clueless. Painfully clueless.

And that's how Nicola justified holding onto the flowing, off-shoulder caftan from Roberto Cavalli for an extra day. Kat would never notice. She'd worn the incredible item for exactly two hours to a luncheon and then tossed it on the floor for Nicola to collect. No respect for the execution or design. Nic, on the other hand, knew art when it called ot her. The caftan was made for Nic's long, thin frame. She'd modeled an earlier incarnation for Roberto back in the day. The item wanted her to wear it.

With her official duties done, she maneuvered the car into a gas station. Fifteen minutes in a bathroom changed her from ignored personal assistant to the woman you can't ignore. She slipped the expensive silk over her head and left her long legs bare, hopeful that the ensemble didn't scream *sleep with me* so much as *please notice me outside my relationship to my employer.*

And perhaps, *I'm really not always as drunk as the last time we spoke.*

She smoothed her long, blonde hair over her shoulder. Sexy but classy. Then she pushed her breasts up just another inch. Couldn't hurt, right?

She stepped out of the bathroom, let her gaze sweep the store. Her look was for one man alone but each appreciative head nod or outright leer meant she still had some sparkle. She needed sparkle. Loads and loads of sparkle.

Carefully, she melted down to the seat. The Ford Focus matched how she felt. Dull and pedestrian. But she had to believe in the sparkle. She threw the car into gear and pulled back into traffic. She'd meet Philip not far from here. At O. For a nice drink on a quiet night.

That he'd agreed to meet her—for a possibly date-type situation—at all, that was promising, right?

No, it wasn't. Philip had never been anything but friendly. Never. Kat had been his *it* girl. Nic was just the woman who made the phone calls. Nic didn't have whatever it was that Kat had. Honestly, Kat was an enigma. A golden something. But Nic pushed down her irritation. If she didn't, she'd blow this chance to be something *other* than an appendage to the great, all-important Kat Porter, who never noticed anyone or anything.

Oh, was this as hopeless as it felt?

Nic guided the car into the valet line, grateful for the backup. *I must breathe and believe. That's what nonna says. Breathe and believe and the world will be yours.*

But breathing and believing didn't guarantee happily ever after.

The valet smiled softly as he helped her from the car. Nic nodded back and smiled when he winked at her. A touch of confidence wouldn't hurt. She let the man hover over her hand as she passed him the five-dollar bill. The she rushed into the hotel and toward the marble-covered bar of the Orchid room.

Philip waited with his long fingers wrapped around a wine glass. Nic's heart slammed into action. She'd felt the same the first day she met him, before Kat arrived and spoiled it all.

Nic paused to breathe and believe while looking at her hopeless love. Philip epitomized tall, dark, and handsome. He was beautiful, and he dressed the part, but he didn't act it. A true rarity.

She waited a moment too long. Philip felt her stare, turned and caught her eyes as she made her way to the bar. Everything felt faked. Nic coached herself along. *If this weren't Philip, I'd reach out and graze his shoulders with my hand. I'd lean in. I'd kiss his cheek.*

Philip accepted her kiss with a friendly kiss of his own. "Well, it's the famous Nicola. How've you been? Still running the world?" He pulled out a bar stool. She slipped in, breathing him in and letting herself relax.

"No. Not in control of myself or the world, I'm afraid. About that phone call—Philip, I'm so sorry. I was . . ." *Drunk. In love. Stupid.*

Philip waved off the apology and then called over the barkeep. "No need to worry. At times like these, any friendship is a blessing."

Nicola noted the downward turn of his mouth, the extra-tight grip on the glass. *If I were me, I'd comfort him,* she coached herself. She reached a trembling hand out to his arm. The touch felt so right. Her smile softened, not forced or fake. Philip was real. She squeezed his forearm again and absorbed his warmth before she spoke. "And you? How've you been?"

"Overwhelmed. Business is good. Booming, actually." Philip poured her a glass of wine from the bottle the barkeep delivered. Philip listed off a long line of pilots and casting calls as Nic sipped her wine. "So that's all my boring nonsense, Nic. Tell me about you. I was sad to hear about the end of Monkey & Me. Have you stayed on with—?"

"—my old boss? Yes." She didn't want to speak Kat's name and potentially spoil this moment.

But Philip laughed. "We can say her name, Nic. Maybe we should each say it ten times so it feels normal? I know you're not in Vancouver with Bea because you called me from London last week."

"Kat. Kat, Kat, Kat." Nic laughed. "I work for Kat. I'm her personal assistant. Apparently with plans to become the assistant to one of the production assistants in New Zealand this year. I used to be the executive assistant for a production company." A sigh interrupted her good humor.

Philip leaned forward. "Feeling like it's time to move on?"

"Yes. No? Yes? Ugh. And I don't want to ruin tonight by talking about the whole big mess."

"Nic, you won't ruin anything. Talk about the whole big mess or not, it's up to you. I'll listen to whatever you want to talk about."

Oh, that was a terrifying bubble. Nic was caught in the middle. The real middle. Of everything. She knew where all the bodies were buried and right now, everyone had a shovel.

"How about I just spill everything and then we have dinner and act like it didn't happen?" Metaphorical screaming and crying on Philip's literal broad comforting chest, that sounded good.

Philip clinked the edge of her glass with his own. "I could handle that."

"Alright. In a nutshell. Big nutshell maybe, I don't know. Monkey & Me tanked because Kat didn't bring Bea along to her movie project, and then Bea sold everything that wasn't nailed down so Kat will have a shiny 'Executive Producer' credit on her name. And now, oh my god, now! The shit is about to hit. Because the great Ian Graham filmed a movie with his ex-wife, who Kat hates, and it's premiering at Sundance next week, and it is so not innocent. And Kat has no idea! Because her boyfriend is kind of a lying bastard. I have to be at Sundance. Because it's going to explode in all our faces, even if it's just the Kat temper tantrum of the century. So that's what I'm trying to prepare for." Nic downed the rest of her wine. "So, yeah. That's the big fat mess. Except I didn't even start on the Bea stuff." Nic dropped her head to the bar.

Philip put his hand briefly on hers. The touch reverberated everywhere. "Nic. I can almost guarantee Bea takes care of herself. And Kat's—well, Kat is going to do whatever Kat wants, right?"

The silence between them crowded out the increasing noise of happy hour. Philip poured himself another glass of wine. "I'll be in Sundance. Taking a week to ski and see some films. So let's get together to commiserate at least. That a plan?"

"That sounds good." A real smile invaded Nic's overall pall. Philip's strong, calm presence made the prospect of film festival disaster less disastrous. Or maybe more survivable.

And his hand still rested on hers. Nic stretched her fingers a little, enough for a bit more contact.

She wanted to kiss him. Here. Forever. In the middle of a room full of people—the where didn't matter. But, that would be weird, right? Precipitous, hasty, probably unwelcome.

He raised his hand off hers to signal the barkeep again. The bottle wasn't done, so it must be the check. This moment was over.

But someday—someday, she would have all the moments. Maybe. As soon as she quit her job. Once she quit, she could sit with Philip and not talk of Kat.

First, though, the problems at hand. "Would you come to Ian's movie? I know it's a lot to ask, but I have the worst feeling about it all. I just know something awful will happen."

Philip's attention snapped to her.

"I'm sorry, too much?" Nic tried to laugh it off, but his face didn't change.

"If . . . if you think . . . ," he cleared his throat. "I'll be there if you think I should." But his face was full of conflict. His brow knit. His mouth pressed together.

She'd done it. Raised the specter of Kat too starkly.

Still, Philip squeezed her hand. "I'll be around. Cheer you on. It probably won't be as bad as all that."

"I hope so." But experience over the last year had taught her it would be as bad as all that, and probably worse.

Philip scribbled his name on the receipt. "Ok. So how about dinner? I could use some overpriced onion straws."

The floor dropped three feet. He meant dinner *now*. Not in a distant future. *Now*. Nic grasped the stool to steady herself. Not good-bye, not yet. She nodded and hoped head-bobbing landed closer to chic than desperate. "Definitely. Though we'll need more than onion straws. Have I mentioned I'm Italian and know how to eat?" *Oh, Nic, pull yourself together*.

"Something I've always appreciated about you, Miss Nicola." Philip gestured towards the dining area.

Color rose in her face. The way he said *Miss Nicola*, saints help her.